UNEXPURGATED? DEFINITELY.
UNINHIBITED? ABSOLUTELY.

HEROTICA® 4

"Behind the Mask" by Serena Moloch
A Victorian aristocrat and her lady's maid explore the true meaning of the word *mistress*.

"Electricity in My Bed" by Calla Conova
When the utility company comes to check your water heater, you may be in for a more thorough inspection than you expect.

"Breaking and Entering" by Susannah J. Herbert
Fact and fantasy become one and the same when you're finding your way around a strange man's bedroom by moonlight.

"The Café of the Joyous Women" by Mary Maxwell
Jennifer gets a deliciously unexpected present when a beautiful Frenchwoman lures her away from a dull birthday dinner with her husband.

AND 24 MORE EROTIC TALES BY, FOR,
AND ABOUT WOMEN

Marcy Sheiner writes fiction, poetry, essays, and journalism. Her erotic stories have appeared in *Herotica® 1, 2,* and *3, Virgin Territory, On Our Backs,* and *Penthouse.* She was editor and fiction editor at *On Our Backs,* and her nonfiction has appeared in *Playgirl, Mother Jones, High Times, Girlfriend,* and *Lilith.* She lives in San Francisco and is working on her fourth novel.

HEROTICA® 4

A New Collection of
Erotic Writing by Women

Edited by Marcy Sheiner

A PLUME BOOK

PLUME
Published by the Penguin Group
Penguin Books USA Inc., 375 Hudson Street,
New York, New York 10014, U.S.A.
Penguin Books Ltd, 27 Wrights Lane, London W8 5TZ, England
Penguin Books Australia Ltd, Ringwood, Victoria, Australia
Penguin Books Canada Ltd, 10 Alcorn Avenue, Toronto, Ontario, Canada M4V 3B2
Penguin Books (N.Z.) Ltd, 182–190 Wairau Road, Auckland 10, New Zealand

Penguin Books Ltd, Registered Offices: Harmondsworth, Middlesex, England

First published by Plume, an imprint of Dutton Signet,
a division of Penguin Books USA Inc.

First Printing, April, 1996
10 9 8 7 6 5 4 3 2 1

LIBRARY OF CONGRESS CATALOGING-IN-PUBLICATION DATA:
Herotica 4 : a new collection of erotic writing by women / edited by Marcy Sheiner.
    p.   cm.
    ISBN 0-452-27181-9
    1. Erotic stories, American.   2. American fiction—Women authors.   3. Women—
Sexual behavior—Fiction.   I. Sheiner, Marcy.
PS648.E7H476   1996
813'.01083538—dc20   95-36094
                                                                           CIP

Printed in the United States of America
Set in Caledonia and Serif Gothic

This book is dedicated to my teachers,
Marco Vassi and Susie Bright.

ACKNOWLEDGMENTS

I am grateful to Leigh Davidson for her unflagging sense, sanity, and support.

If she ever gets the time, I owe Linnea Due a Chinese lunch for her generous feedback.

Shar Rednour, treasure of the Bay Area sex scene, provided editorial assistance, literary acumen, lessons in diplomacy, and fashion expertise. She calls me her mentor, but really she's mine.

One of the bonuses of editing this book was working with the extraordinary Joani Blank. Without her vision and energy, there would be no *Herotica*®, no Down There Press, no Good Vibrations, no Open Enterprises.

A smile for Phyllis Christopher, the only photographer who can make me do it.

Everyone thanks their partners for putting up with them, so . . . I thank mine, although seeing me through the process of *Herotica*® has probably been one of the more pleasurable aspects of Jamie's life with me.

Contents

INTRODUCTION

The first time I wrote a pornographic story, I was amazed to find my pen flowing across page after page in a nearly seamless movement from beginning to middle to end. In twenty years of writing fiction and journalism, this had never happened to me. It seemed that the freeing of my sexual voice had loosened my creative voice as well. I learned, on a kinesthetic level, about the connection between sexuality and creativity. Not only do the creative and sexual impulses emanate from the same source, but the two are also synergistic.

In writing fiction suffused with sexual content, I became more prolific and proficient at my craft. This kind of symbiosis between creativity and sexuality is not limited to writing; it's the reason that so many artists—dancers, actors, photographers, painters—inevitably delve into the sexual arena.

Still, while pornography provided a fountain of creative inspiration for me, after a hundred or so stories I began to wonder just how many ways I could possibly continue to say "They (or we) did it." In editing women's erotic fiction, I've learned that the number of ways to say "They (or we) did it" are in fact infinite.

Since the first *Herotica*® collection appeared in 1988, a supportive atmosphere has developed in which women can express and communicate exactly what arouses us sexually—but until this recent explosion of women-created erotica, our sexual voice had been largely silent. Men, of course, were permitted, even encouraged, to articulate in graphic and loving detail the myriad ways of getting it on, and so the pornography industry inevitably reflected their sexual tastes and behavior. More significantly, the parameters of male sexual expression widened to fill the space it was accorded, while we women remained in the dark about one another's, and often even our own, erotic proclivities.

We are rapidly moving out of these dark ages; although there are still some who question whether or not it's all right for us to write, much less read and get off on, sexual words and images, women's erotic writing has become a fact of life and a hot item in the publishing industry. Our stories are sold in national chain bookstores, promoted at international book fairs, and distributed through mainstream book clubs. The more we publish, read, and talk about what we think and feel concerning sex, the more the boundaries of our sexual imagination expand.

The *Herotica* series continues to lead the way in mapping the still largely uncharted landscape of female desire. The subjects in this, the fourth collection, range from a precocious student's seduction of her English teacher to an evening with a couple of high-class call girls. What strikes me most about the collection is the richness and complexity of the plot lines surrounding or interwoven with the sexual encounters. Some of the work in this collection is as literary as anything you'll find in *The New Yorker* or *The Paris Review*, but because overt sex is largely compartmentalized in our culture, you can bet your multiple orgasms these stories won't be winning any Pushcart Prizes.

And literary quality, as these authors prove, does not have to be sexless: "I take his cock in my mouth, sip from it, drink from it in the same fashion that I consumed the beer in the bar." "Wet, wet, so very wet, the delicious friction made me erupt volcanic, shuddering against her, inside her, through her." These lines are eloquent without being euphemistic; the erotic charge is clearly the springboard for the writing.

In other ways as well *Herotica* stories differ from the kind of wham-bam pornography that focuses primarily on the physical act. What exactly is it that distinguishes these stories?

Context

From the moment she lays eyes on the electrical repairwoman, the heroine of "Electricity in My Bed" wants to sleep with her—but this desire is rooted in the context of a long-standing wish to make love with another woman. At the other end of the relationship spectrum, sex in "Giving and Receiving" occurs within the context of a long-term affair.

Judging from the way women write about sex, one of the most important paths to our arousal is the context in which sex occurs. Some might cite this as proof of women's long-alleged inability to enjoy sex outside of a relationship. But context does not equal relationship; context simply means there's a dynamic between the characters that gets expressed sexually. Whether our heroine is sneaking a furtive hump in the ladies' room or riding the emotional waves of a long-term relationship, the sexual encounter is but one thread in a tapestry that may incorporate various aspects of her history. As the Parisian lover in "Real Pleasure" puts it to her obtuse American counterpart, "Just because I have emotions doesn't mean I want a relationship. It only means I'm not a machine."

This is the reason so many women remain unmoved by porn videos: there's rarely any kind of tension between the characters, or any context for the sex act. Mainstream porn videos tend to focus on organs and orgasms rather than on people and their interactions. Analysts have concluded that women simply don't respond to visual stimulation. Well, it's not that we don't respond to visual stimulation—it's that we don't respond to vapidity. How else to explain the uproar among *Playgirl* subscribers when the magazine decided to put clothes on its male centerfolds: their readership demanded that the models disrobe immediately!

Erotic literature leaves room for the reader to reshape the specifics to her own tastes, something that's more difficult to do with moving pictures on a screen. And from what I've heard women say about the ways they use pornography, we seem to be less immediate—an image "lifted" from porn might come back to us months later, sliding right into our fantasy to send us a notch wetter and wilder. If *Herotica* stories don't always fall under the heading of "one-handed reading," that's because women generally don't read porn one-handedly. Rather, we raid pornography for images and ideas, then adapt them to suit our own sexual quirks. We want mental as well as sensory engagement.

Thus, *Herotica* authors take their time developing plot, character, and setting before inviting us into bed. They tease us with the promise of arousal and satisfaction, then leisurely go about creating a universe, whether it's centered in Hollywood or in Victorian England, in a city's red-light district or on another planet. This exquisite attention to detail plays an essential role in the sexual schema: the authors create an erotic environment, and they don't quit at what may be a crucial moment for either the characters or audience. They don't leave us hanging just outside the bedroom door.

The Forbidden Zone

Pornography is not polite—that's one of the reasons it's continually under attack. To be effective, sexually explicit writing must break society's rules. That's why most attempts to create sweet egalitarian erotica are misguided; sure, some gals or even guys may get off on sunset-drenched scenery, but for most people very soft-core stuff just doesn't pass the wet test. Sex is about exploration and discovery, and that frequently involves entering some forbidden zone.

What's forbidden depends on who you're talking to. For some women, fantasizing while with a partner feels wrong—so guess what? The very act of fantasizing turns them on like nothing else. For many women, thoughts about physical or emotional mistreatment during sex seem politically if not morally incorrect—and so violence and humiliation fill their fantasies. The element of danger—physical or emotional—is a powerful aphrodisiac. Fear of social censure is another, so anything verboten in the culture is guaranteed to excite. Interracial sex. Intergenerational sex.

Adultery. As every teenager knows, any situation requiring se-
crecy is inherently exciting.

Since lesbians have been historically stigmatized, the very
portrayal of two women making love defies a taboo, and the act
itself is imbued with a sense of danger, as well as rebellion—
another potential aphrodisiac. For a Japanese woman, the public
expression of female sexuality is such a no-no that when the narrator of "My Dance at Juliana's" displays herself in public, "a
surge of power rushes through my body and I feel high." For a
heterosexual American college girl the ante gets upped consider-
ably: in "Make Me," the young heroine's attraction to a father
figure skirts around the territory of incest.

But while these stories shine a light into some dark corners,
the door to the female forbidden zone is only slightly ajar. The
Herotica series is part of a movement still in its infancy. We're
only beginning to explore, much less speak publicly about, these
hidden areas of desire. We have barely begun to articulate the
interior processes we undergo during sex and in our fantasy
lives.

Exactly what goes through her head and heart when he grips
her shoulder and pushes her to her knees? What complex com-
bination of jealousy and excitement inspires her to orgasm when
she watches her lover fucking her best friend? What psychic
shift occurs when, for the first time in her life, she has her way
with a passive man? What familial or cultural ghosts hover
around her bed when she surrenders totally to a dominating
partner? These are the kinds of questions that women, at this
stage of our sexual evolution, still frequently shy away from.

If we're not willing to look at our own responses and share
them with one another, we'll do a better job of limiting our sexual expression than any censor. It's ironic that women, notorious
for consulting therapists about everything from insomnia to fail-
ing relationships, don't do the same when it comes to sexual behavior. We're going to have to crawl as deeply into our sexual
psyches as we do into other aspects of our lives. We're going to
have to look honestly at the reality, rather than the ideology, of
sex, even if what we find turns out to be humiliating, mundane,
or—*surprise!*—politically incorrect.

We are beginning to see glimmers of this kind of exploration. "My Mother's Body," for instance, looks at a woman's childhood erotic feelings toward her mother and how they affect her adult sexuality:

> Your breasts are beautiful, like my mother's. . . . I was
> fascinated by her breasts. They were large and very dense
> with nipples in perpetual erection. The thought that my body
> might one day look like hers thrilled me. I watched in awe as
> she put her bra straps over her shoulders, bent over and shook
> all of that pink flesh into the white cotton cones of her 36C
> Maidenform.
>   Bend over and shake for me.
>   Freud had it all wrong. It's the mother-daughter
> relationship that's so titillating. Women are either lesbian or
> bisexual; how can we be anything but, when our first and
> primary love object was our mother?

Entering another forbidden zone, the narrator in "Night Talk" admits a penchant for hearing abusive, even misogynistic, language during sex:

> "They were being way too polite. I had to tell them
> to talk filthy to me. They started out pretty tame, but
> they ended up whispering things like 'Come on, bitch,
> come for us. You know you want to. Let's hear you come.
> You like having two cocks in you, don't you? You like
> getting fucked by two dicks at once, you slut. Oh, you're
> such a little whore. What a sweet little snatch you have.
> Your ass is so hot and snug. You better come soon, bitch,
> 'cause I can't hold back much longer.' Once they started
> talking like this, I totally lost it."

Women's Love Affair with Words

My passion for language developed around the same time as my passion for sex. In high school I began writing essays that knocked my teacher's socks off: during that same time period I began making out with boys in the backseats of cars. The day after one of those steamy encounters, I'd recall delicious details that made my stomach flop—but it was not the remembered feel of an erection through layers of clothing, or even the occasional hand on my breast that I conjured up to turn myself on. No, what I turned over and over in my mind, savoring them like precious jewels, were the *words* he had whispered in my ear. Whether he'd promised eternal love or begged permission to unsnap my bra, his words moved me on a deeper level than his touch.

A popular song at that time, "Things I Wanna Hear," resonated with the girls and instructed the boys in the art and importance of sweet talk. That quintessential "girl group," the Shirelles, insisted they needed a constant barrage of "pretty words" if their lovers expected to get to first base with them. That song told me I was not alone in my hunger for erotic or romantic words.

Herotica 4 authors do the same. Sometimes they create a subtle undertone of language as foreplay. At other times they allude explicitly to the erotic power of words, as in "Amazing Grace," where a lover's sweet talk is "one of the best parts, the slow run of his voice like sugar syrup, over her head and around her ears." Then there's the metaphorical "Tasting the Sky," in which a woman hides in a library cubicle and squeezes a book full of words between her legs. Sometimes, as in "Coming and Cumming," two little letters can mean the difference between long, leisurely sex and quick release:

> Cum ... is the short form of the verb, for boys who bounce up and down on you and cum in three minutes.... Women are built for the long haul—watch what comes.

Pornography, like sex itself, has a way of revealing us to ourselves, and as you read *Herotica 4* you may find yourself responding to images and situations you've never thought about, or dismissed as out of bounds. Just be sure to watch what comes.

Susan St. Aubin

꧁꧂

Coming and Cumming

I was nineteen and the oldest senior in my high school when I found my first lover. Because I was slow learning to read, I'd repeated first grade, but once I caught on, nothing could hold me back. By the time I was a freshman, I had a reputation for intelligence: history teachers would check their facts with me; English teachers would ask me obscure points of grammar. *Lay* or *lie*? I always knew the appropriate form.

In my senior year I took an honors course called Early English Literature, a survey that covered everything from *Beowulf* to Milton's *Paradise Lost*. The teacher, Miss Wilson, probably wasn't more than three or four years older than I was. This was her first job, and in her short skirts, flat shoes, and little gold earrings, she looked younger than most of us.

I wanted to shine for Miss Wilson. She was brilliant: she could recognize a line from the most obscure Elizabethan sonnet and tell you the name of the poem and who had written it. Though I knew I was no match for a mind like hers, I was hopelessly in love. I was sure she'd never guess what a girl like me could feel, hiding in the fortress of my body: fat face, stringy blond hair, hunched and rounded shoulders, heavy legs. Even my feet were fat in their sandals, the white straps cutting into the abundant flesh on my heels and toes.

In Miss Wilson's class I put out. I kept class discussions going when no one else would say two words, and I worked hard on my essays, though I could easily get As in most English classes just by plopping down words on paper.

It was late May, two weeks before graduation. No teacher would admit it, but we knew our grades were decided before final exams. It was a time of movies in all our classes: films on the periodic tables in chemistry or on the digestive system in biology—stuff we already knew, but our teachers liked to pretend there was a great danger that we'd forgotten. One day, Miss Wilson showed an old black-and-white film of *Romeo and Juliet*, a condensed version in just two reels. Now they'd have a color video, but this was back in 1965, when all we saw in school was old movies, the reels spinning, the black-and-white images flickering, and the whole class half asleep in the dimness of the lowered blinds.

When the bell rang, everyone stood up at once. The first guy out the door hit the lights, flaring the room into brightness. I stayed in my seat next to the projector, watching the shadows of Romeo and his lover continue to glide across the screen. I was the projectionist, which girls never were in those days; running movie projectors was considered highly technical. But I'd taught myself how to thread one (which wasn't all that different from threading a sewing machine), how to fix it when it jammed, and how to rewind the films when class was over. I shut the projector off and watched the image freeze as the film stopped mid-reel, then turned off the projector light, loosened the film from its wheels and pulleys, and moved the reel to the rewind position. Miss Wilson still sat at her desk staring blindly at the screen above her head.

"Patricia?" she said, as if awakening from a dream. My zombie hands continued their motions. In the hall, lockers banged. It was Friday, last period of the day, so everyone was leaving as fast as they could. I put the reel of film into its metal can and snapped the lid shut, then slowly wheeled the projector to the door. Alone with my idol, I was speechless.

"Patricia," she said again. "I'd like to talk to you a minute."

"Yes," I answered, "of course."

I locked the classroom door so no one could interrupt our conversation, which I imagined would be so intellectually esoteric I'd remember it forever, and went to the front of the room to stand before her desk.

"It's about your paper," she said.

Then I saw she'd been correcting our essays while the movie was running.

"It's really quite remarkable."

For extra credit I'd written about slang as a sort of shanty language that grows up around the established city of the main language. I was daring: I talked about sexual slang, especially about the word "to come," spelled "cum" the way the boys wrote it on the walls, in the gym, and on the door of the girls' bathroom, sometimes along with "fuck" and "cunt."

In gym class, I'd be down on the floor doing those silly leg lifts they made girls do to reduce the size of their hips, and there it would be, carved into the expensive wood floor we weren't even supposed to walk on in our street shoes: CUM. Though I couldn't find this word in my pocket dictionary, I had an idea what the boys meant. I knew the suspense as my fingers danced over my crotch, the waiting and waiting and wondering, is it going to happen this time, is it? And then it comes, yes, there it is.

In the school library I'd found an edition of the *Oxford English Dictionary* in two volumes, with the hand-held viewing glass you had to use because the print was so tiny. Some guy had actually scratched "CUM FUCK" into the plastic handle in minuscule letters right under the name of the optical company. It must have taken him hours.

Why did I assume it was a guy? Because back then I didn't think girls did what I did. No one ever said anything. Girls were there for guys, as the objects of their desire. It seemed strange to me that girls never seemed to like each other much, because they were also the objects of *my* desire, and, I assumed, each other's.

I ran the viewer down the miniature columns of the *O.E.D.* "Cum: Latin, meaning 'together with.' " Yes, that made sense, though I always did it alone, but how much better it would be with another girl like myself. Beneath that was "Cum, obs. form

of come." A verb, cum as in come. Obsolete. Old English. I pictured generations of Anglo-Saxons and their heirs cumming and
cumming. While the rest of the language moved ahead, into
coming, the sex part stayed back in the more primitive, obsolete
form. That was how I pictured it.

I wondered if Miss Wilson was a woman who knew what she
was waiting for, who knew about cumming, who knew in a rush
what that word meant when she passed it on the walls of our
school; a woman who wouldn't cover her mouth and giggle when
she saw it, like the girls did, or run to get the janitor to clean it
off, like Miss Richardson, the Dean of Girls. I guessed that Miss
Wilson might be like me because she was so smart. Most of the
girls I knew, even the other two in the honors English class, just
didn't seem very bright. I had some idea that it might be plain
intelligence that made a person "cum."

In my paper I explicated the verb "to cum," and the noun,
too, because yes, this versatile word had become a noun, though
I didn't know quite how. Once someone dropped part of an ice-
cream bar in the hall under my locker, and wrote "Jim's cum"
with an arrow pointing down at the viscous puddle the melted
ice cream had left. Jim had the locker next to mine, but I never
had a class with him because he was a real genius who took
nothing but advanced chemistry and math.

I had some vague idea that when boys came, something came
out of them. In biology class, this was called the orgasm, or so
I thought. I was remarkably ignorant for someone who knew so
much about language and literature, but there it was: I believed
men had orgasms, which I defined as stuff coming out, but when
women came (which few did), they just got a little wet, like I
did. As usual, men had more of what we had.

Now Miss Wilson was shaking her head. I wasn't worried; my
solid A in her class couldn't be destroyed by one extra-credit
paper.

"It's very good," she said, "but I think you're wrong about several things."

Did she know how wrong? She ran her tongue over her lips
and shuffled the pages.

"I don't think you can assume high school boys are in fact using Old English," she said, laughing. "That's too much. I think they just can't spell. Do you know how often I've seen 'cum' for 'come' in an ordinary misspelled paper?"

I smiled. "They could be teasing you," I suggested.

"Not much chance that would work," she said, and her eyes locked with mine.

She stood up, letting my paper fall back onto the desk, and stretched her arms over her head. Her breasts lifted beneath her thin cotton blouse. I saw for sure that the rumors I'd heard were true: she didn't wear a bra. She was so small and firm you couldn't tell from a distance. Blushing, I lowered my eyes. She put a hand on my shoulder.

"I didn't mean to laugh," she said. "I like the way you think about language, even about what you see written on walls. But I still think 'cum' is more of a cute spelling, like 'thanx' with an 'x,' or dotting your 'i's' with circles. Kids tend to do those things. I always spell it 'come,' the modern way. I'm not sure I believe your theory of sexual 'cumming' dating back to Old English, though it's true most people are so backward about sex it's logical that the words they use for it wouldn't have evolved with the rest of the language. 'Fuck,' as you know, goes straight back to Anglo-Saxon, and so does 'cunt.'"

As we stood side by side I felt something coming to both of us. In my mind, I spelled it the modern way. Come on, I silently prayed. I willed her to move closer to me, and she did.

"Come," I think she whispered, and her lips were on my shoulder next to her hand.

Our arms slid around each other, easy as cream; her mouth on mine had the sharp sweetness of berries. We slid to the floor under the desk as though we'd dissolved to water, our basic body fluid. There we were, liquefied, flowing into each other. The liquefaction of our clothes: Robert Herrick, seventeenth century. I remembered at once everything and nothing; the liquefaction of my brain.

Suddenly I felt her body solidify against me. "I locked the door," I whispered into the short curls above her ear, and felt the tension flow out of her.

"You think of everything," she whispered back. She didn't

know the half of it. My brain and body were both ready to explode.

Her expert fingers slid down my sides, massaging and squeezing my flesh. "So nice," she murmured.

Nice? I thought I was just fat. Guys followed me in the hall, laughing. "Look at Pat's ass," they'd say, coughing and wheezing into their clenched fists.

She was so light on top of me, with her hands underneath me, inside my underpants, on my ass, rippling across my flesh, massaging and teasing. She spread my legs with one hand on my mound, two fingers rubbing between my lips.

Cumming, I thought. It's coming. I felt as though a tidal wave would burst through the classroom door.

Her fingers stopped and the tide receded. I gasped in disappointment.

"Not yet," she said. "I want you to wait for it."

Once again she brought me to the edge of that rough ocean, then stopped.

"Wait," she hissed.

Each time, what was coming felt larger and rounder.

"Do you feel it coming?" she asked. "Patricia, tell me, is it coming?"

"Yes, yes," I panted.

"And not 'cumming' with a 'u'?" she asked.

This was certainly the most vivid grammar lesson I'd ever had.

"No, no, it's round, like an 'o,' " I wailed.

And then it came, like wings flapping high over the sea, then swooping under the waves.

"It came," I laughed. My "a" was round and liquid on my tongue. Not the short hum of "cum," which had no past tense, but "came," as in something that certainly happened.

When my breathing slowed, she moved herself over my body, unbuttoning my blouse and removing my bra so skillfully I hardly felt her. She was like a small animal—a cat or a dog or even a human infant, crawling over my soft belly, which beat like a drum, my thighs, and my breasts, which she took, one after the other, into her generous mouth, kneading them with all her fingers spread as she sucked, like a kitten kneads its mother.

Her skirt was off, and her underpants and shoes. It was so hot neither one of us wore stockings. I reached up inside her blouse to feel her small breasts, the tiny nipples hard as seeds beneath my fingers.

She lowered her wet crotch onto my knee and moved up and down, her lips spread so wide it almost felt like my knee was inside her. I moved it back and forth, following her rhythm. I could feel her cunt start to twitch, but then she stopped.

"Why?" I asked. She sat still on my knee, looking down at me, and put a finger to her lips. A hot rain of sweat dripped from her forehead onto my breasts. I was afraid the windows of the classroom were steaming behind the blinds, and that someone would notice and break in, but the halls were quiet.

" 'Cum,' " she said, "is the short form of the verb, for boys who bounce up and down on you and cum in three minutes. The noun for that is also 'cum'—that's the stuff they spurt out before they know it's arrived. Women are built for the long haul—watch what comes."

She drew the vowels out long and liquid. "Long," she whispered as she moved herself on my knee. "Long and longer. Let me show you how long."

She moved forward then, until her cunt was over my breast. Carefully she lowered herself until her soft wetness surrounded my nipple. I felt something rising in me, coming. My nipple was a hard knot inside her while her pubic hair tickled my breast as she pressed herself upon it. Everything I'd ever felt between my legs was concentrated in one wet, engaged nipple. When I twisted beneath her she held me firm, not stopping now but riding up and down on the saddle her weight had made of my breast. Both of us were hanging from the same wave, suspended over the ocean.

Whenever I took my breast in my hand to push it deeper inside her, she put her hands firmly on my shoulders and murmured, "Wait, wait."

"I can't!" I nearly screamed. She put one hand over my mouth and then screamed herself, so loud I was sure every teacher and hall monitor would be instantly upon us. But over an hour had passed since I'd locked that door, so the school was deserted.

I felt a throbbing in my breast, and an echoing pulse between my legs. I was wet all over my chest, as though my breast had leaked. My teacher had fallen forward on me so that my nose was in her navel. I reached beneath her to wipe the clear, sticky liquid off my breast. What was it? Did it come from me or from her? Was it what the boys called "cum"?

She pushed herself up and sat beside me. "See what can come if you wait long enough?" she said, wiping my breast with one hand. "I don't always do this, but it's wonderful when it comes."

"Is all that from you?" I asked.

She looked into my eyes. "It can come from women, too, you know, from deep inside." When she brushed her fingers across my lips, I tasted her rich sour cream.

" 'Cum,' " she said, her "u" short and clipped, "is for boys who never want to wait. We come, we arrive, and come again," she murmured in her round voice, moving her hands down my body, expanding with her fingers that timeless afternoon, that lesson in the grammar of the body.

We were in no hurry.

Stacy Reed

Night Talk

Madison had gotten her tiny hands on Jack's cuffs again. She held them near her ear. Clickclickclickclickclick. They sounded like glass or ice.

"Tonight?" Madison asked.

"Tonight we are going to sleep."

"I'm not sleepy."

"But I am." Jack padded around to his side and eased between the flannel sheets. "Tell me a story."

Madison took up his challenge. She had been carefully escalating their bedtime ritual. "You want to hear a true one tonight?"

"Madison," Jack gently chastised. He had taken to using her name casually. A command, a plea, a silly comfort noise.

"Mace and Danny came over last week," she began.

"Who are they?"

"Friends. Like you."

"Right," Jack quickly conceded. "We are friends. I don't want to get involved right now. It's not you, I just need to remain autonomous—"

"You're obviously on your own," Madison interrupted. She wouldn't be snared in his dramatics. Madison realized then that when they finally parted, decency would compel Jack to smear the blood around. He had not yet learned that abandoning a person takes nothing. Any threadbare phrase would do.

The inevitable grated at her, so she hollowed out a nook between Jack's arm and chest. She furrowed her brows at his milky skin and swallowed the impulse to desecrate it with hickeys.

"Madison? Tell me your story."

"All right. Mace and Danny had come over to study *Frankenstein* for our English exam."

"What were you wearing?" Jack interrupted. He was the most aesthetically inclined man Madison had ever fucked.

"I was wearing sweats when they came in, but Mace asked me to change. He told me to put on that white eyelet gown you gave me. He and Danny were in smoking jackets. They had gotten this wacky idea that we'd all do better if we really got into the material. You know, kind of study in the novelist's own style."

"Uh-huh."

"So I changed and made jasmine tea. Mace had brought chocolates and oranges. We lit every candle I had and then sat on the rug in a nest of books and food.

"Since we were playing at romance, I had Mace lie down with his head in my lap. I fed him slices of orange while Daniel read us the important passages. Every time he finished a paragraph, I rewarded him with a chocolate.

"We studied that way for a while until only wrappings and peels were left. Then Danny read us some notes reporting that Shelley and her consorts prided themselves on their liberal sexuality. So Mace up and says, 'Why not take off our clothes?' And he strips."

"Not one to miss an opportunity, is he?" Jack asked.

"Are you?" Madison countered.

Jack kissed Madison behind her ears, smirking into her charcoal curls. "But this was all to enhance your studying."

"Presumably."

"You and Dan were still dressed?"

"Uh-huh. But soon we began to feel left out. Mace was having more fun. So I told Danny to undress me.

"The buttons on my gown ran from the collar down to the hem. He stood behind me and started at the top. I could feel his

cock straining at my ass through his trousers. He kept asking me
if he was doing it right, placing his mouth close enough to my
ear for me to feel his lips moving. His breath on my neck made
my nipples hard. He began rubbing them gently with the insides
of his wrist.

"Mace knelt in front of me and started unbuttoning where
Danny had stopped. His fingers against my stomach tickled.
Once he got to my panties, he forgot to keep going. He let his
hands rest against my thighs and bent his head toward my pussy.
While Danny was still fondling my nipples, Mace started kissing
my panties. He ran his tongue under the elastic and cuddled his
whole head against my crotch. He went on and on like this until
I asked him to stop. I thought I was going to fall over."

Madison caught Jack squeezing his balls. He met her gaze. He
was brave and intent, like an enthralled child. Madison smiled.
She loved to watch him. His Santa Claus eyes looked foreign
against his biting features. She traced them with one finger as
she talked so he could better hold himself quiet. Jack knew better than to interrupt these stories.

"Mace started kissing my pussy through my panties," Madison
continued. "They were soon soaked through with my wetness
and his saliva. Danny uncupped my tits and shoved his hand into
the back of my panties. He reached around with his other hand
and pulled my panties up completely so that I was exposed to
Mace's scrutiny.

"Mace looked up at me and asked if he could play with it. He
put one finger inside me and prodded and poked until he found
my G-spot. He pressed on it while Danny's finger slid quickly in
and out of my ass. He leaned into my pussy and began kissing
it very softly. After caressing every inch of my lips, his tongue
began massaging my clit. His circles got faster and smaller and
I felt an orgasm welling up inside of me, but just as I was about
to go over the edge, Danny said, 'Slow down, man. I can feel her
ass muscles tightening up. She's about to come.' So Mace went
back to his slow deep sucking and kissing. I tried to keep quiet
and still, I tried to come without their noticing, but every time
I was about to, my ass muscles clenched involuntarily, and

Danny told Mace to ease up. I knew the only way I was ever going to get to come was if I got one of their cocks into me."

Madison suddenly felt overwhelmed. She let her heavy lids fall and ground her pelvis into Jack's favorite pillow. "When Mace started flicking my clit again," she continued, "I begged him to put his cock in me. Danny said he wanted to put his in too. I thought he meant my mouth, and I nearly squealed when he sat down on the sofa, pulled his pants and briefs down to his ankles, and told me to ease his cock into my asshole. I wanted to shove it in, but Danny made me go slow because he was worried I'd hurt myself. It took about five minutes. When I had him completely in me, Mace knelt in front of the sofa on a pillow and put his cock into me too.

"I started to giggle because I wasn't sure how we could move with two cocks in me like that. But Mace told Danny to hold me around the tummy while he held the small of my back. Then they both started moving me up and down their cocks. It was a little clumsy at first, but they soon matched each other's rhythm. I felt like I was flying. I let my body totally relax as they lifted me up and down their pricks."

Madison faltered. She wondered whether she ought to describe their cocks to Jack. Men were so weird about their dicks. She loved Jack's; it was, in fact, exactly the size of her favorite vibrator. Danny's was perfect for ass-fucking: small. But Mace's was as thick as her delicate brown wrist.

Jack must have thought her mouth was dry because he handed her their bedside water glass. "Go on," he urged sweetly.

"Where was I?"

"You were flying, I believe."

"Oh yes. I wanted to come so bad by now I could have cried. I begged them not to stop. I knew I was going to start coming if they kept it up, and I started moaning. I worried they might slow down to tease me again, but I couldn't keep quiet.

"They started talking to each other about how they thought I was about to come all over their cocks. They were being way too polite. I had to tell them to talk filthy to me. They started out pretty tame, but they ended up whispering things like 'Come on, bitch, come for us. You know you want to. Let's hear you come.

You like having two cocks in you, don't you? You like getting fucked by two dicks at once, you slut. Oh, you're such a little whore. What a sweet little snatch you have. Your ass is so hot and snug. You better come soon, bitch, 'cause I can't hold back much longer.' Once they started talking like this, I totally lost it. I came so hard and long. I guess my pussy and ass clenching around their cocks sent them over the edge, too. They both had come by the time my orgasm subsided."

Madison was jolted from her reverie by Jack's finger working its way up her ass. She had almost forgotten him.

"What happened next?" he prodded.

"Isn't that enough?"

"Uh-uh, I want to hear everything."

"I took a shower and the guys ordered pizza."

"That was out of period," Jack said.

"I thought the very same; after they had eaten, I suggested studying, but Mace and Danny started going on again about how good my pussy felt and how tight my ass was. Soon they both had hard-ons."

"Were you turned on too?"

"Yeah, but I didn't want to let them know it. I wanted to mess with them for a while. I told them to stand up about a foot apart. Then I ordered them to look directly at each other and not let their eyes wander, no matter what. I knelt between them.

"It got me hot to imagine how deliciously awkward Mace and Danny must have felt. Two straight boys staring bravely at each other while a girl they knew only vaguely knelt between their engorged cocks. I bet that turns you on too."

"You know I love your taste for atrocity," Jack conceded.

"I told them to keep their eyes open and tell me how they felt at each moment. Then I began sucking Mace's balls."

"Did you press on that little spot right behind them?" Jack asked. "That's my favorite."

"You don't want to spoil the plot, now."

"Never," he laughed. "Tell your story." Jack pulled Madison on top of him and ground his cock into her.

"I thought you were exhausted."

"I *am*." He yawned theatrically. "You better tell me what happens next before I fall asleep on you."

"Well, Mace did exactly as he was told."

"What did he say?"

Madison giggled. "First he said, 'Oh Jesus, I'm gonna fail English.'"

Madison dragged in her breath and tried to send up an accurate delivery. "Then he said, 'Oh, girl, you really know how to make me want you. My balls are starting to tighten up. Your mouth feels all slick and spongy. I hope you start licking my cock soon.'"

"What did Danny say?"

"Danny begged me to do him too. But I told him to shut up and wait his turn."

"How vicious." Jack grinned.

"I made him listen to Mace describe how good I was making his cock feel while he waited."

"And what did Mace say after you started playing with it?"

"Let's see . . . 'Lick my cock all over, baby. Yeah. That's it. I love the way you hold my balls for me. They feel so safe. You cradle them just right. Oh god yeah work your finger up my ass. Uh-huh. You got it nice and wet first. What a sweet girl. Ooo, not so fast baby. Yeah like that. Put it in your mouth now. I need to get inside. Come on. Please, baby. I can't stand it. Come on, bitch, suck me. Oh yeah. Oh yeah. Ah Jesus. You really know how to suck cock, don't you, girl? You can really take it in. Follow your mouth with your hand now. It's so slippery. You squeeze just right. Oooo. Make it last, baby. Slow down. Slow down now. Yeah. Lick my balls some more. Mmm-uhm. That's it, girl. Uhhh. Get your hand real wet and run it up and down the shaft. Oh god. That's good. That's how I like it. You're a good girl. You're gonna make me come, aren't you baby? Oh yeah. Come on. Put it in your mouth again. I want you to swallow it for me. Suck it, whore. Oh yeah. Make me come now, bitch. Harder. Harder.'"

Madison took Jack's index finger into her mouth.

"Then what did he say?"

"Then," Madison smiled, "he didn't say anything at all."

"Madison!" Jack slapped her ass playfully. "What a nasty girl you are."

"I know. My name is Madison Vasquez and I am a sex addict."

"The first step is admitting you have a problem."

"The second?"

"Telling me more."

"And corrupt you with this filth?"

"You need to work through it."

"Such an altruist! Well, Mace had to brace himself against Danny while he came. When I looked up, I saw that he had collapsed onto Danny's shoulder.

" 'You stopped looking at Danny,' I said. He told me he was sorry, but that wasn't good enough. I asked him what he thought he should do to make up for it."

"What did he say?"

"He told me he would help me get Danny off."

"Mace said that?" Jack scooted up against his pillows.

"If you had seen how pretty Danny's cock was, you would have wanted to help too. His balls had already drawn up and little beads of semen were dripping off the end. Besides, we were still honoring the Romantics' daring sensibilities."

"Oh yeah. I had almost forgotten about those."

"Well, Mace hadn't. He knelt behind Danny and started stroking his ass while I kissed the inside of his thighs. Before I had even touched his cock, Danny started to moan."

"My god. What was Mace doing to him?"

"While I had been kissing him," Madison explained eagerly, "Mace had spread Danny's cheeks and was licking his asshole. I reached my finger behind his balls and felt Mace's tongue darting across it like it was a girl's clit. It was so slippery that I just eased my finger in and out while Mace kept tonguing around the edge."

"Then you went back to sucking his balls," Jack offered.

"Yeah. Just like I suck yours."

"But you weren't mean. You didn't make him wait too long. When he started to beg you took his cock in your mouth. You put it in all the way and took it to the back of your throat. You didn't move, you just held it in your mouth for a while."

Madison took up the thread. "But then I moved up to the head and sucked on it while I tugged gently at his balls. Before long he laid his hand on the back of my hair and started pushing against my lips in earnest. I could tell he really needed to come."

"So do I."

"But this was supposed to be your bedtime story, Jack. Aren't you ready to go to sleep?" Madison reached to turn off the light.

Jack grabbed her arm. "Hey!"

"But baby, you're so tired."

"Don't tease. Sophie used to tease."

Madison rolled onto her tummy and let her lips brush the head of Jack's cock. She thought of Mace. She thought of Danny. She flicked her tongue across his opening and thought of her other lovers. Jack pushed himself into her mouth and she thought of all the men who had found solace there.

Madison loved nothing more than giving head. It made her feel secure for a little while. She knew that as long as her mouth held his cock, Jack needed her. Her lips held him captive. His cock was heavy with blood. No man would float away while she was sucking him.

Jack wasn't thinking about Sophie anymore, but Madison was. Sophie was Jack's excuse. He thought he had to get over her. I need time to recover, he would say. Whenever he spoke that way, Madison wanted nothing more than to say, I won't do those things. Let me hold you. Be my baby. I will never, never leave.

But Madison's sense of decorum kept her silent. The dignity she had assumed would not let her succumb to the banalities of passion. Neither would it let her haggle in flea markets or ask for autographs.

Madison's most biting desire was thus her most humiliating secret. She dreamed that Jack would dissolve her identity, crush her faults, distill her down to a small pure lump he could slip into his pocket with his keys. She wanted him to fall on her and eat until all that remained was her hair and her rings.

Madison swallowed back her longing like she had swallowed Mace's insistent semen. When Jack blundered into Sophie, all Madison could allow herself was, "Yes, baby, I know, I understand." Then she would spread her legs to him. This was all the comfort he could accept. It was all she would spare.

"Open your legs for me."

Madison drew her lips up the length of Jack's cock, sucked the head for a few moments, and released him. Then she did as she was told.

"Oh yes," Jack sighed. "What a beautiful little pussy you have. May I kiss it?"

"Handcuff me first," Madison pleaded. He had been promising for a week.

Clickclickclickclickclick. Her hands froze to the wrought iron behind her.

"Who am I tonight?" he murmured into her pussy.

"Daddy."

He couldn't help laughing. "That's sick!"

"I know, Daddy. You should spank me."

Jack drew himself up onto one elbow and began massaging her clit. It pushed out from its hood to meet his fingertips. He liked how it was hard and soft at the same time.

"Now why would a good daddy ever spank his little girl?"

"For fucking two boys at once!"

"That was naughty," Jack agreed with mock disapproval.

"Yes, Daddy. Spank me, please."

Jack hooked Madison's knees behind his arm and pulled her legs up. Her thighs were now on the same plane as her stomach and her ass was bared to Jack's fancy.

He nudged his tongue between her lips until it met with her clit. She felt it rest there as he positioned himself. Then he began to let his fingers caress her Renaissance ass. Just when she was afraid she'd start giggling, he brought his hand down hard against her right cheek.

"Daddy," Madison ventured. "Would you suck my nipples please?"

Jack brushed his lips against Madison's nipple. It tightened against his chapped lip, and he began teasing it lightly with his tongue. Madison tilted her pelvis hopefully. Her clit throbbed with blood.

"Daddy?" Madison crooned.

"Hmm?"

"Play with my pussy, Daddy. Just for a little." Madison sighed with gratitude when she felt Jack manipulating her clitoris. She started to moan. The handcuffs cut into her wrists.

"Come for me," Jack encouraged. He rubbed her more vigorously. "Go ahead, baby—oh yeah. That's it. Stay with it, baby. That's my girl ... Madison ... Oh no, baby. Don't stop now. Keep coming for me. Don't you still feel a little tense up in your pussy? Don't my fingers feel good? Oh yeah. I knew they did."

After Jack had licked the last of Madison's come from his fingers, he asked ritualistically, "How did you like it?"

"I didn't think I was going to come twice," she said. "You can unlock me now."

Jack complied, rotating her wrists slowly. "Don't make me start liking you."

Madison took his familiar prick in her hand. "I won't."

Cecilia Tan

Porn Flicks

The first porn flick I ever watched was with the first woman I ever dated. I know, I know, you'd think to look at me now, perched on my bike in my leathers, that I'd been licking pussy all my life. But not so long ago I had just one foot out of the closet and was living a sheltered life. Mona taught me the right way to appreciate porn movies, among other things.

I met her at a bar. Not a dyke bar, just a regular smoky loud rock and roll club where my friend Derby's band was playing. I first caught sight of Mona in the back of the crowd, talking with some other women who hooted out comments toward the stage from time to time. Derby's band wasn't that popular, so the crowd was thin. I wandered by, trying to get a good look without being too obvious.

She wore all black, biker boots, with a loop of dog chain hanging from her neck. Now that I think of it, that's how most people in those bars dressed, but something about the way she stood or the look in her eyes tipped me off, I don't know—I wanted to go home with her the minute I saw her.

It wouldn't have been the first time I wanted to: I had been an avowed bisexual for years. That is to say, it had been at least six years since I told my parents I might bring home someone of the same gender for Thanksgiving. But I never had. I'd had my crushes, my flirtations, my passing acquaintances—but I just didn't know how to meet women.

I still hold that the only way to meet women is through Fate. And that night Fate was with me. I went backstage after the show to congratulate Derby and the band on another searing rendition of "The Brady Bunch Theme," and there she was. A friend of hers was a friend of Derby's too, and that's just the way Fate works. Mona and I talked at the bar until they threw us out and then we ended up at her place.

She lived in a one-room studio apartment, which means that the kitchen and the bathroom are only a few convenient steps away from the bed. We spent all the next day in that bed, getting up only to answer the various calls of nature and to pay the pizza delivery man. After the workout she gave me, it was heaven.

At first I hadn't been real keen to reveal that I'd never slept with a woman before. But after I found out that she'd never been on a motorcycle, nothing was held back. She grinned evilly as she pressed me down into her futon. "I'll be happy to teach you everything I know. But you have to promise . . . promise that you'll do everything I say from now to sunrise."

I promised. She kissed me, her smile wide open, and hugged me. I remember thinking, wow, women are so curvy.

She was, as she put it, a big girl. I loved the shape of her hips, her jiggly thighs, her mounds of breasts; I couldn't wait to get my hands on them.

"Strip for me," she said, lying back against the pillows.

I stood up, my striptease abbreviated by the fact that I was wearing a one-piece catsuit and not a lot else. I stood in front of her naked, and turned myself around for her to see.

"Not bad. Now come here."

She enveloped me in softness, her hands like silk all over my arms, my back, my breasts. She felt me all over like a veterinarian would a cat.

"I like your nipples," she said, circling them with her fingers so they stood at attention. "Nice and dark." She slid her hands down over my pubic hair.

"Now let's see what you like." She searched over the hood of my clit, so hot it felt like it was burning. As her fingers slid down into the wetness, her eyes lit up. I gasped and clutched at her as she put two fingers deep inside me.

"Ooh, you like penetration." She wiped her hand on a bedside towel and pulled my mouth to her breast. She coached me very strictly on nipples.

"No teeth to start with," she said. "And don't suck too hard. Now, about your tongue . . ." Near the end I bit her and she gasped. "Hey, you promised."

"I promised to do what you said, but not to not do what you didn't."

"Smart ass. For that you get the Het Chick Torture. Stay right where you are." She stood on the mattress and clicked on the television set in the alcove at the foot of the bed.

"What's the Het Chick Torture?" My stomach filled with butterflies.

"You'll see." She put a tape into the VCR. "Here are the rules. We're going to watch a het porn flick. Every time a woman gets something in her cunt, you get something in yours. Every time someone comes, you have to come."

If I had to tell you the plot of the film today, I couldn't, but it involved several men and women in various combinations in various rooms of a house. Maybe there was no plot and it just involved the same actors and actresses over and over.

I was surprised to find out that the film was much more comical than I'd thought it would be. I had always heard, of course, that porn videos were dark, evil, misogynistic affairs of a seedy underworld. But then again, I had always heard that lesbians were women who really wanted to be men—and we know how well that story holds up. So much for stereotypes and assumptions. This movie was silly; in one scene a guy getting sucked off by the pool fell into the water when he came.

And the women in this thing, I had to admit, weren't as bad as I'd feared. Sure, they all had bigger tits than their waists would suggest, but I decided I liked a lot of tits, especially Mona's. In fact, I decided that from their necks to their ankles, all the women in the film were damn hot, if only they'd lose the stupid shoes, the makeup and the Farrah Fawcett hair. At least they looked like they were enjoying themselves.

In the first sex scene the blonde and her boyfriend did it in about ten different positions, none of which I had ever seen before, much less tried in the privacy of my own home. They had no attention span, constantly switching from one position to another, with her sucking him in between. I started keeping my head near Mona's crotch, since at unexpected moments the actress would suddenly start gobbling. I would bury my face in Mona's pubic hair, my tongue learning the way through her folds better and better every time. With my face there I couldn't watch the screen, so Mona had to say "Fingers," when it came time to put her fingers inside me. For a long time the couple fucked on the floor of their living room and I floated away while Mona pumped me and tickled my G-spot. We both laughed when the guy's roommate came in, and with a shrug of his shoulders threw off his clothes and joined in. The actress began sucking him without climbing off the other guy.

"Put your own fingers in," Mona said, pushing my head down between her knees.

I moaned while I licked her. I was close; it was hard not to make myself come. But I knew if I was going to come once for every orgasm in the film I had better save them up. Lucky for me, while my head was down there the first guy came all over the actress's back.

"Come now," Mona said, luxuriating underneath my tongue. My nostrils filled with her salty smell, I came, my noises muffled by her muff.

The next big scene involved the women in the bathroom. Mona pulled me up beside her saying, "Watch this, you may learn something."

The two women rubbed each other's breasts, sucked each other, fingered each other. Mona put her fingers inside me whenever one of the actresses did it to the other, and told me to do it myself whenever they were doing themselves. Like the male/female couple, they switched positions and activities faster than a cable TV junkie switches channels. Now they were cunt to cunt, bumping and grinding against each other.

"Will we do that?" I asked.

"Maybe later, if you're good," she said, kissing me on top of the head. Now they were sixty-nine, side by side.

"That?" I asked.

"Definitely," she answered. The women came simultaneously and she made me come twice in a row, not letting me pause in between to catch my breath or rest my clit.

"Why is the music so cheesy?" I asked later, during the big orgy scene in which every actor and actress was involved, and the cuts from one shot to another were fast and furious. By then I had come about seven or eight times. I was on top of her, my head between her legs, pausing in my licking to talk.

"Who knows?" she said. "If you wrote good soundtracks, would you sell them to porn flicks?"

"Ah," I agreed, letting my tongue fly. By the time the credits rolled we had forgotten the game and were just licking and fingering and sucking each other as much as we could.

Two days later I got a membership at the local video store. And I took Mona for her first motorcycle ride. Neither of us has been the same since.

Jo Manning

❧❧❧

By the Rivers of Babylon

Musky sweet, pungent, the bar of hand-milled sandalwood soap released its fragrant oils as I unwrapped it from its bed of crinkled brown tissue. Amazing! After all these years, the smell still brought forth memories. I laid it against my cheek and closed my eyes.

The Government Sandalwood Oil Factory in Mysore, India, sold its wares in a large, airy room redolent with the pervasive scent of sweet heartwood. Displayed on oddly bare-looking wooden shelves were vials of the oil itself, bars of soap, incense, sachets, perfume in glass bottles, hand-carved beads and other jewelry.

I inspected them all languidly that morning, like every morning I had so far spent in India: hot, indolent, tropical hours, full of nothing to do. Jake had his research and writing; I had Jeff to look after—no, not really—Ayah looked after Jeff. I looked after myself, gave orders to the cook, the gardener, the *dhobi* who did our laundry.

I was bored to distraction.

Mysore was a small, quiet Indian city. It had been a princely state before independence, ruled over by a fabulously wealthy maharajah. The south of India is beautiful and green, blessed with abundant wildlife and lushly forested. We were lucky to be here rather than in the dry desert city of Hyderabad, another former princely seat in central India, or in noisy Bombay, crowded with the dregs of piteous humanity, oppressively humid. Delhi could be cold in winter; Calcutta was a mess, by any objective standard. The only place I would rather have been was Kashmir, in the Hindu Kush, a Himalayan paradise to the north.

Or home. Yes, I would rather have been home. But I'd come, in the wake of my best-selling novelist husband, Jake Fuller, who was here gathering material for his next blockbuster, trailing our three-year-old son behind me, hoping to save my marriage.

After six months, the marriage was no closer to being saved. And having nothing to do was driving me out of my mind. I knew no one here—few Europeans or Americans passed through—and Indians were private people, shy of strangers. So I did nothing. I was simply here, waiting my husband out.

It had been 1,100 days since we had last made love.

Jake hadn't touched me since Jeffie's birth. After a normal vaginal delivery a woman is supposed to abstain from sexual intercourse for six weeks, to give those sensitive, birth-traumatized parts a chance to heal. When I came back from the hospital with Jeffie, I discovered that Jake had moved all his things out of our bedroom and was sleeping on the convertible sofa in the living room. He never moved back. Worse, he claimed he was impotent.

I was mystified, then hurt, then angry, pleading with him to see his internist, a psychiatrist, anyone who could help. His retort was that it was his problem and he would deal with it himself; he made it clear that he wanted to hear nothing from me on the subject. I retreated in pain, lavishing the attention that was once his on Jeffie.

Result: one extremely spoiled son. Poor Ayah! He gave her a run for the few rupees we paid her each month.

Now he had broken away from her grasp and was hurtling through the showroom of the sandalwood factory. Terrific! He'd collided with a tall stranger whose back was to me, and had conked himself on the head. He let out a loud, peevish wail. I sighed, gesturing to Ayah to pick him up while I apologized to the man, who'd been almost knocked over by the surprise missile attack of a three-year-old—I had to admit it—a three-year-old brat.

"I'm very sorry. Please accept my apologies. Jeffie gets a little rambunctious sometimes."

The young man turned. He was broad-shouldered, handsome, dark-haired, and sported a dapper mustache. "Maybe you should carry him around in a cage, madam," he replied, smiling. "But, no harm done. And . . . my condolences."

I winced at his cutting reply. Some people clearly did not like children. Well, I understood. I was rapidly becoming one of those people myself.

"Do you know where I could get that cage—cheap?" I asked him.

Surprised by my rejoinder he began to laugh, shaking his head. "If I knew, I'd be glad to buy one for you myself." He extended his hand. "Tony Borden. And you are . . . ?"

"Camilla. Camilla Fuller. Nice to meet you, Tony, and to hear those American vowels. Not too many of us pass through this town." His hand was warm and he had a good, firm grip. I liked that in a man. With a pang, I realized how long it had been since Jake had even touched me. How infinitely long it had been since . . . I let the thought die, stillborn.

Tony pointed in Ayah's direction. "Can your servant deal with your child so I can buy you a cup of coffee? I'm beginning to miss American English too."

I nodded, walking over to Ayah and instructing her, in my basic untutored memsahib Kannada, to take Jeffie home, feed him, and put him down for a nap. Let her deal with it. She took off on her slightly bowed legs (a relic of childhood rickets? I'd often wondered), the end of her ragged green cotton sari trailing in the dust of the factory floor. Jeffie was still crying. What a terrific mother—I could care less.

We walked to the Kwality Restaurant and Coffee Shop, a few doors down from the factory on the dusty main road, and ordered steaming cups of frothy sweet Mysore coffee. Chai is the drink of choice everywhere else in India, but coffee plantations ring the low hills surrounding Mysore, and their beans are among the best and most highly prized in the world.

In the background a tape was blasting out the latest Boney M. hit, "Rivers of Babylon." The popular black singing group—we heard this song everywhere and saw posters of the two women and one man in all the shops—was either African or British, depending on who you asked. When Boney M. sang "Babylon," it sounded as though they were saying "Bobby-lon." Interesting, and annoying, too, because it was one of those tunes that stuck in your mind.

I caught myself humming it several times a day. It tended to sneak up on your mind when it was otherwise unoccupied, which, in my case, was most of the time. *By the rivers of Bobby-lon . . . where we sat down . . . Oh, yah, yah, yah . . . and there we wept, when we remembered Zion.*

I sipped at the foam on my hot coffee and studied Tony Borden. He was a fox. Or was it just because I was sex-starved? I had to face it, I was embarrassingly horny. No, he really was a very handsome man, around my own age—thirty-one—or younger. He was taking a full, detailed inventory of me, too. The interest in his dark eyes was beginning to warm me up. I shifted in the hard wooden seat and parted my thighs slightly. I felt moist where I hadn't been moist for a very long time. Was it the humidity? It was disconcerting.

"Why are you here, Tony?" I asked.

"I was just about to ask you the same thing, Mrs. Fuller. I'm an architect on a Fulbright travel grant. I got here a few days ago to teach a three-week seminar at the college on Indian architecture and its influence on the western tradition. I work in New York City for Berrill Skidings, the firm that did the Paxmore Building at Battery Park City. Perhaps you know it?"

The Paxmore was a controversial office building that had raised quite a few of the more conservative eyebrows in our own Gotham City. I personally thought it was one of the most innovative structures I had seen in a long while. At nightfall, the setting sun blazes over its taut aluminum skin in dark purples and orange; sunrises are even more spectacular, gold striking the building in an epiphany of shuddering light.

"Yes," I answered. "I really love it. We live near there, in an old loft building in TriBeCa. I saw the Paxmore going up. Did you have anything to do with its concept?"

"A little." He shrugged modestly. "It was the first project I worked on when I joined the firm, just after I graduated from Harvard."

Oh, dear, he was young! The Paxmore had been up a year, under construction for almost two. Even given the extended period of study the discipline of architecture demands, Tony Borden wouldn't see thirty-anything for a while. A baby. A damned good-looking baby. I sighed.

"Pardon?" He'd heard my too-audible sigh. I had to watch it; I was alone too much, sighing out loud, talking to myself.

"Nothing," I lied, trying to cover up, "I was just wondering what time it was."

"Time for me to take you to lunch. Is the food here any good? Or can I treat you to a meal at my hotel, The Majestic?"

I admired his decisiveness. It was an admirable trait in one so young. He seemed used to organizing, planning, giving orders. He certainly could give me a few, I fantasized. Yeah, I could take quite a bit from him. I wondered, rigidly willing my gaze not to seek out the area of his crotch, how much he had to give. Stop it, girl! I admonished myself. Stop it before you make yourself crazy.

Recovering my equilibrium and responding quickly, pushing aside my hot, naughty thoughts, I answered. "They have good Chinese food here, steaks, too. However, there are a few items on the menu I would watch out for—for instance, their cream of chicken and corn soup tastes and smells like freshly squeezed piss. But, otherwise, it's okay."

Tony chuckled. "I like you, Camilla Fuller. What in hell is a sharp girl like you doing in Mysore?"

"You've heard of Jake Fuller, the novelist?"

He nodded. "Who hasn't?"

"Well, Jake's my husband. He's here to research a book about the glorious and colorful last days of the former maharajah, his conflict with the British, his eccentricities, and so on. He spends a lot of time in the archives of the old royal palace and is actively seeking out people to interview who remember those days of glory and empire. I had the choice of staying home and perhaps advancing my own career—I used to edit young-adult fiction at Dell—or coming here and going crazy. As you can so clearly see, I made the wiser decision."

I was being blunt and reckless in my speech and manner with a stranger, a man I didn't know at all, but funny things happen to you when you're living in a Third World country, where so much that goes on seems bizarre and foreign to your very nature. You tend to confide in anyone who sounds as though he or she could be someone you knew from back home. It was happening with me and Tony Borden, except, of course, he had not been in India long enough to foolishly confide his deepest secrets to me.

"Jake Fuller." Tony couldn't seem to get over the connection. A new look came into his eyes. It does tend to floor everyone, my being Jake Fuller's wife. "I read one of his books, the first one, I guess, *Savage Sinner.*" He shook his head in amazement. "All that graphic sex and gratuitous violence. I guess it sells a lot of copies, but he must be hell to live with."

I traced two esses absentmindedly on the scarred wooden tabletop as I replied to his frank comment. "He saves up all the violence for his books. The sex, too." I looked steadily into Tony Borden's appraising eyes, blatantly spelling it out for him. He was a smart boy. I wagered he would catch on quickly, but the thought both terrified and excited me. I couldn't blame the moisture between my upper thighs on the humidity anymore.

"Lunch at The Majestic sounds fine to me," I heard myself saying in a voice almost alien—low-pitched, husky, last heard in Jake Fuller's bed in the early days of our once sexually exciting marriage.

The Majestic Hotel is at least a hundred years old. It's small, in a style I'd loosely describe as Victorian Gingerbread, with its many cornices and pillars painted white. It's so airy and spacious on the ground floor of The Majestic that the room seems to float and shimmer in the hot sun. The few tables in the dining area are set apart; waiters and majordomos hover everywhere you look. The tablecloths and napkins are stiffly starched, and someone had taken the trouble to fold the napkins into fanciful shapes resembling birds or flowers.

Our lunch was light: masala dosai, those south Indian pancakes made of sour, fermented whole wheat batter stuffed with hot, spicy vegetables, a side order of dal and chutneys, and two large glasses of chilled Eagle brand beer. The icy liquid quenched my thirst but could not cool me off.

Tony Borden invited me to his room after lunch. "But I have no etchings to show you," he warned, smiling. He had a nice smile, good teeth, and a very sexy mustache. Ever since I fell in love with Clark Gable at age eleven watching the uncut version of *Gone With the Wind* on television, I've been a sucker for a man with a dark, full mustache. What followed was inevitable.

Looking back on my state of mind that day, I can justify everything that happened. I was bored; I hated my life; I was fed up with my child; I had been roundly rejected by my husband. Tony Borden was tall, dark, handsome, and, best of all, interested. There was no way I could have changed any of it. Nor would I have wanted to.

Tony latched the door to his suite, locking it securely, and took off all my clothes, then all of his. They made a small, soft heap on the polished hardwood floor of his bedroom. "You're beautiful," he told me.

Maybe not beautiful enough for Jake Fuller, but, yes, I still had enough self-confidence to take pride in my looks—my long, curly hair and my small but curvaceous body with great legs. I get my fiery auburn hair and green eyes from my Irish parents.

Meanwhile, I was having my fill looking at the unclothed Tony Borden. My wanton gaze devoured him, inch by promising inch. His crotch area was no disappointment, not in the least. And growing even more interesting by the second. "Well-hung" didn't begin to describe the majesty of his groin. I trembled at the thought of all that tantalizingly engorged flesh inside my body, those heavy balls batting and rubbing between my legs. Subconsciously, I was already opening to receive him, so excited I could barely stand.

I thought Tony would take me to bed immediately, before my

trembling legs gave out, but he had other ideas. Interesting ones. He pressed me against the wall of the bedroom, raising my legs so that they encircled his waist. With his two strong hands he shifted my buttocks and slowly, teasingly, rubbed my crotch against his hot, stunningly erect cock. His mouth found mine and our two eager tongues grappled wetly and fiercely; he won, swallowing me up entirely. I had not been kissed that way in a long, long time.

We didn't say a word. Our eyes, fixed on each other, said it all. His were smoldering, passionate, heavy with desire, as he lifted my hips and impaled me on his stiff shaft, penetrating me to the very core of my being, taking possession as if it were his right. I cried out with the suddenness, the wonder of it, but he hadn't hurt me. I had the fleeting image of a hot knife cutting through butter; I was the butter, melting on impact.

Tony was in complete control of the situation, watching my face intently as he lifted my hips up slowly and brought them down in a rhythm that increased in tempo, his tempo. He moved away from me a bit so he could lick my aching nipples with his warm, wet tongue. Ecstatic to be brought back to life after such a long, cold hiatus, my nipples became as rock hard as his cock. Waves of feeling ran down my torso, from my breasts to my cunt, hard tingles of excitement I could barely contain. My long pent-up passion rocked me from within. I felt as if I was falling into a void, my only reality the strong arms and legs of this exciting stranger.

I swooned in ecstasy and started to come. I came, and came, and couldn't stop coming. My hands, in a frenzy, clawed at his shoulders and raked his broad back. And still I came, and came, and never wanted to stop coming. I trembled and shook and couldn't stop, not even when, finally, he did. He held me close and tight as the last wave crashed over me and I cried out against his hand cupping my mouth, fulfilled, filled to bursting. I had waited such a long time.

When it was over, I wept with relief and abandon.

Tony Borden cradled me in his arms and carried me to his bed. The linen sheets were cool against my perspiration-filmed back. I sighed contentedly. It was so peaceful, so quiet. I dozed for a few minutes.

My lover woke me. Balanced on one elbow, he was licking a long, wet, sensuous trail from my throat to my belly. He looked up at me and smiled. I smiled back, lazily, shifting slightly, raising my knees.

"Don't stop," I whispered, my voice a soft purr.

He needed very little direction. Grinning mischievously, he teasingly licked my belly button, causing my stomach muscles to tighten involuntarily.

"Oh," I whispered, half to myself, "that feels so good."

His talented tongue continued south, slowly, snail-like, through my nest of tight red curls. Suddenly, the tip of his tongue flickered against a small, sensitive nubbin of flesh. I jumped.

"Easy, easy," he cautioned, his free hand stroking my breast, causing the nipple to stand to attention. He shifted to my other breast and did the same. I was quivering in anticipation. His mouth, his hands, his cock, all of him, were sources of immeasurable delight. This time, in contrast to our initial fierce, tempestuous coming together, he was taking it slowly, so slowly I thought I would die.

"Easy, love," he crooned. "No need to rush. We have so much time." He went back to lavishing his attention on my clit, licking, sucking, stroking, squeezing, until I could barely stand it. I was whimpering shamelessly.

"Oh, please, Tony, please."

"Patience," he admonished, shifting his weight onto both his elbows and nuzzling my aroused nipples. They were so hard they hurt, and I groaned, my hips moving under his.

"Shush, darling, hold on," he whispered, his breath warm and sweet against my temples. He laid his mouth across mine to stifle my moans. His thick mustache tickled. I sucked on the soft hairs and opened myself to him. His tongue sought mine again and this time I could taste myself, hot and salty, on his tongue. It made me insane with desire. His body strained against mine.

Tony slid two long fingers inside me, and I arched my body in quick response, my hips grinding against his. He chuckled softly at my impatience as he probed my slickness, reaching deeply, making my insides ripple. I reached for his cock and squeezed; he groaned as I rubbed his shaft, feeling the silky skin pulling against the bulging vessels encased within. He withdrew his sopping fingers and gripped my buttocks. I guided him into me, gasping as again he pushed to the hilt and filled me.

I grabbed at his hair and offered him my mouth. He pressed his mouth on mine and plunged his tongue between my lips, as deep as his cock was between my legs. The outside world didn't exist for me any longer. There was just this man, this stranger, pumping between my feverish thighs and possessing my hot mouth.

I forgot everything: Jake, Jeffie, India, my unhappiness and boredom. They weren't real, not now, perhaps not ever. My pulse raced, my heart thrummed loudly in my chest, and my screams would surely have woken up half of downtown Mysore if Tony hadn't swallowed my cries in his throat as he came with me.

Later, spent but exhilarated, we had a last cup of coffee at the Kwality Restaurant. I perched gingerly on the edge of the cheap wooden chair, all too conscious of the lovely tenderness of my long-unused female parts. My body was alive again, alive and singing. I had loved every fierce, exciting, adulterous minute of it. I tingled and sang with the knowledge that my body had been well and deeply pleasured. The feeling would last a long, long time.

Tony Borden, my skillful young lover, looking not much the worse for wear, his dark eyes full of the knowledge of me, of my body, perhaps of my soul, took one of my hands and turned it palm up, kissing it passionately. His voice was low, throaty, soothing, and he made me an offer no sane woman could refuse.

"I start teaching this seminar tomorrow, Camilla, every day from ten to one. I want to see you again, make love to you again, hear you make all those delicious noises just for me. Can you arrange to be at The Majestic every afternoon at two o'clock? I'll get you a key to my rooms. We'll order in room service. And you can get home in time for dinner. Every afternoon, for three weeks. Are you game?"

I thought of my trim little Raj-era bungalow on the Old Palace Road, competently run by Ayah, Cook, and the *mali* who cared for the extensive rose gardens. Every Monday and Thursday the *dhobi* came for our wash. Jake left the house at six A.M. and returned at seven or eight in the evening. Some nights he didn't come home at all. He had been after me for some time to do something with myself, annoyed at the way I moped about the house with a long, unhappy face every day.

I would make Jake happy and tell him I had signed up for an architecture seminar at the college from two in the afternoon until seven at night. It would keep me busy. And the readings for the course—which I'd have to do in the college library—would occupy my weekends, when he was rarely home. It would make both Jake and me happy that I finally had something to do.

Such an incredibly lovely, pleasurable something to do.

"Three weeks," I agreed, nodding, "three weeks." I squeezed his hand, then kissed it. We were coconspirators, partners in crime, coupled for the nonce.

And after the three weeks? What then?

No. I wasn't going to spoil this idyll for myself. I refused to think that far ahead. I would live for the moment, in the moment. The future would have to take care of itself. The present was more, so much more, than I had ever ventured to dream.

Boredom, deadly, soul-draining boredom, would be held at bay. Tony Borden had come along at just the right moment, saving my life. For that alone, I knew I would never forget him.

Behind us the overworked tape deck blared on: *Oh, yah, yah, yah, when we remembered Zion.*

I took a last deep breath of the brown oval of sandalwood soap, remembering that sweet, short, faraway time. Oh, yah, yah, yah, how well I remembered Zion.

C. A. Griffith

Necessary Lies

Where do I begin? Here? It's 5:27 A.M. and I can see a few cars, cabs mostly, from my terrace. Twelve stories above the city and you can still hear the sound of horns honking and the wind trying to find its way. After a while, you forget what the night and crickets sound like and the cacophony of New York at night seems almost quiet.

There are nothing but secrets and dreams at this hour of the morning. I cannot sleep, therefore there will be no dreams. That leaves secrets. Tomorrow, I will cancel lunch with Ashley, again. We've been friends for years and she still wonders if it is to my memory that Michael makes love, if I was the woman who kept him away from his daughter's birth. All the while smiling, confiding, crying, "Angela, Angela. What would I do without you?"

Walking arm in arm with Ashley, I have often felt the harsh admonition of other black people, especially black men, the luxurious warmth of soft, old church ladies, and the fascinated envy of strangers. We are frequently mistaken for sisters, sometimes for twins. Often for lovers. It is easier to let people believe what they will. We are the closest of friends, but sometimes seeing her is painful. We both know that in some perverse way, we are implicated in too many lies.

And Michael. Still hoping for absolution in my voice. Still trying to make it up to me—because I am only godmother to his daughters, because I can't hurt Ashley by confirming her suspicions any more than I can forgive him for hurting her with his affairs. Because our friendships hang in the balance, everything is too complicated. One day, it will be too late.

I woke up this morning singing the blues. I woke up this morning with the blues wrapped around my heart, and scattered all around my bed. Thinking about things I should have done, should have said.

I have a photograph of Ashley and Michael's girls, my godchildren. These two beautiful brown angels smile at me from atop a shelf full of books I've reread too many times on sleepless nights such as this.

I also have a photograph of my ex-husband, Roberto, that I keep tucked away in a drawer. I take it out when I wake up with the blues all around my bed—not so much to look at him, or at a happy time, but to remember happiness itself. It was the only time in my adult life that *anything* seemed possible. I didn't have a care in the world. And it was the only time he wasn't fucking a very wide circle around me while I pretended not to know. It's amazing how small that circle became in five years. On paper, we stand together, dry, colorful leaves whipping around our ankles. He is kissing my neck. We look directly into the camera, wondering if the self-timer will take the picture before the wind knocks the tripod over. I don't recognize the woman as myself.

I close my eyes. I am in California, eighteen years ago, in the dorm library. It's very early in the morning and I am laughing out loud, reading St. Augustine's *Confessions*. I am startled by the voice behind me; I thought I was alone.

"That's the first time I've ever heard you laugh," a guy says, leaning against the door. I am annoyed by his grin and arrogant good looks. I don't have time for another rich white boy trying to flirt with me. I'm too busy trying to finish the book before I go to work.

"How am I supposed to respond to that?" I ask.

"Good morning, Angela, my name is Michael Sloan." He sits on the table, takes the book from my hands. "I lived down the street from you. I just moved off campus." He tries again. "I helped you move your trunk upstairs a couple months ago. Remember?"

If he tries to ask me out and looks deep into my eyes before he asks what I am—black and what?—or tells me I'm interesting looking, I don't know what I'll do. I wait for him to flash his perfect teeth at me and say, *Excuse me, but I just have to ask you something* . . . but he doesn't say a word. He's waiting for me.

"Do you want me to thank you again?" I ask.

"No. I wanted to thank you. For what, right? Well, I'm in your Western Civ class, the one where you got up in front of five hundred people to ask the professor why he—what did you say—'consciously and maliciously skipped the fact that St. Augustine, one of *the* major contributors to Western thought and civilization, was a black man from Africa.'" He looks at me, waiting. Where the hell is he going with all of this, I wonder. I just stare at him, waiting. "Well," he says, "I was one of the few pale faces applauding you."

"And I'm supposed to thank you for that?"

"Did you know that your nickname around here is Ice Princess? Of course not. Well," he says sarcastically, "I guess anybody who can risk the scorn of a pompous, malicious, tenured professor and find *anything* humorous in St. Augustine can't be all that bad."

He hands my book back to me and I open it, reading aloud. "Lord, grant me salvation, but not yet!" He looks at me skeptically and I show him the words on the page. Laughing, he extends his hand.

The memory fades there, after I shake his hand and go back to being busy. I remember that he was not easily fooled, or put off by my coldness. From that day on he made a point of saying hello, visiting me at work in the library, trying to make me stop and talk, even when he could see I was in a rush. Eventually we became friends.

Another memory. We are in my bedroom. He has filled it with plants, made an aquarium for my bookshelf, and put fat, black goldfish in it. A piece of stained glass we found at an abandoned house in town covers the tank and catches the afternoon light.

But it is night now and he is reading *The Great Gatsby* aloud to me as I rest my eyes. I have an exam in the morning and am fighting sleep. He toys with the belt of my robe and says that we should sleep together. I tell him that we do sleep together and he explains the difference between falling asleep on the same bed and sleeping together. I poke him in the belly button.

"I don't fuck my friends," I say, and he pretends to be shocked, drops his jaw. I tell him, *"En boca cerrada no entran moscas."* It was something my mother used to tell me. "The closed mouth swallows no flies." Mrs. Johnson, my pretend grandmother, told me the day I left for college, "Not too much academics, not too much beach, and not too much courtin'. Them's your ABCs." I think of my mother and Mrs. Johnson as I smile at Michael.

"Speaka-da-English." He frowns, raises one eyebrow.

"Goodnight, sweet prince." I kiss him on the cheek.

"Here." He points at his lips, puckers them. Laughing, I kiss him on the lips.

"I want another." I give him another.

"Satisfied?"

"Never." And every night after that, and whenever we first see each other, the same dance.

Several weeks later, I am approached in the girls' shower. Friends, and others, want to know why I don't "stick with my own kind," why I have "betrayed the race." Those who know me, or simply know better, want to know why I am not jealous of his other women. Still others are jealous because it is presumed that I am the "other woman." I am not sure how I would respond to their questions even if I cared to do so.

Do I insist upon fidelity to my class, my race, my people, and say that Michael and I are not lovers to appease them, knowing that they still won't believe me? Or do I tell them in a hushed, confidential whisper of the day I borrowed his car and came back well after nightfall to return the keys, unlocked the door to his apartment, called out his name softly—and heard another woman's voice echo my words in a deep, sensual moan?

"Umm . . . Mi . . . chael."

Do I tell them that I left the keys on the table and quietly

closed the door behind me and walked home? Or do I tell them
the truth? That I found myself outside Michael's bedroom, staring at another woman's breasts through the veil of her long,
black hair as she leaned forward. How I stood mesmerized by
the soft light of a bedside candle illuminating her taut stomach
and gently rocking hips as she moved slowly up and down, her
strong, smooth thighs tensing and releasing, Michael's body beneath her, almost imperceptible in the shadows but for the outline of his thigh, his hands moving around to hold her waist, the
base of his cock slowly moving in and out of sight? Do I dare tell
them how I longed to see her face, that the sweat glistening
from between her breasts and along the curve of her neck was
not enough? I had to see the lips that made that sound that
washed over and through me, leaving me wet and trembling and
afraid. Not afraid of being caught watching them; I was camou-
flaged by the darkness of my skin and the shelter of the shadows.

Yes. There. Those are his hands moving into the light to stroke
her arms, dig his fingers into the soft flesh of her breasts,
squeeze her hard, dark nipples together as she tosses her head
back, her eyes closed tight, her hips jerking in tight, tight circles.
Yes. That is her, calling out to God with the face of an angel,
wearing a vivid mask of pleasure and pain, her eyes suddenly
wide, her breathing a deep staccato as she looks in my direction,
looks right through me, as her body shudders and a moan es-
capes our lips and we come together. Michael rises up, embracing her in the light. He cries like a wounded beast, breaking the
spell.

I close the door behind me, walk home, and lie down between
cool sheets. I tell myself that it was Michael I wanted between
my thighs, not her. That is what I tell myself, over and over, until
sleep comforts me and helps me believe it.

Over the next few months I keep myself very busy. I have to
work. I have to catch up on reading. I don't have time to waste.

I don't see much of Michael. When he calls, I tell him that
nothing is wrong, I'm just busy. I bury myself in my studies and
work. By the time I come up for air, freshman year is over and
I am free.

At home in Chicago, I miss Michael more than I can admit.

I miss his hello kisses. I miss him playing his guitar, keeping me company in that spooky dormitory basement as I did my laundry. I am wondering if he thinks of me, if he misses me also, when the phone rings. My mother picks it up and hands it to me. It's Michael.

He asks how I'm doing. I talk about everything except how I miss him. He tells me that he has made four thousand dollars in profits on investments he made a couple of months earlier. I tell him he is turning into a capitalist bastard and he says that I'm too ambitious to still be such an idealist. I ask him if he used his daddy's money and if he's sitting with his feet up on his daddy's desk. In the background, I hear the chair squeak loudly as he tells me that it takes money to make money, but he doesn't answer the part about whose desk his feet were on. I say that I love him and there is silence. I want to tell him that I love him as a friend, as a brother, but I am no longer sure that is true.

Several weeks later he calls again and ends the conversation whispering, "I love you." I am afraid to ask him what he means.

At the end of the summer, I visit him in his parents' New York apartment. The cab stops in front of a large Upper West Side building—very West End Avenue, very regal, complete with a uniformed, elderly black doorman who opens the cab door for me and offers me his hand.

"Michael told me you were real pretty, Angela. My name is Smiley." He reaches out to take my bags and I give him the lighter of the two. I stand there, feeling utterly lost. He touches my arm lightly and leads me inside. A short, round man with a ruddy face holds the elevator door open for me.

"I've forgotten the apartment number. I'm sorry."

"Don't worry, he knows the way," he says, handing my bag to the elevator man.

"Thank you, umm . . . I can't call you Smiley."

"Then don't you call me that, Sistah. Call me Benjamin. My friends call me Benjamin." The elevator man pulls the iron gate closed and Benjamin leans forward.

"It'll be okay, Angela," he whispers.

The wood-paneled doors close and the elevator man takes me up past the numbered floors to level P in silence. He opens the

gate and the elevator doors open directly into the Sloan family's
foyer. He deposits my bags at the edge of the living room as a
grinning Michael opens his arms to hug me. Behind him are his
parents—their smiles drop flat. Michael picks me up and swings
me around wildly, the two of us laughing and laughing. I have to
beg him to let me down. I am dizzy, and the room is still spinning around me as Michael introduces me to his parents, but I
am certain that I see Mr. Sloan nudging his wife. She tries to
smile. It looks like a muscle spasm at the corners of her mouth.

Later, I am in the shower. Steaming, soothing heat. I turn off
the water, expecting silence. I am not so fortunate.

*Mr. Sloan: . . . how to live your life. We're glad you're so close.
So, she's not Jewish, she's a lovely girl, but—*

*Mrs. Sloan: But nothing! You talk about her constantly and
forget to mention she's a Negro? She's lovely, but friends, you're
not. Don't you lie—I'm not stupid. It's bad enough you bring this
schvartza into my house.*

Oh, how I wish I hadn't turned off the shower just in time for
that. I also wish I could come out and ask Mrs. Sloan why she
is so obtuse, and so damned middle-aged. How could a woman
who survived the war and escaped with nightmares and numbers
tattooed on her arm *dare* to call me a *schvartza*? Instead, all I
do is brush my teeth. As I exit the bathroom, Mrs. Sloan is in the
hallway, a bowl of melting pink ice cream in her hand. I smile.

"You're keeping the guest room so neat and clean, Michael's
room is such a mess! I wish I could find a girl to clean this apartment as well as you do." I smile, convinced of her ignorance—
she couldn't *possibly* look me in the eye and say what she said.
But she *did* say it. And before I have a chance to tell her how
offensive it is, she disarms me.

"You have such a beautiful smile, dear. Have some ice cream.
There's plenty in the freezer."

I decline.

"Goodnight, Angie. Sleep well."

In a few steps I am at the threshold of Michael's door. He
stares at me for a moment, then says, "You heard." He takes my
hand and sits me down on the bed. Looking down at his hands,
he apologizes for his parents, then abruptly rises and closes the

door. Barefoot, bare chested, bare legged; his rugby shorts fit him too loosely.

"You're losing too much weight, Miguelito," I say. He rubs my shoulders. "I should get going to bed. Goodnight, sweet prince," I whisper, leaning back against him. I start to get up but he hugs me. He won't let go. "I love you too," I tell him. "It doesn't matter. Really."

"It does matter," he says. "Sometimes, I really hate them, I do." He stands, walks across the room, and looks out the window. I call him, and he comes to me. I hold his face in my hands, waiting until his tears stop. I lie down and his fingers, hot and guitar-callused, massage my hands, arms, shoulders. Ten years of music stroke my back, from the nape of my neck to the curve of my spine. I try very hard to stay awake. I know I have to comfort his parents with the click of my door.

I awaken near 5 A.M. to the sound of cars whizzing by below on West End Avenue, and the pattern of Michael's aquarium light playing on the ceiling. Michael's head is on my stomach. The towel his mother gave me, red, with an ornate *S* stitched in white, is draped over the back of his chair. I do not attempt to cover my nakedness or to escape quietly into the guest room until morning. Will I have lox and bagels, averted glances, silence, or a little talk, perhaps an early return home to Chicago for breakfast? No. I simply let my hands twist and part the soft, full head of hair upon my stomach. I let my fingers trace the curve of his ear, neck and shoulder. He stirs, and looks at me, unsure. I see my fear reflected in his eyes. What can I do but silence his question with a kiss? He says, "I want another." And the dance begins.

I am not dreaming. Nor do I offer his parents the click of the guest room door. I offer them a song. Not an old Negro spiritual, but something entirely different. I sing in a voice so sweet and deep, a voice they could only dream of and hope for their only son.

But they won't understand this song. They will hear this song and turn it into something dirty, something raw and distorted, a challenge, a dare, a phase . . . something it's not, anything but what it is. I stretch, gripping the stereo dial, turning it on. This song is not for them.

As I bring my hands back to Michael's head, he begins to lick tiny circles around my nipples and suck from each breast.

Soon his head is where it began when I awakened and in a moment it will be lower. He makes a trail of wet kisses along my hips, inside my thighs, teasing me with the secrets he whispers between my legs, stroking my lips in a language we have spoken only with others, a language we have never shared as friends.

He asks me if he should stop, and I moan, my hands pushing his head lower and deeper, my hips rocking, my clit hard against his tongue and lips in response. He moves his fingers inside of me and my mind goes blank. When I begin to tremble, he whispers, "Not yet." Tossing my head back, I close my eyes.

Suddenly, there is no bed, no night, no music, no sound. I see him, not much bigger than my two hands, a tiny Michael, premature, sliding out from between his mother's pale legs. And now, with my honey thighs guiding him in the darkness, I gasp and the warm weight of his body covers me as I urge him deeper, back into my womb—back to the beginning, back to where I too longed to rest. Before the ignorance of hatred, to the safety of home.

A month or so later, in the amber light of the darkroom, I watch my image taking shape under water. On paper, Michael stands behind me, his face nestled against my cheek, his arms around my waist. He doesn't know that I am pregnant and scared, but it shows on my face. I switch on the light and the photograph turns black in the tray.

That brief moment, when the image was sharp and clear, just before the silver reacted to the light and turned it jet black, still haunts me all these years. I had seen my mother's face in my own and it frightened me. I had seen her "No hablo inglés" eyes, her "Baby, estoy cansada" eyes. I'd seen that look in the eyes of every too young, too tired, poor and desperate teenage mother. I didn't want to have their eyes or my mother's eyes. I could not have this baby. I did what I had to do. I aborted her ghost. I graduated from college three years later and laid her tired body to rest the next year.

The telephone rings and startles me. It's Ashley, apologizing for waking me before ten on a weekend. I tell her I've been awake for hours and she is concerned. I make it easy for us both and tell her that I'm fine. She reminds me about lunch tomorrow and I tell her that I have to cancel. She is disappointed.

"Angela," she says softly, "I have to see you." I want to tell her that I'm not good company, that I have work to do, and my own shit to deal with. Instead, I ask what's wrong. She tells me that they ran into Michael's parents that morning, coming back from breakfast with the girls.

"They kept walking as they looked at us, and then down at the girls," she says bitterly. "Not one word. They just walked right by as if we were total strangers." She tells me of her rage and Michael's silence. I ask if the girls are okay, if they knew what was going on.

"They had no idea. And—" Suddenly, she is crying.

"And what?" I ask softly. "Ashley, try and tell me what happened."

"He just left."

I tell her I don't understand.

"We walked home, he called somebody—some woman—and said he'd be back later."

I resent having to say it, but I know she needs to hear that I'm not the other woman and that Michael hasn't told me who she is.

"Do you still love him?" she whispers.

"Michael? Yes, I love him. I love you all."

"No. I mean Roberto. Do you still love him? After everything?"

"Yes," I said quietly. "But I'm over it."

I don't want to think about these things so I tell Ashley that my relationship, separation, and divorce didn't make me an expert on any of those matters, but I did learn something of use to her. I tell her that she must get out of the house, come here, or do something—anything but wait for him to come home. I tell her that I can take care of the girls for a while, if needed. When her tears have stopped and she is calmer, I ask her what she wants, what she needs, and for a long time, there is silence.

"I want to be happy, Angela. Is that too much to ask?"

I have no answer for my sister. I have no magic to scatter the lingering pain of unbearable truths, necessary lies, deep rage, heartbreak, or the blues.

"No. It's not too much to ask," I tell her, my voice cracking with emotion. And this is what I tell myself as I hang up the phone and step outside to lie in the warmth of the sun. I close my eyes to the city rising up around me, just beyond the sanctuary of this terrace garden. No, happiness is not too much to ask for.

I am haunted by the simple, elusive promise of these words. I say them over and over again, until anger comforts me, and helps me believe.

Jolie Graham

Tasting the Sky

I don't want to starve to death, she thought, when she first made the decision to rent the room in the library. I feel like I could starve to death. She nodded to the man who was leaving his cubicle as she entered hers for the first time.

The next day the carpet had changed colors. It was woodsy green instead of gray. She didn't notice. She wanted the right book.

She touched the cookbook tentatively, as if making some big decision. He noticed the way her hands held it and turned it over, examining the binding. While she was in the reference section a river sprang up between them, so he reluctantly returned to his little room next to hers. He could hear her door lock click. He could detect subtle movements coming from their shared wall.

She pulled more books into her cubicle every day, creating a mountainscape within it. The READ poster on the wall now said EAT. As she became more engrossed in her search for sustenance, he became more engrossed with her. She was a thin and plain-looking young woman, with a serious face. She usually wore jeans and a T-shirt. But whenever she was near he caught a whiff of something, some perfume or aura that made him want to climb the big oak tree now growing in the middle of the library. Or climb her.

Climbing. Climbing up her body. He contemplated it as he leaned back in his chair. There was a row of narrow windows near the ceiling between their rooms. They hadn't been there before. With trembling eagerness he climbed on top of the table. The light was off in her room. But with the light streaming through those upper windows he could see her. She was naked, examining a fresh stack of books.

She selected a large volume, one with a rough leather binding and no dust jacket. *Tasting the Sky: A History of Flowers As Food.* She squatted on the grassy carpet, her legs spread. As he watched, she slowly rubbed the spine of the book between her legs. He could hear the sound of moisture, smell the heavy scent of rain in the air. She moaned. The room was becoming darker. Night was falling despite the light in his room. In a few moments he would lose sight of her entirely. He could hear her little grunts and groans as she pushed herself onto the book.

Quickly he shed his clothes and climbed through the open window, dropping from the stack of books to the ground beside her. She looked up in surprise. A naked man in the paper mountains.

"Oh," she whispered, "I've been so hungry." She opened her mouth to him. The book fell open to some unseen recipe.

She licked his balls, sucked his cock until he came, until he thought he would never stop coming. Like a silent rain, rose petals, violets and chamomile fell steadily from the dark sky. They rolled in the flowers, becoming drunk on the scent, drunk on the liquids from their bodies. He ate her, ate the flower that bloomed between her legs. With joy and laughter, their voices echoed off the walls of this banqueting hall. The room had grown spacious as their bodies moved, opened, and consumed each other in every way. They tasted exotic fruit and created new books about it.

When the flowerfall ceased they stepped out into the now darkened library. From all around them came the whisper of

pages being turned in the dark, the sigh of volumes of naked
bodies being opened. Some inarticulate choral music rose in
concert from the floors, tables, chairs, and shelves. And everywhere, ankle-deep flowers bathed the arching bodies as they
sang and sighed and tasted the sky.

Emily Alward

Honeymoon on Cobale

They had sauntered through her dreams ever since she could remember, these handsome and confident Cobalean men who existed to give her pleasure. Melerie struggled fitfully to remind herself of those dreams, while her nerves screamed and the wedding guests babbled on around her.

"You don't really want dessert, do you?" she heard her cousin Nikalla ask. "You'll be getting lots of honey later." Nikalla grinned at Melerie and, without waiting for a reply, waved away the server.

Melerie stared longingly at the rich pastry with its golden crust and toppings of fragrant honey and spiced cream. Finally she decided her cousin was right: she was too nervous to enjoy it.

And that's all right, she told herself, echoing her upbringing on faraway Earth. *Brides are supposed to be nervous on their wedding night.*

But not on Cobale. Here, in this culture that comprised the other half of her heritage, women were self-confident and sexually assertive.

"Everything is for the woman's pleasure here, you'll see," her aunts had said when they'd first started making marriage plans for her. Melerie was willing to grant the theoretical truth of their statement—at least no one had suggested that she give up her graduate studies or anything else to conform to a husband's whims—but it hardly helped reassure her about tonight. Her nerves were jangling with apprehension and her stomach was so clenched that she wished she hadn't eaten anything at all during this interminable wedding banquet. It wouldn't do to be sick in the arms of one of her new husbands.

She ventured quick glances toward them now, masking her interest by pretending to watch the musicians. Dillin aq Dubraiz sat at the table nearest hers, his slate black eyes jewels of intensity. She wondered how he worked that trick, of following her steadily with his gaze while carrying on a serious conversation with the friend at his side. Tall, dark-haired and urbane, he clearly was not a man to be trifled with. When he noticed her studying him, he raised his goblet in a silent toast. Melerie nodded in polite recognition, but the exchange brought her no further knowledge of the man: mystery was wrapped around him like his elegant cloak.

She looked around for the other two men to whom she had just pledged her bond and body. Simen mir Gower stood in a corner of the hall, his hand resting lightly on the hilt of the ornamental dagger on his belt. For comfort, she guessed—Simen looked as if he'd rather be anywhere else but here at his wedding feast. The forest green suede he wore and the copper circlet in his dark brown curls were suitable enough garb—yet they subtly conveyed that he belonged in the woods and open spaces, not in an ancient hall where politics and revelry thickened the air. When he felt Melerie's attention on him, he shifted his lithe body uneasily.

Across the room a clump of followers surrounded Rafe xi Torrin; they were tossing dice and coin-jewels in insouciant disregard of the more sober guests. Rafe looked up and grinned when he felt her scrutiny, then turned back to settle a squabble among his henchmen. Blond, broad-shouldered and convivial, he radiated an easy mastery that knocked Melerie's poise into the violet Cobalean stratosphere.

Three men, as different as the separate fields of stars that marked their shields. They shared nothing beyond the pledges they had offered her this day, pledges originating in the need for a truce among three powerful families. Each man was strong and determined in his own way. She need not try to bring them together; simply by their sons each having bonded with the same woman, the families were expected to reach a degree of amity.

But that assumed that she, Melerie, would attain some degree of attachment to each man. Could she do it? Doubts crowded her mind; she shivered at the daunting task before her. Her new husbands were not known to her except by their pedigrees and the formal meeting held before the announcement of the match. And they were not men she would have picked had she done the choosing.

Not that she had ever been so lucky or knowledgeable about choosing men: she had gone for sex or for friendship, but never both from the same man, a common custom of the culture she'd grown up in. The friendships had proved less disappointing than the sexual encounters. But never had she felt an inclination to evaluate a male as "husband material," by either society's standards. So when it came time to do so, she had been willing to defer to the Cobalean tradition and let her maternal relatives make the choices.

Still, she could not let go of the notion that one should find rapport with a husband—or even husbands. She had no clue as to how to go about establishing a relationship with any of these formidable men, let alone what to expect of the formal Cobalean sexual ritual.

"He's supposed to bring some game or art to entertain you," Nikalla had told her, and chuckled as she added, "but you won't need it."

Her cousin nudged her now. "Do you like what you see?"

Melerie blushed; Nikalla had probably been watching her all along, entertaining the bawdy speculations that were standard observations of a Cobalean bride. She stole another quick glance around the room, pausing at each of her new husbands.

"Yes," she said reluctantly, admitting to herself that all three were very attractive. The flush spread from her face to suffuse her body in a soft sheen of desire. She took one more look, but really looked this time, first at Rafe, then at Dillin, and finally at

Simen, and an urgent emptiness tingled in her cunt. She found herself wondering which of them might best fill it.

Melerie reached out to take a sip of the golden ale, to steady herself and mask the excitement she suddenly felt. To have three attractive men legitimately make love to her—for once to have as many delights as her body craved—there *were* some advantages to the Cobalean family system beyond the obvious political ones. How was it she had not thought of them before?

Because I don't know how things will go with any one of them, she reminded herself, *and rightly so.* Pursuing her periodic desires had always brought more trouble than pleasure. Why would pledges make it any different?

Despite her part Cobalean heritage and having lived on the planet for half a year, there were moments when it seemed incredibly alien to her. Especially the men.

She took another sip of mead. Its tiny bubbles tickled her throat. Her sensory boundaries were falling. As she leaned across the table to put her mug down, the gems decorating her gown's bodice brushed her nipples with promises.

Shaken by the flood of sensory input, she knocked over a candle. Nikalla and two guests leaped up to smother it, and Melerie stood, apologizing in half-coherent phrases for her awkwardness.

"Never worry," Nikalla told her. "No one expects a new bride to be a model of poise."

"I think I'll go now," she murmured, picking up another candle to light her way. Nikalla's eyes widened, but she gave her cousin an understanding smile. It was only when a cheer went up from the crowd that Melerie realized the implications of her sudden flight. Scalded by embarrassment, she fled down the ancient stone hallways.

She sat in her darkened suite, gazing out on a lake through the tall windows. Tiny points of light glinted on its onyx surface, reflections of the torches set into the castle walls. They called this place the Lake of Dreams, and it was famous in Cobalean history and legend. It seemed as good a backdrop as any to face down the haunting questions and gather courage.

How had she ever gotten herself into this incredible situation?

Three new husbands, and absolutely no idea what to do with them—beyond the obvious, of course.

Maybe the obvious is enough, said a mocking little inner voice.

Impossible! She sighed. If that were true, her whole life would have gone differently. And better.

But maybe Cobalean men are different.

Impossible, she snapped at the inner imp. But then, because it held out a hope she sorely needed, she entertained that possibility.

They had been in her dreams ever since she could remember; as a small girl she had known that somewhere, circling another star, was her other family, with uncles and brothers who would give her toys and patiently play long games of chance or strategy with her. As she grew, the delights offered in her dreams changed.

Melerie's mixed-race heritage brought her more than the usual teenage troubles. Taunts of "alien" gave way to uneasy male attention; on certain days the bolder boys followed her with doggish persistence, like hounds trailing prey.

"Bitch," the other girls called her. For all her efforts to stay modest and invisible, her stubborn body, with its pheromones and gossamer shimmer, kept proving them right. Even worse were her impulses, which built relentlessly, until every few months she would go off with any agreeable mate and fuck and fuck, until her cycle burned itself out and she slunk home.

Her father and grandmother had greeted these episodes with hurt and sympathy. Knowing how she hated the biological double bind their culture put her in, they did not scold or shame her. Both became adept at apologizing to the outraged mothers of teenage boys. It was only when she returned home with a black eye and cord burns on her neck that they sent her to a renowned xenogynecologist who gave Melerie drugs to suppress her cycles.

No longer did Melerie send out tantalizing signals once a month, and her body's impulses lost their urgency. For the first time she was able to concentrate on her studies. The next year she went to university and majored in planetary ecology with the

vague idea of visiting Cobale and claiming her other heritage—
her mother's half—some day.

Most of her fellow students in the course were men. Without
the threat of cyclic hormonal demands, she was able to befriend
several of them. They'd take long walks through the subtly tinted
exhibits in the holographic gardens, talking about the Meaning
of Life and the new horizons they intended to explore. Melerie
never took it beyond friendship, nor did she want to. Even if her
body had been willing—and it hardly was—her past bewilder-
ment at being rejected after sharing pleasure haunted her. She
wasn't going to risk that hurt again.

Then she attained her dream; she traveled to this planet and
met her Cobalean relatives. An important and protective noble
family, they showered her with so much warmth that she natu-
rally fit herself into their culture—which included, she discovered with mixed shock and fascination, polyandry to cement
political alliances.

The details blurred in her mind now; all that mattered was
that she'd ended up with three of those handsome and confident
men dreamed of long ago. They were supposed to give her pleasure. Would they? All she knew for sure was that as an adult the
games would be played on her body—and theirs. And the next
move was hers.

She must have drifted off, because suddenly thunder was
booming across the lake and through the massive castle walls,
then receding to a loud pounding on her door. Nikalla eased the
door open and whispered, "Melerie, are you all right? Everyone's saying that you have no liking for your new husbands."

Melerie moaned softly. She saw, with wonder, that her skin
was radiating a slight glow into the room. Between her legs she
felt warm and damp and faintly throbbing.

"*Nyai*, that's not true. One of them can come in."

"Which one should I call?"

She wasn't sure about the proper etiquette; she truly didn't
know which one to call. With a mix of fear and delight she realized that she didn't really care.

"Um, I don't know. Why don't you have them draw lots?"

Nikalla scurried away. Melerie stretched lazily, leaned over the casement to make sure the two moons had risen above the Lake of Dreams, and waited in a strange world for a husband she didn't know.

He came in to her in the darkness. She felt the tension in his shoulders when he embraced her, and was relieved that he shared her anxiety about this first encounter.

But his touch was sure and stirring. Strong hands tangled in her hair. Lips found hers and brushed a quick tantalizing kiss across them before sliding down to trace her body. Fingers caressed her throat. Hands gently cupped her shoulders. As they reached her fingertips she muffled a ripple of laughter and delight: his technique was exquisite. Her cells were tingling with excitement and desire—how long must she wait while he paid homage to her fingertips and other assorted body parts?

She turned her face and pressed her lips searchingly against his, then burrowed in and claimed the velvety welcome of his tongue. He tasted like salt and honey.

She felt the swell of his erection. Her hips circled in response and she pushed against him. His hands found her breasts and scribbled questions across her nipples; she answered with small wiggles that teased his penis. She shrugged off her loose gown; a moment later his tunic and trousers tumbled to the floor. She leaned into his embrace and their bodies touched, all along the line from shoulder to thigh. Against her heat his skin was cool and warm and smooth and rough all at once.

Then her arms were holding empty darkness. Kisses parted her legs and flickered over her clitoris, growing ever stronger, his mouth becoming the driver and Melerie the giddy rider. Just as she melted under his tongue, he gave her a last slow lick and stopped. His hands released her buttocks and traced their way down her body as they had done earlier.

He went all the way to her feet this time, then stood and reached out his hand. Her desire flared higher than ever, but this interruption of their love game seemed right. As she followed him to the bed she looked back to where they had just embraced. A faint light shimmered in the night air.

He paused to make sure she was ready, then plunged into her, sure and intense. She rose to meet his thrusts with her own, seeking, matching his intensity. The world faded away and the darkened room blurred into insubstantiality; all that remained was her body and his, rocking across the chasms that had separated them.

On the brink she cried out. He paused; a shade of uncertainty hung between them. But it was joy, not pain, that had elicited her cry. She clutched him tightly, letting her soft throbbing cunt caress his cock.

He came a moment after she did. Melerie, still basking in the sweet descent, felt ripples of aftershock stir her womb. She smiled. The ripples were pleasant, a quiet bonus to their lovemaking. Exaltation drenched her, spreading like amber honey through her veins, bubbling into every cell like the points of light dancing over the inky lake outside.

The promises she had heard about Cobalean men were true.

In the early morning Dillin stirred and spoke to her for the first time. "Were you pleased?"

"Oh, yes," she murmured. Still groggy with sleep and satiation, she tried to find words to express her wonder. "I didn't expect—I mean, there are so many differences between us."

He stroked her cheek tenderly. "My dear, don't you know that's why the Creatrix made us this gift? So the differences can bring us together?" He put an arm around her and trailed kisses across her face and shoulder.

Melerie had to remind herself twice that it was all right to enjoy the kisses and still look forward to encounters with her other husbands.

That afternoon she was unpacking her books and holodiscs when she suddenly felt a hand tracing the flare of her hips. Surprise and sudden new desire rippled through her. She turned to look into the warm brown eyes of Simen mir Gower.

"Oh. Can you stay?" she asked, feeling awkward.

He nodded, and took the cup of licochat she offered, saying nothing. Melerie began to worry that she'd broken a taboo. Was silence a required part of foreplay? Then Simen muttered, "It won't work here, not this time," and grabbed her by the hand.

He led her down the castle's corridors until they found a door leading to a lakeside path.

Birdsong like merry glass bells followed them. Simen pointed out the tiny crystal birds, almost transparent, revealing themselves as their wings flashed silver through the air. He picked delicate blue flowers for her hair. He called to a strange furry creature, who came right onto the path and snuggled up to Melerie while Simen explained how it fit into the life of the forest. Melerie's heart warmed, but at the same time she burned with reawakened need. Was he going to give her a course in Cobalean ecology before he made love to her?

Finally he pushed aside a veil of leaves and pulled her into a glade. Sweet herbs and grass were strewn across the ground, walled off by interwoven branches; obviously he had gone to a great deal of effort to make this place comfortable. Once inside, Simen's diffidence fell away. With a lightning flick of his dagger he cut the fasteners from her gown.

Shocked, Melerie stood perfectly still. He drew her up against him. His chest was smooth and tautly muscled, his penis suddenly enormous: it fit into the triangle between her legs as if it had always belonged there. To her delight she felt herself wet and quivering, and opened up to him, leaning against a tree while he thrust inside her cunt. He moved back and forth just enough to tease, coaxing her to lead him on. Melerie's every nerve screamed; she wiggled and circled until he stabbed deeply within her, touching the center of her need, jarring layers of tension loose so that she felt herself dissolving. She shuddered; for a brief moment she worried that she was coming too fast—but she didn't care.

On the walk back to the castle he said, "Next time we'll do it your way."

"I have no complaints about this time," she said, reaching out for his hand. Simen beamed, no longer the worried young man who'd lurked in a corner at his wedding feast. Melerie suddenly noticed the cacophony of birdsong and animal sounds surrounding them, and wondered what new secrets their next time might reveal.

o   o   o

They met Rafe xi Torrin on the threshold to her quarters. The two men exchanged a quick suspicious look, but Simen relinquished her. Once inside, Rafe unloaded an armful of objects: a flask of bubbly wine, a wheel of cheese, a large box and a small one. The small box turned out to hold an exquisite necklace of rare chromatic gold. Rafe fastened it around her neck with a flourish, ruffling her honey brown hair. Then he stood back and admired her, making faces as though he had personally put her together and wasn't quite sure what finishing touch he wanted to add.

Melerie giggled. She was already thinking *I know what you should do for a finishing touch,* but her bold thoughts astounded her and instead asked, "Did you expect me to have two heads or something?"

"Aret's hounds, no. Just two extra husbands. It's not much fun to wait until last." He shrugged, as if dismissing the other men from his mind. "Don't you want to know what's in the other box?"

"Of course." She reached out for it, but he held it back.

"Aren't you supposed to bring me games and entertainment?" She felt an urge to challenge him.

"Only if you're gracious. I can tell you don't have much patience for the rituals. That's all right, but at least we can eat first." He poured wine into two glasses and cut wedges of cheese, holding one out to her.

Three men within the same twenty-five-hour day, Melerie marveled. Her Earth memories kept telling her it was not quite seemly, but her body kept purring in delight.

Rafe finally unwrapped the package. It was a version of *kini,* a Cobalean game that mixed imaginary quest with truth or consequences. But what a version! Most of the questions were on preferences, sensory or sexual, and Rafe insisted on checking out each answer. He explored her outer ear. He fingered the lingerie in her dresser drawer. He skimmed kisses across the nape of her neck, and tongued her nipples until she gasped. Somehow no opportunity arose for her to explore him—until he drew a card that made him choke with laughter. He waved it at her. "It says you're supposed to chase me to get your way with me."

She sprang up, but he'd already had a head start. Around the room he ran, and into the enclosed private yard with its grotto pool. Melerie ran after him, cut across to the gate, and slipped on a wet rock. She wasn't hurt, but she seethed with anger. Husbands weren't supposed to behave this way!

A moment later he dashed by. She reached out and grabbed him by the ankle. He fell down beside her and they rolled over and over, tangled in each other's arms.

"I have you!" she cried. "But Rafe," she said, her voice falling, "I won't make you do anything. You're supposed to want me just as much."

"Don't you think I do?" he growled. It was the first time he had been serious. "Is there any reason we can't have fun and love each other too?"

He'd uttered the magic word, the word that supposedly didn't exist on Cobale, or in its marriages. He must have gone to a lot of trouble to look it up.

"So tell me what you want me to do," he said. She tried another word—an obscene word on Earth, but it translated as "joy" on Cobale.

"Fuck me. Oh, fuck me," she cried.

Rafe held her tightly, caressing her arms, her breasts, her labia, letting her put an arm around his broad strong back and do nothing else while he pleasured her. When she was shaking with anticipation he entered her. His tongue explored her mouth so that her glad cries bubbled up like the sweet wine they had drunk. One hand was still doing crazy things to her nipples, while his cock moved deliberately inside her, almost meeting her need, giving it time to build and build. She raged and smiled and simmered silently, knowing she could change that if she wanted to. Finally she could stand it no longer, and responded, challenging him to match the rhythms. He took a few oblique strokes to tell her he'd picked up the challenge, then confronted her moves with hard thrusts. She careened with him through somersaults of ecstasy, until they shuddered to a breathless stop.

Her skin soaked with sweat and the planetary night mist, her womb drenched from lovemaking, Melerie decided she had never been so happy before.

Three husbands! Long after Rafe fell asleep, she was still daydreaming about the next round with each of them.

Stacy Reed

Holiday

They always met for lunch at *Coeur Carré*—Elizabeth hated the steaming mounds of meat and slippery cabbage dished up in most other Berlin restaurants. She grinned at Drew around a mouthful of *crêpes d'épinard*.

"And how's Jeremy?" she asked.

Drew tongued the rim of her thick-glassed mug. "Very accommodating."

"I can't imagine any man could accommodate you."

"I wouldn't have come here if he couldn't," Drew replied.

"Yes. New Orleans is overflowing with the merely adequate."

Drew cautiously set down her mug, as if the heavy glass might splinter in her pale hands. "This is ridiculous, Elizabeth."

"What? You actually falling for some guy?"

Drew sucked in her lower lip and teethed it lightly. "Elizabeth, have you ever seen me like this before?"

"You were like this about Noel."

"And since him?"

"No. It's true. I haven't seen you this unrestrained in years. You have yet to offer me a battery of reasons why you ought to be with Jeremy."

"I can't think of any."

"Well," Elizabeth began methodically, "there's the sex."

"Yes, there is that."

"And then there's compatibility."

"You're making us sound like a personal ad."

"And finally there's this completely inexplicable fondness he has for you."

Drew smiled openly at Elizabeth so the small space between her teeth showed. "That's easy to explain," Drew countered. "He's after my best friend."

"That's another thing! Three weeks I've been in Berlin and he hasn't so much as flirted with me."

"I'm so sorry," Drew laughed. "I had no idea he would be this unswerving."

"He's very focused, this one."

"I know," said Drew ruefully. The thought of Jeremy's simplicity quieted her. She tossed back the last of her beer and watched the city traipse by.

"Whatever will we do?" teased Elizabeth.

Drew reached across the debris of their lunch and smoothed her friend's rebellious black curls. "We'll have to do what's only decent."

Elizabeth leaned forward conspiratorially. "Yes?"

"Approach him on his own terms."

Jeremy stared intently toward the window at a point suspended approximately five feet in front of the blurred U-Bahn wall. The advertisements swished by him too rapidly; they might as well have been American. Only the angry graffiti inside the subway car distinguished the train as German.

With his weak grasp of the language, it was easy for Jeremy to ignore the monotonous calls for the various stops. He fantasized about Drew. It embarrassed him that she had become his favorite transit material. Wasn't he supposed to be dreaming of some woman who didn't want him?

He looked across the aisle at a young woman in a sundress. Her breasts moved easily against the floral print as the train bumped around corners. He imagined what her nipples might look like after he had sucked them hard. He tried to think of how she might taste, what she might whimper as she came.

He laughed at his contrivances and looked back out the window. Drew loved to come. He had made love to her this morning before leaving for the firm, as he had every morning since they'd immigrated. Their life together had uncoiled along a series of rituals, rituals that never disintegrated into unruly habits.

During the past week Drew had taken to hiding herself just before he arrived home from work. The first time, he had assumed she was out with Elizabeth, until he'd stumbled across her crouching behind his woolen suits, wearing nothing but the leather gloves she'd given him for Groundhog Day. She gave him some quiet gift on every holiday she remembered.

He exited at Thielplatz and strode up Habelschwerdter. It was a long walk. He studied the crumbling remnants of the older buildings and imagined how they might have looked before the war. He saw their simple row of new apartments down the block and imagined them cut at a cross-section, their interiors exposed. He envisioned all the rooms and nooks where she might be. He thought of her scurrying naked through the flat, looking for a new hiding place. He tried to remember all the places he had found her.

He greeted the downstairs tenant and loped up the three flights to their flat. He fumbled his key into the hole, turned the stubborn lock, and kicked the base of the heavy door lightly with the toe of his shoe.

"Hi, baby." Drew pressed herself against him.

"You're not hiding."

She took his awkward portfolio from him and with a pointed finger traced his jaw, willful beneath its gauzy cloak of olive skin. "You're not disappointed in me?" she asked.

He shook his head slowly and knelt in front of her. He petted her fine-threaded cotton dress reverently. He closed his shadowed eyes and leaned his head against her crotch.

"Jeremy, Elizabeth has come over for dinner."

He furrowed his brows dramatically but held his eyes shut. "Tonight?"

"Yes. She's here now."

He nuzzled Drew's thighs, inhaled patiently, and rose. "Where?"

"In the dining room."

He quietly kissed Drew's flaxen strawberry hair. "Let's not have dessert tonight."

The three sat around the table. Jeremy chewed purposefully, resolved to either take Drew or work on his drawings, depending on what time Elizabeth left.

He watched Elizabeth and Drew exchanging glances. They were more like an old married couple than best friends. They talked to amuse themselves, but it was extraneous to their communication.

When Drew left New Orleans, she had promised Elizabeth that she would be gone no longer than the year Jeremy took for his preceptorship. In the winter, she and Jeremy would return to New Orleans and he would join an architecture firm in the city. They had invited Elizabeth to come to Berlin with them, but her grant at Tulane kept her in the States most of the time.

Jeremy set his fork prongs down at the edge of his plate, propped his chin against the heel of his hand, and looked quizzically from Drew to Elizabeth.

"Look at him," giggled Elizabeth. "I told you he'd know."

"He's quite astute," Drew conceded, looking not at Elizabeth but at Jeremy.

"You say that's what you like about me," said Jeremy.

"So I do." Drew raised her fine eyebrows and spoke to her glass of wine. "We have a proposition for you, Jeremy."

"You're blushing."

"Elizabeth would like to fuck you and I would like to watch. Does that strike you as an agreeable way to pass the evening?"

"Why, yes. It does." Jeremy smirked affably at Elizabeth. He cut his eyes sideways toward Drew. "But I thought you planned to finish Chapter Six tonight."

"She finished it this afternoon," Elizabeth interjected. "She even began outlining Chapter Seven."

"How industrious you are."

"You should reward her, Jeremy."

"Come here, then." Jeremy pushed his chair back from the table. Elizabeth went to him. "Now sit down so that Drew can see you."

She sat down cautiously on Jeremy's lap, resting her back across his shoulder so that Drew could see them both. She leaned her head back and whispered something in Jeremy's ear. Drew smiled proudly.

Jeremy drew Elizabeth's short pleated skirt up so that her white mesh panties showed. Holding Elizabeth's waist with one hand, he stroked the insides of her thin tan thighs with the other. He looked directly at Drew while breathing into Elizabeth's ear.

"Pull her panties aside," said Drew. "I want to see her pussy."

Jeremy pulled Elizabeth's panties over so that her lips were exposed. "Like this?"

"Yes. Now ask her what she wants."

"Tell me what you want me to do to you, baby."

"Tease my nipples," said Elizabeth.

Jeremy pushed Elizabeth's burgundy silk blouse up over her full round tits and pulled down the cups of her lacy bra. He flicked his thumb and forefinger against his tongue for moisture before rubbing them over her eager dark nipples. She squirmed helplessly against his hardening cock.

"You're doing beautifully," said Drew. "I think she's enjoying this. I bet she wants you to play with her pussy."

Jeremy politely ran his hand down Elizabeth's smooth tummy and over her black curls. He scooted back in his chair, propping Elizabeth's legs further open. Drew could see how wet her friend had gotten; a spot appeared on the dress slacks she'd bought Jeremy for St. Patrick's.

"You're making a mess on Jeremy's favorite pants," Drew chided.

"Isn't Labor Day coming up soon?" asked Jeremy.

"I promise I'll find something special for you if you play with Elizabeth's pussy for a little while."

Jeremy flashed Drew his finest little-boy grin and placed an index finger at Elizabeth's opening. "How should I touch her?"

"Like this," Drew whispered, scooting her chair into an especially viable angle beside Jeremy's. She placed her hand over his poised finger and moved it up the length of Elizabeth's lips to her engorged clit. She moved his finger around in tiny circles until Elizabeth moaned plaintively against Jeremy's neck.

"I think that means she wants you inside her," Drew advised, furtively tracing Elizabeth's slippery opening with her red-tipped finger.

Still holding Elizabeth by the waist, Jeremy stood and backed her onto their dining room table. She caught herself with her hands and looked up at him expectantly.

From her chair Drew unbuckled Jeremy's belt and eased his pants down. She pulled his boxers gently over the head of his cock and ran her tiny hand over it, pulling insistently to the right, then squeezing as she went back down the shaft. He braced himself against the polished wood and laid his head on Elizabeth's shoulder as Drew tugged impatiently on his hard cock.

"Now put it in her," Drew instructed.

Jeremy held up Elizabeth's ass and bent his knees so that the head of his cock nuzzled against her yawning pussy. Elizabeth arched her back and whimpered for him to push inside her. He exhaled sharply at the feel of her wet lips dragging over his cock.

"Please," someone murmured. Jeremy complied, driving his thick cock into Elizabeth until his balls were nestled softly against her contracting ass muscles.

Drew pressed her hand firmly against the curve of Elizabeth's spine. "Now fuck her very slowly while I watch," she whispered.

She leaned her pixie chin on the edge of the table, right in front of their arching pelvises. It thrilled her to see Jeremy's cock plunging in and out of her best friend's cunt. His dick was slicked in Elizabeth's wetness. She wanted to take it out and suck it, but Elizabeth's cries dissuaded her.

"Fuck me harder, Jeremy," Elizabeth begged.

"Hold on." Jeremy braced himself against her abundant ass. He rolled back his sharp shoulder blades ceremoniously and sighed.

"Are you coming, baby?" Elizabeth asked.

"Don't move," Drew hissed to Jeremy. "Don't come yet."

Elizabeth was desperate to come. "Drew," she pleaded, "please let him fuck me."

"In a minute," Drew said, holding fast to Jeremy's gaunt hips. "I'm kind of enjoying this. You can wait, can't you?" Drew kissed Elizabeth on the lips. They felt thin and tight. After Jeremy's appetite had abated slightly, Drew released him. "Go ahead. I want to see her come now."

Each time the base of Jeremy's cock bumped up against Elizabeth's clit, she felt herself getting closer to orgasm. Drew slipped her finger into Elizabeth's pursed asshole. "Do you like getting fucked by Jeremy's cock?" she asked.

"Yes, Drew." The words came out staccato, shattered by Jeremy's oblivious ramming.

Drew scrutinized Elizabeth's contorted features; the slightest prompting could push her to orgasm or throw her completely. She'd take her chances.

"Come on, Elizabeth. You like to get fucked by my boy, don't you? You like getting your pussy and your asshole fucked at the same time. Show me, baby. Show me how good his cock feels."

Drew's persistent encouragement drove Elizabeth to a spasmodic climax. Every muscle in her body seized up against each of Jeremy's compelling thrusts and she cried out in ecstasy.

Jeremy shuddered. "Oh, Drew, baby, I'm gonna come if I keep fucking her."

"Do you want to come now?" asked Drew.

"God, yes."

"Give me your cock."

Obediently, Jeremy pulled out of Elizabeth's satiated cunt and turned to Drew. "Please suck me."

Drew opened her mouth very wide, inserting Jeremy's cock without really touching it, then fastening her Cupid lips near the base and sucking deeply. She drew her mouth up the shaft and paused at the head, licking the tip quickly with her probing tongue. Cradling his heavy balls in one hand, she sucked and lapped at the head of his cock for long minutes while her other hand pulled at the skin of his shaft.

She let his balls go and pressed her hand against his thigh when he began pushing himself persistently into her mouth. Her thong panties were soaking wet from the thought of his tossing off in her mouth.

Drew moaned gratefully when she felt Elizabeth's hand slip down her panties. She concentrated feverishly on pleasing Jeremy as Elizabeth steadily massaged her protruding clit. Elizabeth's slick fingertips pinched Drew's stiff clitoris, coaxing out one intense orgasm after another.

Drew's muffled cries combined with the sight of Elizabeth manipulating her pussy finally overwhelmed Jeremy. He grabbed Drew's hair, thrust his dick against the back of her throat, and came. He kept thrusting until the last racking blows of his orgasm had subsided.

Drew smiled at Jeremy and licked her lips. "Happy Bastille Day."

Erin Blackwell

Real Pleasure

I had a dildo in my hand when I answered the phone and I nearly spoke into the wrong instrument.

The voice issuing from the receiver belonged to my ex-girlfriend, Candace, the one who got away. We can go months without speaking, but it's always worth the wait.

"How would you like a two week, all-expense-paid trip to Europe?" she asked.

"What's the catch?"

"I'm giving some safer-sex workshops for women, and Jan, my regular partner, is tied up. Literally. Some dominatrix has her in bondage in Berkeley. So I thought of you."

"I think about you a lot, Candace," I said.

"This is business, not pleasure," she reminded me.

"Can't it be a little of both?"

"With you, it'll have to be."

"Should I bring my hardware?" I asked.

"Hardware?"

"Dildos. Vibrators. Ass plugs. I was just putting one away when you called. They travel in their own customized leather carrying case. Those Europeans ain't never seen nothin' like it."

"As long as you can get them through customs."

"They never look in your bags."

* * *

First stop: Paris. I was so excited, the airplane food tasted like *haute cuisine* and the sleepless night made me feel years younger. Arriving at Charles de Gaulle Airport was so *chic* that even the moving sidewalks looked *exotique*. Candace and I pinched each other and laughed. We were going to have fun.

We got our passports stamped, then stood waiting for our bags to emerge from the belly of the plane. We were schlepping them toward the exit doors when a woman in quasi-military drag motioned me to a counter under a sign marked DOUANE. I complied, hoisting up my big plaid suitcase.

So this was France: clear brown eyes, skin like cream and cheeks like peaches, glossy chestnut hair swept off her face in a *chignon* and lips in a pout. Was she in a bad mood or was she being sultry? Or was this the prescribed national expression? She gestured to the leather case.

Uh-oh. I didn't mind her looking through my underwear, but my sex toys were off limits: I may be an exhibitionist but I'm not into humiliation. I unzipped the large plaid suitcase but she only pointed again to the leather case. Oh well, I guess this was an erotic moment like any other. Too bad I couldn't videotape it for the gals back home.

Lovingly, I undid the straps and lifted the lid. There, snug in their leather restraints, were thirteen vibrators and thirteen dildos, plus assorted ass plugs in varying shapes, sizes and colors. A real rainbow coalition. I was proud to be an American, proud to be a dyke, and very proud to be an impeccably accessorized butch top.

Mademoiselle Douane seemed not to know what she was looking at, but she clearly didn't like the look of whatever it was. I grinned at her and she sneered. I started miming what they were used for, but she closed her eyes. A facial tic seized her upper lip and nose, which jiggled like a hungry rabbit's. When she opened her eyes, she wouldn't look at me or my collection.

I caught a glimpse of Candace walking through the double doors to freedom. I waved to her but she seemed not to see me. Uh-oh. The last thing we needed was to lose each other at the airport.

Mademoiselle slammed down the lid. She held up a finger, which could have been a criticism of my collection, but was in fact a signal to another woman, a senior officer. A few counters down, a woman broke into a smile that gave me that home-cooked feeling: I couldn't help smiling back any more than a strip of bacon can resist being fried.

Her brown skin heated up her white shirt. Solar disk earrings and beaten gold bracelets played off the regulation *épaulettes*. A mountainous cascade of tiny braids ending in drops of gold de-fied the colonialist bureaucracy she served. She looked like Cléopatre in uniform, her gait as stately as any Nile River barge.

With a single deep red fingernail, she lifted the lid on my dil-dos. Shaking her head as if she was having trouble believing what she was seeing, she gestured to her sister officer to pick up the case and follow her. I picked up the plaid and we made our way to a small glass-walled office. Cléopatre dismissed her infe-rior and told me in exotic English to make myself comfortable. Coming from her that was quite an invitation, but I wouldn't have known where to start. Besides, she was on duty.

She took a printed form out of a drawer and asked, "What do you do with these . . . *gadgets*?"

"I fuck women," I said.

Her eyelids fluttered, then batted themselves half open. That old U.S. charm had her in its grip.

"You may not bring your paraphernalia into France. However, if you will sign this paper," she said, handing me a form, "we will hold your property until you leave Paris on a plane back to your country. Until then the suitcase will remain in my personal care."

However moved I was at the thought of her personally caring for my paraphernalia, I had to put up some kind of a fight. "It's not as if I'm smuggling drugs," I said. "It's not as if I'm running guns. I came to Paris to taste the joys of *l'amour*." She smirked. "Why take from me the very thing guaranteed to give pleasure to the women of France and inspire their love?"

She moved her lips in the most amazing way. "I wonder why you think you need these *accessoires* to inspire the love of *femmes françaises*. You are cheating yourself. You need a *femme française* to show you what real pleasure is."

Real pleasure? What'd she think I'd been having all these years—*fake* pleasure?

As a matter of formality she asked for my address during my stay in France. When we stood up, I felt like I was still sitting down: this woman was tall. She made an un-Frenchlike offer to shake hands. Her palm was dry and warm. I felt like butter on hot biscuits. I melted out of her office and picked up my plaid suitcase. Walking through the exit doors, I looked around for Candace, whom I found sitting at a small marble-top table.

"You're all right!" she said when she saw me.

"Cléopatre took away my toys."

"We'll just have to do without them," she said, trying to get a waiter to acknowledge our existence.

"It won't be the first time," I sighed.

"We never used those things. When did you start?"

"When was the last time we made love?"

"Twelve—no, thirteen years ago."

"Thirteen years ago, then."

"You started the minute you left me?"

"*I* left *you*?"

"Let's not get into it."

"I was broken-hearted, Candace, you know that. Well, I wasn't going to let any other woman get to me the way you had. Literally. I wasn't going to let anybody else inside."

"But you used to love that."

"I was hooked, but I managed to kick the habit and become emotionally independent."

"You sure you don't mean emotionally dead?"

"Let's just say I grew up."

"And no one's been in there since?"

"I've got my sexuality where I want it: under control. I get pleasure from giving pleasure. My technique is flawless. Just wait till you see me in action."

"Too bad about your collection," she said, turning to the waiter. "*Deux cafés, s'il vous plaît.*"

"Oh my goddess. What am I going to use?"

* * *

Next morning we ate *baguette* for breakfast and visited a *cathédrale* that felt like a public library installed in an antique spacecraft. All the tourists took each other's pictures, grimacing beside the gargoyles that crouched on the uppermost balustrades.

We *rendezvous*ed with the workshop organizers at a small restaurant near the *hôtel*. A sad-looking woman named Véro, who made English sound like Danish, outlined the day's *programme*: lunch, a two-hour workshop using volunteers from the audience, a break for coffee and cake followed by a *débat* on the theoretical implications of the demonstration, then dinner and dancing. Sounded like my kind of *programme*.

Lunch was an inspiration. Everything was *au* something else: *pâté au saumon, canard à l'orange, fromages aux fines herbes*, washed down by a *château au vent*. We all giggled a lot. They stared at us like we were visitors from another planet and maybe we stared at them the same way. The table got very *chaleureuse*, which is to say warm and friendly. If this kept up we'd be asking for volunteers from the audience before dessert: *glace au marron avec sauce au chocolat*.

After a slug of that tar they call *café* we paid and left the restaurant. Sauntering up the narrow one-way street to number 68, we ducked into a doorway designed for carriages and crossed a small cobblestone courtyard dripping with ivy. Up a flight of spiral stairs, we passed through a high doorway into an airy room with plaster molding and *chandelières*.

About forty women were seated in folding chairs, talking and laughing. They calmed down when we walked onstage. Véro introduced us and the audience applauded. Candace started her spiel, explaining why safer sex was necessary even if some *lesbiennes* fantasized themselves immune to AIDS. Véro's translation made everything sound refined but sexy. Candace held up dental dams, gloves, condoms and finger cots. We pantomimed using them and passed out samples.

The audience tested the give-and-take of the latex and discussed the ins and outs of safer sex. Candace asked for questions, but there weren't any. Until the door opened at the back of the room and Cléopatre walked in with my suitcase.

Uh-oh, a raid. Before we'd even gotten started. Couldn't she have waited until the coffee break?

"Bonjour," she said. "I'm Marie-Antoinette de Retour and I have a question."

She had a nerve. I'd signed that form in her office—what was she doing dragging my suitcase all over Paris? Whatever it was, she looked great doing it. A red leather bolero jacket set off a black silk blouse tucked into zebra-striped stretch pants that snuggled her *mont de Vénus* and the curves of her *derrière*. Watching her stride to the foot of the stage made my legs quiver.

Candace asked what was the nature of her question. Marie-Antoinette set the suitcase down and slid open the straps, musing, "Is it true you *américaines* use these things? That you can't make love without them?"

When she opened the lid the audience craned its collective neck and jumped to its feet. Candace looked at me as if I'd planned this little *divertissement*. A few of the women were horrified, most were amused and some couldn't be bothered. Those who got a close look described what they saw to those who'd remained seated. When the aftershocks were over, Candace looked at me like I was supposed to do something. I decided to make Marie-Antoinette squirm.

"What a fine collection," I said. "Is it yours?"

"Non," she confessed. "My Uncle Marcel, a member of the *Résistance*," she lied, with a tremolo, "was caught and tortured by Vichy swine. After the war, he required a synthetic means of expressing his passion. This," she laid a familiar hand on my case, "is the result. On his death, my aunt Madeleine built a chapel to house these *réliques plastiques*. She claimed that touching them had cured her rheumatism." The audience giggled in disbelief.

"I don't claim my uncle was a saint," said Marie-Antoinette. *"Au contraire.* If the workshop is *d'accord*, I will show my uncle's triumph over Vichy's antieroticism. I will inaugurate his legacy of pleasure for a new generation of *femmes françaises*. At the same time, I will demonstrate French proficiency in what is considered a *technique américaine*." There was scattered applause. "If I could have a volunteer."

About six women left the room, yelling what sounded like "Day-Glo ass!" but turned out to be *"dégueulasse!"* meaning "to vomit!" Someone in the back grumbled, *"Typiquement améri-cain"* but stayed. Those in the front laughed as if this U.S. *comédie* wasn't worth the effort of a political analysis. Marie-Antoinette stepped onstage and, when nobody else volunteered, asked me to help her into the harness.

I looked at her like she must be kidding. She looked at me like she wasn't. I didn't have an answer for that. Lest things de-generate, I removed the pad that would massage her clit from inside the harness. She put a hand on mine to convince me oth-erwise and I felt as if I'd stuck my finger into a light socket. Trembling, I reinserted the pad.

Candace began a running commentary which Véro did her best to translate accurately. The audience was on the edge of their folding chairs as I liberated a midsize dildo from its leather stall, but Marie-Antoinette pouted her lips doubtfully. Pointing a recently trimmed fingernail at a model twice the size, she winked. The largest in my collection, that monster had been given to me as a joke. It was never intended for actual use—least of all on me.

"The back row has to see, too," she murmured.

Just a simulation, I reminded myself.

Fitting the unwieldy dildo into the harness, I handed the thing to Marie-Antoinette, who wouldn't take it. That meant I had to move in to where I could smell her body through the silk and leather. Her breath on my ear burned like a desert wind. She leaned a broad palm on my shoulder and I went down on my knees. Her hand slid onto my neck as she stepped through the legholes. I pulled the belt up over her zebra stripes so that the dildo was poking me in the face. Was this real pleasure? I strapped her in.

The sight of her wearing my damn dildo would've been funny if I hadn't felt a little woozy. Probably the wine at lunch. I made the mistake of standing up too fast. My cunt went liquid and started to throb like hot sulphur springs. She, *au contraire*, looked like a long-distance runner at the starting block.

Candace handed me a condom, thereby adding insult to

injury—or was she trying to save my life? That's what we were there for, after all: safer sex. The workshop must go on.

I held up the rubber for everyone to see, then fumbled around on the head of Marie-Antoinette's dick. I couldn't get the thing on. I just couldn't. I mean, those things only stretch so far. I was relieved when the latex tube split, since we could now move on to something else, but Candace produced another condom. Marie-Antoinette slipped it over her member before I could say, "Let 'em eat cake." She grinned at me with the largest, most ferocious teeth I'd ever seen. Then she asked for a glove, which she pulled onto her right hand.

"Close your eyes," she told me.

"Why?" I gasped.

"I'm just a poor *femme française*," she purred. "We aren't used to high-tech sex. If I know you're watching me with all your superior U.S. know-how, I'll be too timid to try." The audience found this funny and clapped their encouragement, chanting in unison, *"Fermez vos yeux!"* I closed my eyes and imagined myself in the *cathédrale* we'd seen this morning. What was its name? Like the football team. That huge, cluttered, candlelit barn seemed like the perfect place to hide.

Her hands are on my shirt, undoing my buttons. My pounding heart is probably visible through my chest. She pulls my bra up over my breasts and just leaves them there, hanging. I cover them with my hands. *O-là-là.*

Her hand slides down to my belt buckle and I feel a tug and hear a clink and the belt's open. I feel another tug and I know Customs is taking care of me. Customs is looking into it. Customs is unzipping my pants.

"This is just a simulation," I remind her.

"But it has to be believable," she murmurs.

My pants are pulled down in my very first striptease for a French audience. Candace can't think what to say and Véro doesn't feel the need to translate. I can hear the door open and close. Are they coming or going? I don't want to know.

The dildo knocks up against my hipbone before being redirected so it's bending into my thigh. She sighs. I guess that's her clitoris getting its massage.

Something brushes my pubic hair. Latex. Preparing the area for entry. Her hand moves down to my lips. I shudder. She kisses me suddenly on the mouth. She's so moist and warm. She sticks her finger in. One finger? Two? She twirls them around as I rock my pelvis. I want it. The whole nine yards.

Notre Dame, that's it! Only they pronounce it differently. Our Lady of Paris. Our Lady of Pleasure. Do it again, do it again. I like it, I like it.

"*C'est si bon*," she tells me. Her mouth travels down my neck to my breasts, to my nipples. She sucks and she bites.

"*C'est si bon.*" Everything she does is so good. So fast, so soft, so hard, so slow. I want her in there. She's in there. I want her to stay. She's gone. Where is she? If she doesn't come back I'm going to scream.

"Relax," she says. She's back and she's bigger than ever. It's not her—it's that dildo! This can't be happening. She'll never get it in. She's insane to try. I'm insane to let her. First she takes away my toys, then she fucks me with them—I've never been so excited in my life! I see stained glass windows depicting blood-engorged labia. A customs officer is examining the contents of my cunt. Instead of stamping my passport, she stamps my clit—with lipstick. That's it! I come and I keep on coming, sweating and crying, and she holds me. We stand there exchanging waves of vital energy. I open my eyes and I can barely focus but I can see her smile.

After a stunned silence everyone in the audience started babbling at once. We were a hit if the idea was to give them something to talk about.

Marie-Antoinette peeled off her glistening glove and threw it to the crowd, who dove for it, shrieking like seagulls. Véro gestured to a long table covered with fruit tarts and announced, "Mesdames, there's coffee in the back." That got them moving.

I started to button my shirt. Marie-Antoinette interceded. "I can do it," I told her.

"*C'est un plaisir pour moi.*"

Oh. Well then. Who was I to begrudge Marie-Antoinette a *plaisir*, after what she'd put me through? She dressed me in silence and I unbuckled her harness. The condom on the dildo was dry.

"Wait a minute," I said. "If you didn't use the dildo, what did you use?"

"These," she said, wiggling her fingers.

"All of them?" I said hopefully.

"Just these two," she said.

"Two? That's all? Are you sure?"

"There are plenty of witnesses."

"It felt so big!" I said.

"As big as your imagination," she laughed. "As big as your desire."

"Two fingers is nothing," I mumbled.

"Two fingers is all that's needed if you know how to use them."

"I thought for sure you'd used the dildo," I muttered.

"Did you want me to?"

"Of course—I mean, of course not. But when I thought you were going to, I got ready to take it. And then the feeling was so intense, I was sure I was doing the impossible."

She stared at me. "Why should making love be impossible?"

I didn't know how to explain. "You wouldn't understand," I said. "It doesn't matter. Let's go get some coffee."

"How long are you in Paris?" she asked.

"Two more days."

"That's not enough."

"The workshop must go on."

"I'm serious," she said.

"So am I," I said.

"When can I see you again?" she asked.

"Look, we just met. We don't know each other. I'm not your type."

"What do you mean?"

"I can't speak French," I said. "You don't know me."

"I know *me*," she said. "I know what I want."

"You can't always have what you want."

"Does that mean you don't want me?" she asked.

"I didn't say that."

She turned away from me and something splashed on the floor. Uh-oh.

"Marie-Antoinette, you're crying."

She turned around to hiss and spit at me. "Do you think I do this for a living? Do you think public sex is part of my job as a French customs officer? Do you think I'm a professional dominatrix? Don't you know, if I wanted to teach you a lesson, it's because I care about you? Do you think because it's érotique, it can't be émotionnel? Do you think—at all?"

Uh-oh, emotions. Where was she getting all this passionate dialogue? Don't tell me she was confusing a casual sexual encounter with the love of her life. I may be cute, but this was ridiculous. I didn't know what to say to calm her down without hurting her feelings more than I already had. Somebody shoved a plateful of berry tarte in my hand and I was frankly grateful for the interruption. Sex is one thing, but complications are a drag. Marie-Antoinette could dish it out, all right, but then she wanted what she'd dished out back. Sex doesn't work that way. If you want to play, fine, but leave your emotions in your bathrobe pocket.

I looked down at the pastry on my plate. It's times like these I wonder why I bother with women at all, why I don't just eat my way to ecstasy. The tarte was a vision of red and purple berries sunk into a firm but creamy custard separated from the crispest of millefeuille by a layer of almond paste. Pretty as it was, the tarte was even better on the tongue, where the various layers of flavor did a culinary version of the dance of the seven veils. I closed my eyes and moaned.

When I opened my eyes, I found myself surrounded by audience members sharing theories and rattling off long-winded questions. They were all cute, they were all excited, and they were all trying to seduce me—so why wasn't I enjoying myself? I couldn't understand what they were talking about. When I looked around for Marie-Antoinette to translate, she was gone. Seeing her suddenly not there made me feel as if one of those

gargoyles had sunk its claws into my chest. I choked on the forest fruit and custard, which is how I knew I was being a jerk.

I handed the *tarte* to someone, ran out of the room and down
the spiraling staircase, threw open the door to the courtyard and
flew over the cobblestones into the shadows of the entranceway.
Out on the street, I swung my head wildly from right to left hoping to catch a glimpse of her, but all I could see were women in
high heels carrying carefully wrapped packages of *charcuterie*.

"*Chérie*," said a low voice behind me.

I turned and saw her, leaning up against the heavy wooden
door.

"You're still here!"

She held out her hand and when I came over, drew me to her.

"I'm sorry I forgot to be cool," she said, looking into my eyes
with a smile. "I know you *américaines* like things to be cool.
Otherwise, you get very *émotionnel*. It was silly of me to make
a crisis. We don't know each other well enough for that. Forgive
me."

I stared at her. How had she gotten so reasonable so fast? Was
this a French trick? "I forgive you," I said.

"We had a nice time together and now you have a *souvenir* of
Paris. That's all." She squeezed my hand and tried to let go, but
I held on.

"Marie-Antoinette," I whispered, thinking the whole street
must be staring. "Nobody's ever fucked me like that. And nobody's fucked me at all for a long time. I wouldn't let them. I
didn't want them to. But you—I don't know—you're making me
feel things I don't know if I want to feel. I'm kind of out of my
mind right now, but I don't see how we could have a relationship
when I'm only here for two days. You see what I mean?"

"Just because I have emotions doesn't mean I want a relationship. It only means I'm not a machine. That shouldn't scare you,
it should reassure you—unless you fantasize about robots."

I was starting to like this woman. "You don't want a
relationship?"

"You please me," she said, like someone addressing a chocolate *éclair*. "I want to take advantage of your presence in Paris.
Voilà, c'est tout."

"Really?"

"More or less," she said, extending her lips in an ambiguous pout. "The important thing for me is to see you again."

"Why?"

She brought my hand to her lips and with her eyes closed, slowly traced between my fingers with her tongue. She opened her eyes as if she were returning from another world. "I want you inside me."

Now I know how an electric blanket feels when somebody plugs it in with the dial on high. "Where do you live?" I'd explain to Candace later.

"The *métro*'s right there—it's only three stops—or we can walk. It's so beautiful out."

I wanted every moment to last.

"Let's walk," I said.

Martha Miller

❦

Hormones

It was the hormone replacement therapy that caused the weight gain. Alexis had always been plump, but the estrogen/progestin treatment did her in. As a child she remembered trips to the doctor—she'd leave with a 1,000-calorie-a-day diet and a grape Tootsie pop. She remembered suppers of broiled hamburgers, cottage cheese and canned peaches. As an adolescent she had been heavy until she'd discovered diet pills and for several years went up and down like a yo-yo. After the children came she settled into a comfortable size 18. Now the kids were almost grown. Billy was working his way through college. Alex was still in high school—he'd lost a year in drug rehab and all that had led up to that.

It sort of happened overnight. One morning she woke up and felt like hell: hot flashes, depression, fatigue and irritability. She thought she had the flu or had eaten something spoiled. When the symptoms didn't go away, she decided to see a doctor. She chose a female gynecologist, thinking that with a woman she'd at least find compassion. She hadn't. The only thing the medical profession seemed to have to offer was a twenty-pound weight gain that sent her already sinking sense of self-esteem over the edge. The doctor, who was probably ten years younger than Alexis and called all her female patients "ladies," minimized her complaints with an "Oh, don't be a baby" look on her face. The hormones she prescribed did help with many of the symptoms, but they also created new symptoms—like the weight.

Alexis finally had to stop wearing even her largest rings. She gave up on blue jeans and bought jerseys and sweat pants.

"I don't have any medication that will make you feel like you're eighteen years old again," said the doctor when she complained. Alex remembered the scene from *Gone With the Wind* where Mammy told Scarlet she'd never have an eighteen-inch waist again—only it was a *size* 18 that Alexis had lost forever.

"I'm gaining weight," she said.

"Are you eating more than usual?" the doctor, a plump woman herself, asked. "Sometimes depression . . ."

"I'm eating the same as I have for the last twenty years!"

"How about exercise?" The doctor's hair lay in damp ringlets on her forehead; her face was rosy and flushed. She looked like a frustrated cherub. What the hell did an angel know about real life anyhow?

"I injured my back when the kids were little," Alexis said. "I used to walk in the park, but last year I got mugged."

The doctor turned away and shuffled through some papers. "A massage will help with the edema. I'm going to give you a booklet about our wellness clinic. They have an exercise program there."

Alexis considered it, then repeated, "Look, I have a bad back. Exercise programs just get me injured."

"There's a trained professional who will monitor what you do. Brian hasn't let anyone get hurt yet."

Oh, great. A man, thought Alexis. "Can't you just give me some hormone that doesn't do this?" she persisted.

"How's your sex life?"

"What?"

"Sex." The doctor turned to face her. "Vaginal dryness? Painful intercourse?"

Alexis felt sweat break out on her forehead and she thought she might be having her first hot flash in weeks. "I'm lesbian."

"Yes?"

"Actually, I'm single," Alexis confessed. "I don't have much of anything." Sweat dripped out of her hair, onto her collar.

"Well," said the doctor with a weak smile. "You lucked out on that one. Many women have problems in that area too."

Alexis pulled a tissue from a box on the white counter and sponged her forehead.

"It was the children that threw me," the doctor said, shaking her head. "And, of course, you don't look lesbian."

"Am I supposed to say thank you?" Alexis picked up a magazine and fanned herself. She was angry. Her body felt out of control. She hoped that she was at least losing some water weight. "What does a lesbian look like, anyway?"

"I'm sorry. I didn't mean to offend you." The doctor stammered slightly, then regained her composure. She handed Alexis a booklet and a yellow sticky note with a phone number and name on it. "This should help. I've written down the name of a good massage therapist. You won't need another appointment with me for six months unless you have some medical problem."

"When I hit three hundred pounds, will you consider it a medical problem?" Alexis shot back.

The doctor was at the door. She turned and said, "Try to get some exercise. Get refocused."

"Are you going to tell me to get a lover too?"

"That wouldn't hurt a thing," the doctor said over her shoulder.

Alexis tossed the magazine at the closing door. It thudded and slid downward, pages fluttering.

The following Tuesday Alexis left work early to keep an appointment with a massage therapist. She sat in the waiting room on a wicker chair, reading a magazine. The lighting was soft, relaxing. The curtains on the windows were sheer and ruffled, like the ones her favorite aunt Midge had when Alexis was a child. A small desk held a phone and an appointment book cluttered with scraps of paper. The desk was the cheap kind you get at Kmart and put together at home; her kids had had them and usually dismantled them within a year. A couple of two-drawer filing cabinets with a door across the top sat against the opposite wall, serving as a desk for a small printer. A metal office chair that looked like it came from the Dumpster was stacked with thick manila file folders. Hanging plants and a large potted palm added a homey touch.

A woman came in. Alexis smiled. She looked a little older than Alexis. Plump. Attractive. She sat on a wicker love seat across the room. It snapped and gave slightly under the woman's weight.

Alexis looked at her watch. The woman had pulled a book from her purse and started to read.

"My doctor sent me," Alexis said. The woman looked over the top of her glasses, smiled and nodded, then returned to her book.

"Hormones," Alexis said.

The woman looked up again. Was she annoyed?

"I started gaining weight." Alexis realized the woman was larger than she was and probably wasn't interested. "Every day another pound." Why was she talking? Why couldn't she shut up? It was probably the progestin; it was that time of her cycle.

The woman closed her book and set it in her lap. "Isn't it hell, what we have to put up with?" she said.

Alexis nodded. "If someone had told me ten years ago, I wouldn't have believed them. A lot of the time I don't even feel like myself."

The woman smiled. Not a big smile, but a small smile of acknowledgment. She said simply, "I know."

Alexis's heart leapt—they had connected.

Late-afternoon sun slanted through the window, falling across the woman's shoulders. Alexis noticed her graying hair, long, salt-and-pepper-colored. She felt some envy. She'd started coloring her own dark hair a year ago. She hated it, but couldn't seem to make the decision to stop. "My name's Alexis," she said at last.

"Rose," the woman said.

They were quiet for a minute. Alexis checked her watch again. Her appointment was for ten minutes ago. "She usually runs late," Rose said. "She takes extra time with someone who really needs it, and that screws up her schedule for the rest of the day." Rose shrugged. "No one really minds. Especially when they're the one who needs the extra time."

"Are you here to see Sandra?" Alexis asked.

"Her daughter Dana," Rose said. "They're in together. I usually try to get Sandra, but this is an emergency. I took what I could get."

"You had a massage emergency?"

Rose smiled. "Sounds silly, doesn't it?"

"No sillier than a hormone emergency."

"Now, a hormone emergency," Rose said. "That's a real emergency."

Alexis liked Rose—so much, in fact, that her nipples were getting erect. Damn progestin.

A young man walked through the waiting room, and a barefoot girl in cut-off jeans and a red T-shirt that said "Chicago Bulls" followed. "Did you want to make a next appointment?" the young woman asked.

The man seemed groggy. "I'll call later in the week," he said.

"Okay." The girl smiled. Her teeth were white. Perfect. She turned to Rose. "I'll just be a minute. I need to change the sheets." She left the room at the same time the man went out the front door.

Alexis stared after the girl.

"Dana's very pretty, isn't she?" Rose said softly.

"Takes my breath away," Alexis said. "God, I'm salivating."

In Rose's silence Alexis realized what she'd said. How could she have forgotten herself? She looked across the room. Particles of dust swirled in the sunlight, and Rose's face was in shadow. Alexis wasn't sure, but she thought Rose was smiling.

"My, my," Rose said, clicking her tongue. "You *are* having trouble with hormones, aren't you?"

Alexis slid down in her seat. Sweat broke out on her forehead and ran down the side of her face. When Dana returned to call Rose to the back room, Alexis couldn't look at her.

The massage was wonderful. The room was dim, with soft light and music. Sandra was a big blond woman who spoke in soft tones and had strong hands. Alexis had to excuse herself to pee halfway through the treatment and stopped at the bathroom again on the way out. When she got home she shut herself in her bedroom, threw off her clothes and masturbated. For the first time she noticed that her vagina *was* dry. She needed K-Y jelly even for self-pleasure. Was this her body? The one she'd known all these years? What the hell was happening to her?

The exercise room had emerald green carpets and several shiny chrome machines. Alexis chose the early morning class that met twice a week at 6:00 A.M. Most days the slightest exertion caused sweat to drip from her forehead and run down the valley between her breasts, but the hot flashes were subsiding; they were fewer and farther between. The hormones were working.

Brian, a middle-aged gay man, hovered over her. Alexis hated it. The first day of class there were four women and two older men. Brian favored the men and fussed over them in a way they seemed to love. At the second class two of the women didn't come and a new woman started. It was Rose.

Alexis was thrilled: now there was someone in the class larger than she was. Also, she was happy to see Rose again.

At first Rose didn't recognize her. How could that be? Their meeting had meant so much. They had shared so much. Hadn't they? She gave Rose a big smile, which Rose politely returned. At the end of the class, sitting in the bubbling hot tub with the other two women, Rose asked, "Do I know you?"

"The massage therapist," Alexis answered. "You were seeing Dana that day."

"Oh, yes." Rose laughed. "Menopause."

The other two women, who were probably in their twenties, stared at Alexis as if Rose had mentioned leprosy. Alexis sat in silence, the water bubbling around her, a smile pasted on her face. Was it her imagination or did the women actually slide a little farther away from her?

Weeks passed and though Alexis watched the scale religiously, her weight didn't drop. It did stop increasing, though, and she felt a little better. She started looking forward to the morning workouts. She was always glad to see Rose. Everyone in the class except Alexis and the two men, Paul and Richard (who she was soon convinced were lovers), had a terrible attendance record. Rose missed at least every third session. Alexis hadn't missed a class, but the morning of the storm she almost stayed in bed.

She awoke with a slight headache. She could hear thunder and rain. The room was cool. She pulled the covers up and turned over on her belly, opening one eye. It was 5:30. She had just enough time to brush her teeth, pull on her shorts and T-shirt and get to class.

She lay there for a minute, calculating. Rose would probably miss today. Alexis could use the sleep. She wanted to lie in bed and listen to the storm. But first she needed to pee.

On her way out of the bathroom she stepped on the scale. She was five pounds lighter. She blinked. Stepped off and on again. Five pounds less.

She put on her shorts, pulled her tie-dyed T-shirt over her head and grabbed her gym bag and umbrella. Rain beat down noisily, splashing in puddles. Lightning streaked across the dark gray morning sky. The wind blew her umbrella inside out as she ran from her car to the door. By the time she was inside, her wet hair was plastered to her head, and the shoulders and back of her T-shirt were soaked.

There were four of them that morning: Paul, Richard, Alexis and Rose. Alexis was glad she'd come.

"I lost five pounds," she mouthed to Rose during the warm-ups. Rose put her thumb and forefinger together in an "okay" sign. Alexis felt a warm rush. Was it a hot flash? She waited for the sweat to start pouring. It didn't.

Halfway through the workout Alexis realized that she and Rose would have the women's hot tub and sauna all to themselves. She put extra energy into the workout that morning, feeling good for the first time in months.

Brian had to slow her down at one point. "Have you forgotten your bad back?" he said, patting her damp shoulder.

"Fuck off, Brian. I've lost five pounds!"

"Just be careful, honey," he said. "We don't want you to be the slimmest person in traction."

At the end of the workout Alexis rushed into the dressing room, grabbed her gym bag and unzipped it.

"Shit!" she shouted.

"What's wrong?" Rose was behind her.

"My swimsuit. I left it at home." Alexis pictured the black suit hanging over the shower rod.

"You don't need it."

"What?" Alexis turned. Rose was closer than she'd thought.

"It's just the two of us," Rose said. "You don't need it. Hell, I'll leave mine off too."

"Do you think?"

"Sure. Come on."

Alexis stepped into a changing stall and slowly pulled off her damp clothes. She looked in the narrow mirror. Her body was full. White. Glistening. She was scared and excited. She wanted to get into the water before Rose. Peeking out the door, she saw no one and made a dash for the hot tub.

Rose was standing there, testing the water with her toe. Her body was round, her breasts full with pale brown nipples. Her pubic triangle was dark and feathery. "Water's fine," she said, and stepped in.

Alexis sat in the tub with the warm water bubbling around her. "I can't believe I'm doing this," she said.

"There's no one here but us. Brian and the boys are busy. And you can bet they're not in *their* suits."

"Really?"

"Why the hell do you think they're so religious about attendance?"

Alexis laughed nervously. "Do you think they're making it over there?"

"We can hope."

"Boy, I haven't done anything like that for ever so long," Alexis said wistfully, breathing in the steam from the noisy, churning water.

"Well, you should." Rose moved closer.

"That's what my doctor said."

"Sounds like a smart doctor." Rose was right next to her.

Alexis exhaled slowly. Purple shadows gathered in the corners of the locker room. Rose's gym bag sat on a bench, two white towels folded beside it. Waiting. Alexis felt her muscles relax. "This is nice," she said.

Rose pushed a strand of hair off her damp forehead. "When I was a kid, the neighbor girl and I played in a wading pool in the backyard. On hot days we swam naked. I guess our mothers thought we were too young for that to matter. We'd play out there for hours. Get sunburned all over. I was always a fat, healthy-looking kid."

Alexis tried to imagine the wading pool. Hot summer days. The cool water. Two naked children.

"We'd touch ourselves," Rose went on. "It was great. By the time I was nine I was coming. I think that's early. But we had that pool."

Alexis leaned her head back and let her body float slightly off the marble bench.

"When I was twelve, I was coming with the shower massage in my mother's bathroom. Spraying it at my cunt."

"Didn't you run out of hot water a lot?" Alexis asked, thinking of her own teenaged kids' long showers. Her youngest would stay in there as long as the hot water lasted.

"Oh, no," said Rose. "It didn't take long."

Alexis laughed.

"Sometimes even now I like to position myself under the running water in the bathtub," Rose said. "Of course, I'm older. Fatter. I must look a sight with my legs in the air like that. But what the hell?"

Alexis closed her eyes and tried to imagine Rose in the bathtub. "Sex was always easy for me," she sighed. "These last few years have been hard. A big breakup. Menopause. I feel like I've lost my place. Like I have to start all over again."

As if from a long way off, just over the sounds of the bubbling water, Alexis heard Rose say, "We could touch ourselves here. We could use these jet streams."

Alexis opened her eyes. Rose already had one hand working under the water.

Something deep in Alexis's middle ached. She slid her hand down her belly, separated her folds, touched the flowery edges of her labia. The water was swirling. She pushed and kneaded her swollen lips. She held her breath.

"I'd like to kiss you," Rose said softly. She had moved very close.

Alexis nodded.

Rose's mouth was warm and moist. Alexis leaned into the kiss as Rose embraced her, pressing her soft flesh against her. The kiss lasted a long time, moving, soft pressure, moist tongue. At last Alexis pulled away to breathe. A low moan escaped her throat.

"Turn around, move this way," Rose whispered.

Alexis turned sideways on the bench and pulled one knee up. A jet stream of air flooded against her cunt. Rose cradled her from behind, reached around, and gently moved Alexis's fingers away, replacing them with her own. Slowly Alexis moved her head luxuriously from side to side. She stretched and wiggled against Rose's fingers. A tingling sensation spread. How could anyone touch like that? How did Rose know just what was needed and give just that, no more?

Alexis willed herself to let go and with a rush of exhilaration her climax, a mixture of pleasure and pain, beat through her. She felt one with the churning water, spilling, flowing, warmly melting.

Alexis turned to Rose. Sweat dripped off her face and she was panting. "Wow," she said.

"You're so articulate." Rose smiled.

Alexis kissed her and touched her voluptuous breast. "Come sit on my knee," she said.

Rose shifted her body. The warm water made her light, buoyant. With her arms around Alexis's shoulders Rose straddled her thigh and moved in a gentle fucking motion. Alexis felt the water sucking and swirling, the pressure of Rose's cunt, somehow warmer, wetter, more slippery than the churning water. Rose was right. It didn't take long.

The jet stream timer ended and the room was suddenly quiet. Rose cried out, clinging to Alexis. She rested her head on Alexis's shoulder and whimpered softly.

After a minute Rose said, "We'd better go. Brian will think
we've drowned in here."

Rain was coming down vigorously as the two women walked
through the gym. The window behind Brian's desk looked like a
gray waterfall.

"You girls look beat," Brian said.

Alexis nodded. "I think this is helping, though."

"You *look* like it's helping." Brian smiled.

"Thanks." She winked at Rose.

Alexis opened the door and hesitated. Rain splashed on the
sidewalk and street. Rivers of water ran to the parking lot.

"Damn," she said. "I just got dried off."

Then she plunged into the downpour.

Debbie Esters

My Nail Broke: A Story in Four Scenes

Prologue

I broke a nail. Who cares? Well, maybe you need to hear how it happened. I wish you'd have been there to see for yourself.

It all began when I decided that life is too short for me to be walking around as a horny bitchy down-at-the-mouth celibate and I went off the wagon, sexually speaking, in a big way. One issue that had been on my mind during my celibacy was getting it on with more than just one other person. I'm not the type of person who initiates much, but I'll do almost anything once if I'm asked—so when Michael asked me if I wanted to go to a sex party that he saw advertised in a magazine, I said okay.

Now, Michael had been to one such party with another friend of his, but she got cold feet and decided not to participate. Michael told me all about that first party so I knew what to expect when I got there.

Scene One

We drive to Hayward. I guess you got to go to the burbs to find anyone who's bored enough to pay for a sex party. I'm sure there's plenty happening in the city, but by invitation only.

So we go to this house painted green with a neglected front yard. Inside we're greeted by this skinny broad in a robe who asks us to sign in. It doesn't take two seconds to sum up that I'm one of the best-looking broads there and Michael is number one for guys. But he sees one pretty lady he likes, and I'm enjoying all the attention I'm getting so we decide to stay.

We walk to the kitchen and each pour ourselves a glass of the Chardonnay we'd brought along. We meet our hostess, Sophia, and take a tour. I haven't seen so many mattresses in one house since that movie where a mafia gang all live in one place during a mob war. It's a bit too cheap and tacky for my taste: I mean black lights and fluorescent posters are cool, but a sexy scene, in my opinion, must have matching sheets and incensed air, candles and erotic knickknacks on low tables. This was more like plastic flowers and faded prints of blondes with big tits on cars, country western music and stick-on-the-wall mirror squares. But everything was very clean. I like that. Cleanliness makes me less inhibited.

Scene Two

After changing into a towel, the attire of preference at the party, I go back to the deck where there's a hot tub. I have to squeeze my way into the circle of naked strangers, plus Michael who's already there. *New meat* must be emblazoned on my forehead, but hey, that's what I'm here for, meat. I'm not in the tub ten seconds and the guy next to me has his hand up my cunt. An old geezer he is, but his sixty-odd years have taught him a thing or two about hand jobs.

I can't stay in hot water too long—the heat wrinkles my skin and ruins my acrylic nails; remember, this is a story about a broken nail. So I say, "My nails can't take the water," and slide myself off of Mr. Sixty-something to go dry off.

I sit down to finish my glass of wine and smoke a cigarette in the living room. Not much happening. Two TVs going simultaneously; one with the Olympics and the other showing a video of a cock being sucked by painted lips. There may or may not have been people attached to these body parts; I never saw any. You know the type of video I mean.

Michael appears and tells me there's something hot going on upstairs so I extinguish my cigarette and follow him.

Scene Three

It turns out that Sharon, a pretty, tan lady Michael saw earlier, is getting it on with her husband Larry. Michael loves to watch, so we go join them on the adjacent mattress. I don't quite know what to do. Being new to the scene and not much into visuals, I begin to give Michael a massage. I figure that if rubbing those hard, tight runner's legs of his doesn't get me in the mood, nothing will.

Sharon speaks first, addressing us with a simple "Hello, is this your first time?"

It takes us a minute to clarify that it is my first party but that Michael had been to one before because most folks who come to these parties are married couples or at least in long-term relationships. We, being just casual partners, are unusual. After a weird pause Larry asks me if I want Sharon to give me a massage.

I think I need to describe Sharon to you at this point. One very sexy lady. Caucasian. Deep, deep tan with white tan-line breasts that shine in the black light. Very slender, the body type that when turned sideways sort of disappears, but with an unusually soft round ass. And skin: smoothest skin I have ever felt, on anyone. She is like soft brown silk crepe, the kind that floats through your fingers.

I guess she and Larry think that of the four of us I'm the one needing the most attention, being new meat and female; I know the situation of a foursome where the other girl gets cold feet. Must be what they anticipate, because Sharon gets to rubbing me and Larry joins in and Michael takes me in one hand and Sharon in the other—I think. At some point I just close my eyes and start drinking in all these sensations. I mean, six hands rubbing me, three mouths sucking on my tits, licking my ears. I reach out my hands; it's cock to the right of me, cock to the left

and pussy in the middle. My first pussy, other than my own. I
think I'm developing an appreciation for pussy. It's fun to compare shapes and sizes and then it's like driving someplace
familiar—the car, you know, drives itself. I mean, you just know
how to move your hands on the wheel to take the vehicle home.
A clit is a clit and I've spent enough time with my own to know
exactly how she feels and what "ooh" means and what "ahh" is.
We're talking easy. See, with men it's always a bit tricky the first
few times until you figure what does it for them. But Sharon—a
piece of cake, or should I say, coffee mousse.

There is something very sweet about a foursome. You reach
out and your hands find parts and you don't know right away
which is whose but the textures blend; silky skin here, coarse
chest hair there, a slippery cunt, a hard smooth cock, hard balls,
soft balls, tits, nipples of various shapes and sizes. A flesh cock-
tail; each tasty morsel blends in with the flavor of the next.

Nothing lasts forever. Sharon wants to eat me but I don't consider cunnilingus to be safe sex so I say no thanks. Now, Michael
wants to eat me too and had been asking me for it all week but
I tell him no for the same reason, so he goes down instead on
Sharon. Right about here I contemplate asking Larry to suit
up—put on a condom—and fuck me but I don't know if being
demanding is correct etiquette so I don't say a word. Mistake.
He starts watching Sharon but sort of moves away from the
scene, dejected. She notices this and manages to drag herself off
of Michael's face to ask him what's up. He says he's feeling left
out and sure enough his cock is flaccid. Being such a loving wife,
Sharon sets to sucking him back into shape. Now, watching her
suck him is all Michael wants to really get him going so he suits
up and drags my ass to where he wants it so he can fuck me,
which is fine because I'd been wanting it for ten minutes or so
while he was busy with lunch and Larry was feeling sorry for
himself.

Well it gets good because she takes Larry from her mouth to
her cunt and I put my head down and my butt up so Michael
can watch them while he pounds me. But no one's coming yet.
Larry gets to talking about whether he wants to continue at all,
so I climb up on his chest and rub my drooling cunt on him, fig-

uring that's got to make him feel good, which it does, but he says, "I can't feel anything with a condom on."

And I say, "I don't fuck without them."

I do want to fuck the man, so we're at an impasse. Then Sharon says, "I'm not fixed. I mean, my tubes aren't tied and I won't let anybody but Larry fuck me because he is fixed and we have two kids and that's plenty. I don't trust condoms not to break."

I'm still holding to my safe-sex standards. So Michael goes back to eating Sharon and Larry and I just sort of sit back and watch.

It is fun to watch. She obviously is getting off, and getting on and getting off again, just writhing there under Michael's face. At some point I join in, sucking her tits or fondling them. Then Michael moves from sucking her to fucking me full force. She moves on to me too and Larry starts fingering my clit. I think, oh goody, my turn again, and all of a sudden I know it's towel-time. I start giggling this giggle that always needs to be explained because it's not that I'm laughing *at* anything or anybody but just that I'm having a good time and if I don't get something under me I'm going to ejaculate all over the bed and make puddles on the mattress.

Anyway, Michael is fucking me, they are fondling me and the three of them are making me come all over the towel. Larry is finger-fucking me and Michael is back on Sharon and every time I giggle I dribble some more onto the towel and it is getting so I can still laugh but I can't ejaculate anymore and Larry hasn't figured out yet that what I'm doing is coming all over his hand.

So I can't come anymore and Sharon's having orgasms on Michael's tongue again and I glance at Larry, who's looking dejected, like a beached seal. I take that as a challenge. I re-member reading about a woman who puts condoms on cocks with her mouth. First she practices with bananas, then works her way up to cucumbers until she finally gets the guts to ask a friend if she can practice on him.

Well, it's one of those times when I know I should have prac-ticed when I was reading the book, because I want to use the technique on Larry. I think, Can you do it, girl? Hell yes! I answer myself. But this is going to be trial by fire.

So I say, "Larry, I want to suck your cock, but I'm not going to do it without a condom, do you mind if I put one on you with my mouth? You don't have to do anything."

"You can try," he says, "but I just don't get off that way."

Well, I pick one of Michael's condoms out of his variety pack figuring that I ought to use the best, and I suck the reservoir tip into my mouth with the edge around my lips and head for Larry.

"Hey, doesn't she look like one of those inflatable dolls," he says.

Wham! I grab his cock in my mouth, suck him in and push down on the condom edge. He's deep in my throat and I want to gag, but voilà! He's dressed!

I suck his cock hard. He's big and not easy to eat. I still want to feel him in my cunt so I straddle him. He grabs my ass and starts pumping from underneath. He thrusts and twists and makes me want to pump back. He's one of those fucks that can fill your cunt and rub your clit with his pelvis at the same time, no hands needed. Then he comes. Really quickly when you think of it.

"Gives you some respect for latex," I say sarcastically. Sliding off him the condom sticks in my cunt and I have to take it out carefully and carry it to the bathroom, where I wash my hands.

It's pushing midnight. Larry and Sharon have to split; Wednesday is, after all, a workday. They hand their phone number to Michael; it reads *Jean and Arnold* . . .

Scene Four

I'm feeling pretty good about myself. I mean, I always feel good when I come buckets-full, don't you? But I think about Michael and how he sure is a tough nut to crack sometimes. What do you expect from a man who runs six miles just for fun? So I'm not surprised at all when he asks me to go with him upstairs to the *Big Room* for some more action. It's big all right, with about six mattresses all pushed together and a big screen TV continuously running videos.

The room is vacant when we get there. Michael and I get started one on one. But honey will draw flies: the ratio of men to women had been about 2:1 when we'd arrived but by this time many women had left. So a small crowd of guys comes in to watch us. I hear a strange voice say, "I'm next, I . . . I mean if you want to."

I don't answer but I feel hands on my breasts again and mouths on my thighs and I'm feeling too relaxed, too good not to enjoy it all. Now, Michael, he does like to watch, but I'm really surprised when he dismounts and moves aside. Then he whispers to me, "Is this what you want?" and I answer in the affirmative.

The first guy goes to eat my cunt and I stop him and tell him I won't have that without plastic wrap or latex. That gets some laughs from the others but I close my eyes, lying on my back, and what follows is the fulfillment of one of the few fantasies I've ever had: one after the other these four (or five) men line up to fuck me. I keep my eyes shut and it creates a mystery: see, I don't know which cock belongs to what voice or what hand belongs to which face. Michael is right there, jacking himself off, letting me jack him off too. Michael's sweet; even as I'm getting him off he keeps an eye on all the goings (and comings) for me. At first I try to touch each cock to check for dress code, but Michael tells me he's watching them so I can just relax.

A lineup of men, each just waiting his turn to fuck me—that was my fantasy. But the reality is better. I mean, each one is like his own short story. The old guy from the hot tub shows up. He starts something but never finishes and I never see him again. I feel one light touch on my thigh and hear a heavy Pakistani accent: "Oh, I came before I even touched her."

I guess he did because I hear all the other guys laugh. Then someone flips me over, enters me and with one hand on my clit, fucks me and makes me come again. One after the other they sort of come and go. Michael too—only after he comes he goes to the bathroom and is nice enough to bring me a glass of water on his way back. Because, you know, I feel like just lying there, still, for a moment. I reach up for the cup, maybe too fast, and my middle finger jams into the porcelain mug, and my nail breaks.

Epilogue

On the way home, after one last dip in the hot tub and some homemade lasagna, Michael and I talk about how we should have been paid to go to that party instead of paying to be there. But this morning I wake up relaxed and think to myself, Gee whiz, I fucked about eight people last night, including a woman, and I had an honest-to-goodness fantasy fulfilled for real. I might not have given any of these guys the time of day in another situation, I sure didn't give anyone my phone number, but each one was part of my *lineup*, just waiting his turn for me. I mean, this is not something that one or two friends can do for you. It takes a whole bunch to form a line, right?

Anyway, I got to go now and get this nail fixed.

Angela Fairweather

My Dance at Juliana's

Juliana's was a Tokyo disco where women were admitted free to perform erotic dances onstage. In its heyday as many as 3,000 people watched the amateur dancers. Juliana's closed in September 1994, after three years in business, under pressure from an outraged public.

When I start dancing a surge of power rushes through my body and I feel high. I love that feeling; I live for nights at Juliana's. I open my feathered fan and undulate to the music, moving my fan real slow—two big flutters above my waist, two below. I pretend not to notice the men staring up at me; I keep my eyes discreetly lowered, at least at first. But I notice who's looking and who isn't, and when I have an audience, I make small gestures to further entice them.

Machiko and I discovered Juliana's about a year ago. "Kaoru," she said, "let's go see what it's like." "Sure," I said, "we can check it out." The first night there we realized this was the place for us—it made us feel alive.

Machiko and I are secretaries in the same office. We hate our jobs, hate the way the men treat us in the traditional way, as if we were foolish, dispensable objects. Sometimes we talk about it over tea, but really, there's no solution. Mostly we find ways to escape.

I wear my skirts skin-tight, what we call "body con," body conscious. At first I didn't; I was afraid to be too provocative and maybe get thrown out of the club, like Hatsuka did when she wore no underwear. But once I caught on, I knew what was okay and what was too much. We've stretched the rules a lot this year and we have much more freedom now. Machiko says I push the limits and should be more careful, but I think we should rebel, let them know that we have feelings and desires that matter too.

Two months ago I bought a bustier. My breasts are full for a Japanese girl, and the bustier emphasizes them even more. I can't believe how much this attracts the men.

I wear sheer bikini panties that often ride up my hips when I dance. Sometimes I pull the front of my panties tight so the men can see more when they stare up at me from the dance floor. I get wet when I see someone staring; it makes me hot to see how much power I have. I'm tempted to put my fingers down there and let them watch, or even get crotchless panties so they can see me better.

When I was seventeen I was voted the prettiest girl in our school in Osaka, where I come from. Also the most sexy. It's an all-girls school and each year the students vote on the cutest, prettiest, smartest, and so forth. They also voted me the most brash—because one warm spring day when we were in English class, I decided to tease our teacher, who was American. I knew he had a crush on me; actually, we all knew it. He was facing the blackboard, so I stood up on my chair real quietly. When he turned around I lifted my skirt over my head. He was only a few feet from me and he had no choice but to look. He got really red and said, "Kaoru, sit down at once." We all laughed.

Japanese men like their women cute and pert, but also submissive. At least the traditional men do, but frankly I want nothing to do with tradition. Maybe it's because my name is modern, and they say we're affected by our names just like we're affected by astrology. I don't think my parents know about the incident at school and why I was voted most sexy and brash, but my brother does. He heard about it from Reiko's brother, Takeshi. He wasn't happy about it and told me I'd better watch out, but at least he kept his mouth shut to the rest of our family. Being rebellious gets me in trouble, but I don't intend to change—at least not yet.

When I came to Tokyo I was a typical girl from a respectable family. I was trained as a secretary, and since I did well in my studies it wasn't hard for me to get a good job. I found an apartment that I share with my friend from school, Reiko, who also breaks rules, so I'm in safe company. I don't tell on her and she doesn't tell on me. We go home once a month to visit our families and we keep ourselves subdued at work. We don't want to give our families cause for alarm.

I'm starting to socialize with the men who watch me, and I've let a few of them take me home. Frankly, I was uneasy the first time—actually, a little scared—because you never know if they're just going to be a little pushy, or if they might actually force you. After all, they figure you're fair game if you're flaunting yourself on stage.

But the big worry is the Yakuza. They run the gambling and prostitution rings. They abduct women and force them to work for them, especially the American prostitutes who come here to work because Japanese men think they're exotic. But the Yakuza sometimes blackmail Japanese girls. They frequent the clubs to check us out. I can usually tell them from the guys who are just there to cruise; you learn after a while. Besides, the guys at the door are my friends and they watch out for me.

I'm getting bolder. I love how it feels to mix with the men, all the time pretending to be demure. Now that I've had several lovers, I know what to do and how to act to make them crazy for me.

Let me tell you what it's like to be a secretary in Tokyo. We wear dresses or suits to work, sometimes even slacks, but it's always pretty straight and formal. I wear my hair tied back at the neck and not much makeup, just a little blusher, eyeliner and lipstick.

The men expect me to make tea first thing before they come in and I have to serve them while I bring them their phone and fax messages. All day it's "Kaoru, take a letter," or "Kaoru, I need you to call Aishi at the brokerage right away, hurry now," or "Kaoru, I need 30 copies of this," and it's just before the time to go home and they know I'll miss my train. They make jokes all the time, often rude, always sexist, but I pretend not to notice. It isn't lost on them that I'm pretty—maybe even sexy—but I play it down and act like nothing is on my mind except waiting on them while I look for a good husband.

Inside I feel all nerves and frustration. I don't know how we keep ourselves so composed. I guess it's because of how we're raised. You have to hide your feelings from the time you're little—that's just how it is. By the weekend all this tension has built up inside and I feel like I'm going to explode. That's when I go to Juliana's.

First I take a long bath and then I oil my skin and mousse my hair so it's all tousled as it hangs over my shoulders and down my back. I stand naked in front of the mirror and admire myself while I dress. When I wear the bustier I don't do this, but when I have on my leopard skin dress, I pinch my nipples several times to make them stand out and rub against the fabric. Then I put on my bikini panties and a belt that hangs on my hips, or I wear my skirt that's so short it almost breaks club rules. Hiroshi's in charge, though, and he's got this crush on me, so he never says anything; I make sure to talk with him a few times each night, and sometimes I brush my body against his so he feels my breasts through my dress. I make it look like an accident, but he's on to me.

I put on my makeup carefully so I don't look washed out in the light, and then gold spike heels, a pair of long earrings and a few bangles on my wrists. Most of the girls who go to Juliana's change clothes in the bathrooms at the train station because they're too embarrassed to be seen dressed like that in public. I think that's silly, but I have to admit I do wear a full coat.

I go to Juliana's with Reiko and Machiko. The stage at Juliana's is three feet above the dance floor. We dance on the main floor if it's too early and not many of the women who dance are there, but soon enough we climb up on the stage because that's where you're bound to get noticed.

When I do go home alone afterward, I tease myself with fantasies. Sometimes I stand in front of the mirror in a demi-bra and bikini panties and act out my part of the fantasy. Other times I lie in bed in the dark and watch the scene as if it was a movie in which I star.

My favorite fantasy takes place at Juliana's. I am on the stage dancing. I am wearing my tightest, most revealing dress with the low top and the short, short skirt. Other women are dancing too, but the men are all looking up at me. Slowly, one by one the other women disappear, until only I remain in the spotlight dancing.

I am not demure, nor do I keep my eyes downcast. Instead, I look directly at each man, my eyes hard, my mouth in a sultry pout, as I move my hips in rhythm with the music. I put my fan down, and sensuously fondle my breasts, accentuating each one, pulling on my nipples. My hands follow the contours of my body down my hips. I let my skirt ride up so it's resting on the tops of my thighs and the edges of my panties show. Then I slowly look from man to man, pulling my panties apart so they can see they're crotchless and I am open to them.

I slip my fingers inside where it's fragrant and wet like a flower at dawn. My other hand plays with my breasts, and I arch my back, my face toward the ceiling, so they can see how good it feels to have my fingers inside, how hot and wet I am. I bring my fingers to my mouth and slowly suck them, all the time staring blatantly at the men's crotches. They are all growing very hard. Good. That is just what I want.

I ease my dress up over my hips and my waist, then pull it over my head. My hair drops back as I dance, my arms are high in the air, my dress is falling to my feet. I look through the audience and see my bosses standing there, their faces all shock and amazement. Then there's the cute guy down the hall from my office, the arrogant one who flirts with us brashly, thinking we must be dying for his attention. And there in the crowd is Hiroshi, Reiko's brother, Takeshi, and oh, even my brother Riota! I wink at Riota and he stares back, shocked. He wants to drag me off the stage but he is frozen in place—and what? Yes! He is very aroused too.

Some of the women, even my friends, are in the audience.

They admire my total control, the flouting of everything we have been taught to be. They are mesmerized. And, too, they are very aroused. Aroused in the way that our genitals tingle when we are repulsed by but also drawn to something truly scandalous. The way I felt when I saw a picture of a beautiful transsexual.

I am heady with power. I say to my audience, "Expose yourselves to me. Show me what you have that I might want." They all comply, unbuckling belts, unzipping flies, pulling up skirts and discarding panties. The men bring themselves out for me to see; they are hard and moist. I study each one carefully. And the women too.

"Come up on stage with me and spread your lips," I say. "I want to see you unfold like roses." The women boldly come onto the stage, encircle me, and open their lips. I pull my breasts out over the fabric of my bra, then kneel down to look at each beautiful pussy, blushing deep, surrounded by a mantle of black silk. I slip my tongue into each woman, one at a time, balancing myself with my hands on each woman's hips. I run my tongue over their clits as they hold themselves open to me, some sighing, some crying out a little as I lick. I bring one of my breasts up and rub it between their aching lips. I slip my fingers deep inside them. The men are going wild, stroking themselves, eyes glued to the spectacle.

After I lick each beautiful pussy, I turn the women around and they play with themselves for the men. They do it not to please the men but to be totally in control, wearing haughty looks on their faces. This makes the men even more crazy. Yes!

I come down from the stage and walk through the audience. I study each of the men, holding their cocks to see how they feel, cupping their balls in one hand and gently scratching my long nails along the inside of their thighs. Even my Hiroshi, Takeshi, and yes, even my brother! I am so bold, even I am shocked . . . well, actually, I'm shocked only to be telling you this fantasy.

I choose one man and I bring him on stage. I have never seen his face before. And he is very big, especially for a Japanese man. He follows me with his hard cock leading his body.

There is a bed now on stage too; the women have brought it

there, and they flank it on both sides. I lead him to one side and he removes his clothes for everyone to see. The women remove my bra and panties, and then they lay me on the bed, spread my legs open, and caress and lick me all over. The man I have chosen and those in the audience ache so badly they can hardly bear it.

The women stroke me and lick me until I am so hot I must have him to ease the throbbing inside. Two women lead him to me, and another two hold my legs open. He enters me hard, thrusting into me again and again until I come very hard and I scream.

Sometimes I allow him to come, other times, not. It is my choice, after all, my pleasure. The women now may have whomever they choose from the audience, men or women, whatever they want. We are the pagan goddesses, the deities of fertility, and they are simply our vassals. The music returns, loud, and I grab my fan and dance naked in the spotlight as everyone applauds and begins to dance again.

You know, there is one more component to all of this, and that is what will happen next—what will happen to our lives. My girlfriends, even Reiko and Machiko, may talk freedom, but what do they really want? A boyfriend who will spend time with them and take them to the beach. In the next five years they expect to marry and settle down and be good wives and mothers.

There is nothing wrong with that; in fact it is a good thing to aspire to. I wish that could be me as well, but I have a deep secret. I have already told you so much that I will confide this to you too, though now I must say I find it hard to look you straight in the eyes; my head is downcast and I feel submissive.

I have a love for women. Yes, I crave having power with men and I sleep with them. But what I really want is a woman. And that is not something a Japanese girl can speak of. In fact, it is even more unspeakable than my fantasies with men, more even than my desire for power and control.

It wasn't always this way. The pillow books of women in the courts of the Samurai tell of how the women provided comfort and erotic pleasure for one another. Of course, it was within the context of men being away at war. Nevertheless, they could touch and love each other, woman to woman, at least part of the time.

I am not sure of what I should do. But I have read that in America it is different, that the women can love each other there. I found a magazine that tells about it, but my English isn't good, especially to read. Machiko reads English better, but I am afraid to speak to her of this as I don't want to risk losing our friendship. Perhaps someday.

In the meantime I will continue to dance. A short dress and gold spike heels, my fan slowly moving, two flutters above the waist, two flutters below.

Calla Conova

❧❦❧

Electricity in My Bed

At 5:00 P.M., dressed in the standard brown Pacific Gas & Electric work clothes, she stood in my doorway, responding to my service request. At first I only noticed her short sandy hair, wire-framed glasses and a toolbox in one hand. I had been too involved in moving to even think about sex. But it didn't take long for her to bring me back to my senses.

I watched her make her routine check of pilot lights, her competent fingers lighting matches, tools clattering in her toolbox. I had once been an electrician, so I felt some camaraderie. Or was it something else?

"This isn't right." She pointed threateningly to the water heater vent. "Gonna have to turn it off till it gets corrected."

Shocked at this disruption of my plans, I protested, "I've been moving and cleaning for two days. I was counting on a shower tonight."

Her eyes swept me down and back up again so quickly I might have dismissed it. But then they settled on my breasts, assessing me. I started wishing I was wearing something more revealing, something that would tell her I wasn't wearing a bra, that my breasts were real nice with talented pink nipples that stand out with only a whisper of attention. I'd never had a woman check me out like that. Men, plenty of times. It was familiar, that look, but this was a whole new context.

She retreated coolly down the stairs, looking over her shoulder as she spoke. "All right, take it now before the water cools off. I'm working this area all night. Here's my emergency number." She came back up the stairs and shoved her card at me. "Call if the landlord gets it fixed tonight."

She was almost mean. So why was my crotch so excited? I called the landlord right away.

Was I going to pursue this attraction? I was shaking as I hurried into the bathroom to undress. She dominated my thoughts as I stood beneath the blessedly hot water. Mmm, I *am* beginning to think about sex again. After all these months celibate, and now turned on by a woman! *That's* different.

I shampooed and soaped everything, and then shaved my legs, wondering if lesbians liked legs shaved or au naturel. Well, I liked them smooth. This was my fantasy; I was going to have it any way I wanted. Was she lesbian, bi or like me—attracted for the first time? She seemed strong and in control. I'd always envisioned it that way—someone dominant to tell me how to do it all. But what was I thinking? This was a PG&E service person!

Hot water all used. I relished moving through the fresh paint-scented air completely nude. These thoughts of dangerous possibility would last me for days.

My answering machine showed one message: the landlord coming over in a few minutes. Got to get dressed. I put on some baggy jeans, a sweatshirt and tennis shoes. Forget all this; back to my nonrevealing protection.

After three hours of the landlord's huffing and puffing with the water heater and boring me with stories of his six grandkids, it was fixed. I was alone and getting juicy again, just imagining what might happen if I called her. I did, and while the phone rang I flung off my sweatshirt. I wanted her to know, over the phone, that my nipples were standing at attention. Her radio phone crackled, her voice sounded very distant and professional. My voice was kind of squeaky; I couldn't help it.

"This is the person who has the water heater that you turned off. I'm on 16th Avenue . . . Yeah, right. Landlord fixed it. Could you . . . uh . . . come over now and . . . uh . . . turn it back on?"

I laughed nervously, waiting for some signal in her voice. God, I was getting hot, and about to chicken out. There was silence as she checked her list. Still revealing nothing she said, "I can be there in an hour. Did you get your shower?"

That was all she said. My heart was beating hard, and my face was flushed. I wished she would come stomping up the stairs right now, saying something, even something cold—saying it with a look that would take the doubt away.

I tried clothes on, checking myself out in the mirror. I put on the flowered drop-waist dress. Too coy and feminine. How about the black cleavage-creating bra and sheer white blouse? No. What if she wasn't even interested, or had some other woman? What if I was making this whole thing up? Come on now, you know what you felt. I finally settled on black cotton leggings and a black, oversized button-down shirt, unbuttoned a little more than usual. No bra. I told myself I would be wearing this no matter who was coming to the door. But the truth was, I often stood alone in front of the mirror, wearing this shirt completely unbuttoned, my hands sliding over my body. It was my turn-on shirt.

Half an hour left. Earrings? Lipstick? I decided to just go plain, but to add sandalwood lotion.

In the bathroom again, I yanked down my leggings, no panties. I never needed an excuse to smooth the scented lotion onto my hips, butt, and inner thighs, all the way to my pussy. My pussy: maybe I should give it a little attention before she came, just to get the musk in the air. Fifteen more minutes, there was time. If it turned out to be a false alarm I would at least have had my fantasy bubble before it burst.

Getting the lubricant out of my bedroom dresser, I took it, my vibrator and *her* to bed. *She is right here watching me, then helping me, her commanding hands pulling my clothes off, her intense eyes inspecting and approving of my breasts. I'm naked—she is still dressed in her brown uniform. She authoritatively pushes my legs wider. Then her tongue is flicking and sucking. She is looking up from between my legs and asking if I*

*like her doing it. I beg her for more. I am swooning, thrilled to
have her push me around. My hips buck up for her access, for
her viewing, for her poking fingers and tasting, sucking tongue.
She teases me, "I think you want to come in my face. I can make
you come so hard you'll never want a man again."*

*And I beg her, "Yes ... God ... Fuck me ... Woman-fuck me
... oh yeah." Screaming. "Oh yeah ... I'm ... shit yeah ...
coming ..."*

The doorbell rang. I wiped my hands on the sheets, pulled up
my leggings and half-closed the door on the unmade bed. My
face was burning when I opened the door. "So you got your
shower, eh?" she asked, checking me over, almost sniffing to see
how clean I'd gotten. She was not wearing her glasses or her
jacket. I tried not to be conspicuous as I eyed her small breasts.

Our eyes met again. "Yeah, nice and hot, too." I smiled, step-
ping aside for her. She brushed my arm as she passed. I followed
her to the water heater. She did her check in silence; I wondered what she was thinking.

"Okay. You've got hot water now. It's according to regula-
tions." She filled out a form in triplicate on a clipboard.

"Is there anything else you want ... uh, I mean, want to
check?" My heart was racing, my cunt aching, and my tone
slightly desperate; I felt wetness starting to soak the crotch of my
leggings. Did she notice?

"Well, you're the last house on my schedule tonight." She put
down her clipboard. "Do you mind if I wash my hands?" She
moved toward the kitchen sink.

"Sure, but I've got some nicer soap in the bathroom. Smells
like sandalwood."

"Oh, this will do just fine," she said as she picked up the bottle of dish soap.

The fluorescent ceiling light was buzzing. "I hate this light," I
said. "I never turn it on. I only had it on for your work. Are you
done now?" I flipped the switch and the buzzing stopped, leaving a dim light over the stove. She studied me as she dried her
hands on a dish towel.

She seemed to be taking her time so that I wouldn't miss her
drift. "There *are* some other things I'd like to check," she said.

"Care for a soda?" I turned to the refrigerator and began talking rapidly. "How long have you worked this job? Do you enjoy it? Do you always work at night?" She answered in short replies that I didn't even hear.

We had definitely stepped over the line of a PG&E service call. She lifted the bottle to her lips, tipping it up but keeping her gaze on me. Around the third sip her eyes began roving over me again. Yeah, I was right! I leaned on the refrigerator across from her, resting my head back.

"You changed out of your moving clothes. Bet that feels nice." Why didn't I greet her at the door with no clothes on, still wet from my shower? I thought. She jolted me into the next level of intensity by taking two steps toward me, saying, "Yes there is definitely something I need to check. What kind of shirt is this, a girl's shirt, a guy's shirt?" Her clean hand fingered the light fabric of my sleeve. Looking down, I saw the gaping spaces between the buttons, my flesh darkly visible.

"It's comfortable. Feels good with nothing under it. What do you wear when you aren't working?"

"Oh, I like jeans and T-shirts. But you look great in this."

We found ourselves staring alternately at each other's lips and breasts. Her nostrils were flared. I looked away, suddenly shy. Her hand smoothed its way up my arm, across my shoulder. Holding my breath, I watched her hand proceed boldly to my breast. She took my nipple between her thumb and index finger, very intentionally pinching and releasing. I exhaled loudly through my mouth. Heat flashed to my crotch.

"You like girls? Yeah, you are cute with your gumdrop nipples." My knees almost gave out. "You like girls, don't you? You don't have to answer. Test the merchandise first."

Full mouth, juicy kiss, our tongues very involved with each other. Deep throat moans, her hand cupping my breast. Dizzy, I loved her pressing me against the refrigerator.

Amazingly, my hand went to her crotch first. *I know what to do with this. I know what I like.* She unzipped her pants and I reached in, feeling her as wet as I was. It was so easy to find her clit and finger it in hard circles. Her breath heaved.

"Yeah, you like girls," she said as she gingerly caught my nipple with her teeth. Pulling off the rest of our clothes, we stumbled to the mussed bed, where my vibrator lay on the pillow.

"Ooh la la, girl, I am so glad you got over your shyness," she said, reaching for the white plastic vibrator. " 'Cause you are gonna get girl-fucked the right way your first time. Yeah, I can tell it's your first time. You just relax." She pushed me down and pinned one of my hands to the mattress.

Her turn-on patter was doing its trick. "Let me just slide this toy up inside you. I want to watch you. Just slow. Just a little bit at a time. You want this much?" She looked up to watch my face. "How 'bout this much?" Another inch of plastic. "You want a little more?" I spread my knees wider in answer. The vibrator twisted further inside me, sliding easily with my juices. Succumbing to her excited me more than anything ever had.

Without warning she roughly pulled the slippery toy out of me and pushed my legs together. Shocked and desperate, I tried to grab the thing. She calmly held it out of my reach, placing it to her face and taking in its thick aroma.

"More, please," she had me begging pitifully. I would do anything now. I admired her discipline even as I squirmed.

With the vibrator against her clit, she whispered, "Let me have a few plunges." I watched her expert maneuvers. Her eyes told me to look but don't touch. I watched her fucking herself, her eyes closed. The fingers of one hand attacked her clit, the other hand was grinding the thing inside her. The wet sucking sound drove me wild. She opened her eyes halfway and eased off. "Ah . . . yeah . . . Now what else do I need to check?"

A lusty picture of her going down on me gave me a rush. She caught the picture. "I gotta check this part."

Her fingers combed through my triangle of hair. Her breath and fingers became inspectors. Fingers and shivering tongue went sliding, pressing, flicking, entering, probing. A hum from her mouth full on my vulva transmitted a fine vibration that caused my eyes to roll. I clutched her head, encouraging her, and impulsively nuzzled my face into her aromatic and sweaty crotch.

Finally! The act I had always wondered if I could actually do. I started lapping at this woman like I was in a watermelon eating contest. So sweet and soft. We matched tongue thrusts in a rhythm of deep sucking. She made sure I came first, then she exploded in her own orgasm.

But she wasn't done. Commandingly she rolled me around until we were lying face to face, breasts pressing. Her mouth and chin were smeared wet and loose. My prayers were answered when I felt her fingers purposefully separating my labia. She whispered in my ear, "Here's your dessert," her low voice buzzing. "What a sweet slit you have. Bet I can put something in there you never felt before." Two heavily lubricated fingers screwed into me. My nostrils flared, I nodded, my pelvis opened like a flower in the sun. *Do anything to me. I'm your plaything.* Two more fingers joined the others inside. They stretched me, opened me, fucked me. *Make me shiver and squirm like a puppet on the ramming rod of your expert hand.*

"Can you handle it? You want it all?"

"Yes, yes, fuck yes."

"Okay, your initiation awaits." Thumb folded in. Hand in up to wrist. Everything exploded orange and yellow behind my eyelids. Inside me. *I can't hold on.* My body jerking in contortions. I screamed, fire raging to the top of my head.

Sobbing loudly, I gave up with a shuddering breath. Her hand relaxed and withdrew. She held me, cupping my crotch as my crying subsided. A warm stillness enveloped us and she whispered, "Now you know."

The next day I answer the phone. It's a TV cable company representative. Her voice is healthy, athletic, boyish. She is offering discount installations in my neighborhood. I undo my top shirt button as I give a musky call with my voice.

"Sure, can you come install it today?"

Breaking and Entering

How I got into his apartment doesn't matter. Curiosity, not necessity, can be the true mother of invention.

Finding myself outside his front door at 3 A.M. surprised me. I had seen him once or twice before, but always at a strict professional distance. I had no knowledge what, if anything, he knew about me.

Opening the door I was struck by a lightning bolt of sanity. What if he's wide awake? What if he's not alone? What if he has a gun?

For once in my life, pure bravado won out over logic. I took a quick gulp of Cuervo 1800 from a sterling flask in my coat pocket and fingered the doorknob. Cold. After all, even L.A. gets chilly in November at 3:02 A.M. The fact that I was wearing nothing underneath my leather coat but seamed stockings, a lace garter belt, and scraps of silk and lace that someone had the imagination to call a brassiere, didn't help raise my temperature.

I didn't mind. Somehow I knew I wouldn't be cold for long.

Miraculously, I got the door open and no security alarms were tripped. I carefully shut it behind me, smiling at my success, considering a potential career as a second-story woman.

The room was dark. Pitch black to be precise. Even after my pupils had acclimated, I could not see an inch in front of me, proof positive that this entire journey was to be fueled on instinct. With a strong sense of direction that came from I-don't-know-where, I walked through the main room. I decided to remove my five-inch heels, lest they make too much noise.

I crept into the bedroom. The blinds were cracked just enough to paint the room in James M. Cain moonlight.

He was sound asleep in the majestic king-sized bed, beautifully deep in sleep. I took a long look at him, courtesy of my accomplice, the moonlight. His body was naked, only partially covered by a pure white goosedown comforter.

Quietly I removed my coat and let it fall to the floor. My heart stopped as he stirred in slumber. Miraculously, he merely turned onto his side. I drank in the line of his back, the drape of his neck, the lush, masculine curve of his ass.

Women are not trained to enjoy the power of voyeurism toward the male body. Forget the childish gyrations of boy-toy dancers; I followed the waves of his breathing, the strong, quiet beauty igniting a heat that began in my cheeks and quickly flowed to my pussy. His cock, half-hard, undulated, and I tried to imagine what dreams were spinning in his head, how they would measure up to what I had in mind.

My hand moved to my nipples; not difficult since they peeked through the tips of my lacy bra. My little pebbles enjoyed the caress. My other hand slowly slid between my legs and my familiar middle finger found its way into my silky, slippery cunt.

Wild! Here I was, standing in a strange man's bedroom, only steps away from his delicious naked body, masturbating like a hot little schoolgirl!

This luscious voyeurism paled in comparison with what happened next. Slowly, sinuously, I crept into his bed, curling spoon fashion behind him, my nipples pressing into his back, my barely covered pussy snug against his ass. As I'd hoped, he moaned contentedly but didn't awaken.

I let a full minute pass, allowing our bodies to touch, allowing the pulse in my pussy to throb. His ass began to tighten almost imperceptibly and I knew this meant he had grown fully hard.

When I'd removed my coat I had taken a wispy silk scarf from the left pocket and placed it beneath the bed: my initial plan had been to bind his hands. But now I knew that wouldn't do. I wanted his hands all over me—and soon.

Besides, I came up with a far better use for the scarf. Gently, quickly—before he grew fully conscious—I wrapped the fragrant pastel silk around his eyes. In sleep he smiled, enjoying the fabric's caress. His eyes were fully covered.

My hands reached around his chest and gently pinched his ripe nipple. Still more asleep than awake, he reached for my hand to pull it to his throbbing cock.

No. Without saying a word I made it clear we were not going to rush. He seemed content to enjoy the waking dream while I explored his body. His shoulders were firm, his arms muscular. The hollow in his ass cheek—now wet from my pussy—was made to be kneaded, needed and enjoyed. When I moved my finger to his face, he took my hand and licked the inner palm, his tongue darting between my fingers as though licking hot cunt. I fed him my pussy-covered fingers and he sucked hungrily, his ass gyrating against my cunt.

Finally I reached for his cock.

Oh, his cock! Gloriously thick, sensuously full, every vein pulsing against my touch. His balls were magnificent; full and lush and fluid. Wetting my palms I pulled and stretched and scratched the skin, letting his guttural moans conduct my movements.

When he reached his arm around me and thrust his finger into my quivering cunt, I knew he could no longer distinguish what was reality and what was a dream. Still unable to see, he turned his body so we were face-to-face, lying on our sides. Our arms clutched each other and we fell into a kiss or series of kisses that were soft and wet and searching and hot. My hand was squeezing, rubbing his turgid cock; he was wildly fingering my lips and cunt as the kiss went on and on and on. Lips and tongues and teeth created their own language. I could feel drops of cum, hot cum, from the tip of his cock.

I moved him slightly and he turned onto his back. I straddled his legs and leaned forward. His hands traveled across my bra. He seemed surprised—and pleased—when he realized my nipples could be had without removing the seductive lace surrounding them. He licked and sucked their sweetness, moaning. "Cherry hot nipples. Sweet baby titties." I wanted to douse them in rum, dip them in sparkling champagne, dot whipped chocolate cream on the very tips to surprise and assault his taste buds. He was wild, out of control, his every movement telling me I was the hottest fuck in the world.

There was no stopping our accelerating pace. He let loose a moan as I pulled my breasts away from his hungry mouth, but before he could move I buried his cock deep into my hot pussy. We shook and rocked and I rode his cock like a wild woman. My sweet swollen clit, my baby-girl dick, met the base of his cock with every stroke. One of us was gasping, maybe both of us. The equation floated back and forth, hour after hour, as pussy met cock met lips met balls met finger met ass met tongue and back again.

The window let a sliver of daylight into the darkness. I had to go. We had both been dozing. Quickly I got up, threw on my clothes, and left the room. He moaned "come back" in semisleep, but I ran out, got in my car, and drove away.

Back home I had a moment to reflect on all that had occurred before I fell into a deep sleep. Too deep. Reliving everything in my dreams, I overslept, and had to rush to prepare for a business meeting that logic kept telling me to cancel. If I had listened to logic, though, the previous night would never have occurred. So I kept my appointment, foregoing my pink-and-black-checked Chanel suit for coral pants in a cool linen and matching turtleneck.

I arrived, miraculously enough, a few minutes early. I entered the building and looked around for the suite I needed. No one to ask; I was the only one in the lobby.

At that moment a man emerged from the elevator. I'd ask him. We made eye contact and—oh my God!—I felt my cheeks instantly burn. "You're . . ." I said, half-saying, half-asking his name. "Yes," he replied. "You must be Linda."

I nodded, the absolute professional. He extended his arm. "My office is this way."

I followed him, smiling slyly, wanting to burst out laughing. I'd no idea *he* was the man I'd had an appointment with. I loved the fact that I had a secret on him. And *what* a secret!

We sat in his office and reintroduced ourselves. He was impressed with my résumé, my designs, my ideas about how the project should go. We talked and talked and talked, finally ending the meeting knowing we wanted to work together. I rose to leave. I held out my hand in a gesture of farewell. He pulled his hand from his pocket and squeezed something into my palm.

My silk scarf.

"I believe you left this at my house," he said. I smiled. So did he.

"Thank you," I said. I turned to leave. His voice stopped me.

"I'd like you to begin tomorrow," he said.

My reply was swift and assured. "I'd like *you* to start tonight."

Eve Mariposa

Back to the Future with a Vibrator

It's time for another family visit to the suburbs.

From the moment I step off the plane, despite the fact that I came equipped in my uniform of individuation—combat boots, defiantly deteriorated jeans, and as much black as I can manage to cram into one outfit (Mom prefers me in pastels)—I always seem to get swept up in the tide of daughterly duties and expectations. I am everyone's "little girl" who looks "so sweet"—at least from the left side of my face, where you can't see the nose ring.

Mom and Dad are both here to pick me up this time, divorce and all. Mom has the metallic helium "Welcome Home" balloon which I am years beyond being embarrassed about, and Dad is beaming from ear to ear. A strange ritual has evolved around my visits. My parents, who otherwise have little to do with each other, come together in their long-rehearsed role as the ubiquitous, indestructible "Parents"—so that everything can be "like it used to be." Throughout my stay we all play the big happy family game and pretend that nothing has changed. Dad comes to the house, Mom cooks dinner, both sets of in-laws come over, and at the end of the night Dad quietly slips out of the house while Mom and I pretend not to notice.

I like to think of my entire visit as an exercise in make-believe.

I am not really the struggling-to-be-a-poet Generation X funk/ folk neophyte who lives in San Francisco, but rather a prepubescent girl with a Farrah Fawcett haircut and braces who wears whatever she's told and smiles even when she's feeling lousy. I refer to my oversized pink suitcase—a bad choice made in seventh grade—as the time travel machine that links the Rachel of yesteryear to the tall, unpredictable woman with attitude who invades her room a few times a year.

The relatives are waiting for me as we lug my excess of luggage into the hallway. As I wrestle the backpack off my shoulders, Grandpa Hymie pulls me aside and gives me a resounding slap on the rump. "What's the story with this *tuchas*?"

"It doesn't tell stories, Grandpa."

"I mean how'd it get so big?"

"Yes, I know what you mean," I say, and I go to the kitchen to get a drink.

When I return to the living room with a Diet Coke and a piece of pita bread, Grandma Lilly crowds me into a corner of the couch and presses a finger into my chest. "Do you have any boyfriends, Rachel?" As if they come in sets.

"No, Grandma, not currently." They wouldn't approve of my live-in situation—not to mention the convulsions of horror I'd have to endure if they ever discovered that he's not Jewish. I've learned to keep my love life to myself.

"You know why the boys don't like you? Because you're so skinny. You don't have enough curves. Boys like curves." She raises her eyebrows in the direction of my breasts, apparently indicating that they will grow if I eat more.

"I don't date boys, Grandma. I'm twenty-five years old—I prefer men. And who said the boys don't like me?" I give her a devilish wink, and she frets off to the kitchen with pursed lips.

After dinner I clear the table and wipe the place mats while Mom does the dishes and Grandma Shirley wanders around the kitchen trying to remember what she came here to do, asking me again and again what my name is and where I live. I answer her questions while Mom sighs heavily from the sink. Mom's hair is in her eyes, and she looks smaller than I remember.

As the sun lowers over the deck the grandparents decide they are tired and ready to drive home. I kiss everyone good-bye, get some money stuffed into my pockets (along with another resounding slap on my oversized *tuchas*), and we stand at the door waving as the cars pull away. Dad turns on the game and I run up to the bathroom where I sit for about fifteen minutes, staring out the window, answering "Yes" every time Mom yells up to see if I'm okay.

When Dad has gone "home" to the apartment we never mention, Mom takes off her makeup and I feign exhaustion and shut myself in the pink room that has been preserved as a shrine to my adolescence. It immediately envelops me with its cutesy cross-stitched proverbs pockmarking the walls, the mirrored "Rachel," which I'm beginning to find redundant, and my once-prized Bat Mitzvah gift—a satin cloud with my name hand-painted in rainbow colors dangling its silver gauze over my twin bed.

The bed's headboard, pink and white with large wooden knobs on either end, is a significant landmark in my brief history of rebellion. As the story goes, one night I got angry at my parents for letting my brother sleep with them but not letting me, so I chewed on the knobs of the headboard in protest. To this day the knobs remain chipped and scarred, and I smile remembering the gutsy girl who dared misbehave in this suffocating pink room.

I spend a few minutes examining the plants that Mom has been watering in my absence for six years. As always, they are drooping, but alive. I pull off all the dead leaves and water them. Then I browse through the bookshelf that holds an unusual conglomeration of childhood books crammed in alongside college texts; *Shahat the Egyptian* is bedside mates with *Ramona the Brave*. Squished in next to a stack of Cliffs Notes on *Moby Dick*, *Ulysses*, and other such memorable works, I uncover an old diary.

I used to sneak this particular diary into the bathroom to write, leaning the book against the tub while kneeling solemnly on the floor mat and recording my secrets. Now I reread with fascination my epic high school tragi-comedy of failed romance. Was it really this complicated and painful? Interspersed are some elementary rhymed poems about tragedy and loss, two subjects of which I knew close to nothing. Then I come across the following entry addressed to no one in particular:

I want to tangle flowers in your hair and lead you to the river. I want to ambush you with kisses and move through you like trains. I would like to singe your mind with the hunger of your hands, get you sloshed in my vodka poetry. I would like to part your lips over my breasts' enduring pink. Send you reeling like the seagulls. I would have you jellied and raw, the sting pulsing through me the way your guitar travels the floorboards and suffuses my feet with wanting. I would flute you through my silver wand and drink the last kiss of breath from your mouth.

Eat your heart out, Grandma Lilly.

This entry, which could have been referring to any number of passing crushes, looks like it's speaking to the guitar player in the band I sang with during senior year. I loved the way he bent seriously over his guitar, and I also remember liking his bushy hair. His name was Dave and he was very quiet. I deciphered his silences as mysterious. I would invent scenarios in which I would catch him completely off guard and seduce him, thereby revealing his true passion. I imagined that secrets lurked beneath the serene blue of his absent eyes that never seemed to really focus on me. But after months of fruitless advances, I realized that Dave was not dying to be probed or discovered, and that in all probability he was not only uninterested but just plain boring.

Then there was Alec. And Jonathan. And Paul. All recorded faithfully down to the last detail: the small space between Paul's front teeth and his enormous high-top sneakers that were never laced, the red number 12 that was peeling off Jonathan's football jersey, the fact that Alec used to cut eighth period to watch *The Addams Family* in his friend's basement. All of these were invented romances that amounted to at most a few kisses, a ridiculous grope or two, many unreturned phone calls, and endless nights in the bathroom recording the minute details of each interaction.

Rereading the teenage Rachel, I am very sad. So many elo-
quently voiced urgent desires thwarted and frustrated by the
limitations of the clique infrastructure at school, ignorance of my
body, and an unwillingness to deviate from the "good girl" per-
sona. Closing the diary, I find I am walking the delicate tightrope
between Rachel of past and present. Tingling with all the missed
opportunities, all the conquests I did not conquer, all the un-
named stirrings that kept me awake on winter nights, I realize
that I am wildly horny.

I rummage through my suitcase and come up with a long narrow felt bag with a drawstring at the top that accompanies me
on every trip home. I stick my head out the door of my room.
Mom's lights are out. I turn out the lights, extract my vibrator
from its bag, and plug it in.

Using a vibrator in my childhood room is one of my most
cherished activities. I imagine the sensation is akin to what race
car drivers feel when they race—maneuvering a tiny, confining
vehicle around some tricky turns and then taking off at a million
miles an hour. It is at once irreverent, wild, ridiculous, and intox-
icatingly dangerous. After all, Mom is just around the corner.
The truth might get out that I'm a sexual human being, and then
our family's little world of make-believe would spontaneously
combust, leaving me a regular ol' adult and everyone else at a
complete loss.

As I switch the vibrator on and position it in its well-worn spot
just below my clitoris, my head fills with the smell of a damp
football jacket. I am nuzzling soft stray hairs curling behind pink
fleshy ears. Must be Jonathan. I think I still have that jacket in
the basement closet. That's what he gets for dumping me: I keep
the goods. They collect mold in the basement.

I run my hands over my body. I am slightly damp with exertion, buried under three blankets to mute the sound of the vibrator. Jonathan is pressing me up against the rough brick wall
behind my high school. My sweater is unbuttoned but I don't
notice the cold, though I can see my breath fogging the air. Girls
are coming out of the locker room, ponytails bobbing and field
hockey sticks in hand. We are in an alcove hidden behind a brick
partition. The girls don't notice us.

I am panting. Jonathan is whispering something urgent in my ear, his forehead lowered to my shoulder, which he bites with the same urgency. His hand is pressed hard against my jeans between my legs. His face is thinner and sadder in my reinvention than it probably was. And I give him a little more scruff for this go-round. Scruff turns me on, though I couldn't have known it at the time.

Jonathan has just triumphed over the button to my jeans when, against all odds, Sebastian—the French guy I met in Radio Shack one summer when he was trying to sell my mom a set of speakers—walks out the doors we are leaning against. Jonathan does not appear surprised or concerned, and I certainly don't complain when Sebastian reaches into my unbuttoned sweater and firmly grasps a warm breast with his chapped hand, sending chills up my spine. My breasts are always larger in my fantasies than in real life—they aren't big enough to really be mobile, and I like to fantasize the jiggling that real life doesn't make possible. So Sebastian hefts my enormous lobe of breast in his hand, squeezes the nipple into a solid tip, then fills his mouth with me.

Meanwhile, Jonathan has worked his hand down the narrow passageway between jeans and skin into the steamy crevice of my cotton flowered underpants. He has my legs spread open against the wall and is trying to shimmy the jeans down my thighs for a better range of motion between my legs. Unfortunately, these are the days of skin-tight jeans, and Jonathan is hardly graceful, muttering "Fucking shit!" under his breath, and with a tremendous effort yanking both my jeans and me to the ground.

Sebastian goes with the flow, following us to the ground where he lifts the hair from my neck and breathes his milky breath over the goose bumps on my shoulders. I straddle Sebastian, take him by the throat and fill his ear with my tongue, working the dainty lobe with my lips and teeth. My ass is to Jonathan, who places his pointer finger just inside my underpants and traces the indentation of the elastic all the way around my thigh. I gasp as his finger glances over the lips of my pussy and then pinches my clitoris with unexpected force. I fasten Sebastian's hands on my breasts from behind and climb onto Jonathan. His erect cock springs up from behind the zipper as I lower it. My eyes water with nostalgia at the familiar aroma of Zest soap and clean sheets as I surround the tender flesh of his cock with my mouth. He smells like a fresh, well-groomed little boy, and I am going to suck the cum out of him.

I have all but forgotten about Sebastian when I feel my gloriously weighty breasts scraping the pavement. It feels like scruff but even better. Rougher. Sebastian is pressing me to the ground, still with Jonathan's cock in my mouth. He spreads the lips of my labia open to the wind. Then he does nothing—just holds me open and exposed. I wait. Jonathan waits. I notice I am trembling more in anticipation than from the cold. He is doing this exactly as I like it to be done—I have remade him with a profound knowledge of all my preferences. Ah, the advantages of fantasy.

When my lungs are thick with suspense and I can hardly breathe, Sebastian slowly slips inside. He's got on that ever-ready spare tire condom that melts in a teenage boy's wallet for a year or two and is perfectly useless by the time it's called into action. I am so thrilled to have my mouth and pussy full at the same time that I don't object. The three of us merge into a seasick swamp of motion. My hair is sticking to my face, my clothes lie in a rank pile on the cold cement, and I am screaming like I never screamed at those mandatory pep rallies for the goddamn football team. I am screaming because I am getting laid bigtime. They are biting and scratching me. I am thrashing and pumping and grasping and yanking somebody's hair.

We all come at the same time—another luxury of the world of make-believe. Jonathan shoots his sweet cum into my mouth and I swallow hungrily while rocking back onto Sebastian in heaving tides of loose silk. Sebastian is holding onto my breasts with gusto, moaning his final thrusts into my ear.

I get up matter-of-factly and gather up my rumpled clothes. Sebastian and Jonathan are flushed and sweaty, and neither will look me straight in the eye. "Go home and do your homework," I tell them. They duck their heads sheepishly, dig their hands deep into their pockets, and kick small pieces of gravel across the pavement as they saunter off in different directions.

As I return my vibrator to its carrying case my eye catches the chewed knobs of my headboard. I smile deviously. "Good night, Mom," I whisper.

Jane Handel

In Flagrante Delicto

We sat around a table sipping cocktails in the late afternoon, chatting casually about everything and nothing, waiting for the waiter to return and take our food orders. During a momentary lull in the conversation, my friend Gloria turned to the woman on her left, a new acquaintance, and asked, "Do you have a sexual preference?"

The eyes of each of us quickly focused on the beautiful young woman to whom the question had been addressed, and it almost seemed as though we held our breath collectively in anticipation of her answer. We didn't have to wait long; after the briefest of pauses she replied with a firm, unequivocal "No."

"Good," said Gloria, in her inimitably straightforward manner. "We must seize desire where we find it."

Following this rather show-stopping bit of dialogue, our conversation proceeded along a more general path, but a provocative door had been opened. And when, several times throughout the course of the meal, the eyes of the woman who had answered no met mine, I felt they did so with a new implication. Of course, this could very well have been wishful thinking on my part and it's a moot point in any case since I did not see her again.

* * *

But I remember the incident now while lying on a sun-drenched hill in the Napa countryside—reveling in the sultry heat of summer and enjoying a much-needed respite from the stress of urban living. My body, naked and still moist from its shower, is gently dried by a breeze as I massage lotion onto its parched surface. A hawk circles overhead searching for a field mouse or a rabbit, and I wonder if it might also be voyeuristically eyeing me and my nakedness. But no, it suddenly swoops down with lightning quickness and then flies off into the distance with a snake dangling from its beak. Nearby, a lizard is doing push-ups. It reminds me of the ones I used to catch as a child, keeping them in coffee cans and pretending they were pets. Inevitably, they made a dash for freedom in the middle of the night, and the next morning I would be desolate when I discovered the empty can. As I raise my hand to massage another dollop of lotion onto my belly, this one stops his calisthenics, eyes me warily and then scurries under a bush, thus bringing my fantasy of voyeurism to an abrupt end.

To a city dweller this California hilltop undoubtedly seems serene and still, devoid as it is of technology's pervasive hum. It seems that way to me, but as I listen and look more closely, I become aware that it is, in fact, alive with noise and activity: yellow jackets, horseflies and crickets buzz; birds chatter; leaves and grass rustle in the wind; children's voices ring out from the valley far below. I become acutely aware not only of this continuous symphony of sound, but of a drama being acted out all around me, the main character being the light that shifts constantly as the sun journeys overhead; the clouds that change shape and move from here to there; the dust devil in the distance swirling aimlessly and then vanishing mysteriously. In this landscape of flux the only mute and static element is myself—the observer. But no, I too am contributing to this lively interchange: with each intake of breath my chest rises slightly, then collapses as I exhale. And if someone were to press an ear to my heart they would surely hear its beat.

But there is no one to press an ear, no one to observe the rise and fall of my chest. Even the lizard and the hawk have long since moved on.

Another breeze comes up and I catch a whiff of lavender and rosemary and again hear Gloria's voice in my ear. Feeling as though I am being seduced by the insistent caresses of the sun and the wind, languorously and subtly my body begins to awaken. Alone on this oak-studded hilltop, my lovers are the four elements, the four directions, the flora and fauna. Myself. I revel in the purity and simplicity of this moment as my hand joins the wind and the sun and I seize desire where I am finding it.

My hand reaches between my legs and probes the wet, dark place it finds there. As I lick the sticky, pungent wetness from my fingers, my back arches and my breath quickens. With tender precision I press and massage the tiny pink clitoris in a rhythmic, circular motion. I am suddenly oblivious to my surroundings—to the fact that I am naked and exposed and that the gardener may drop by to water the newly planted squash and tomato plants, or a hiker might mistake the driveway for a trail. I am simply immersed in the ruthless, single-minded activity of bringing myself to orgasm. At first it seems elusive and I shift my hips slightly, raising them so that the pressure is at a different angle. My fingers move faster and more insistently until the miraculous explosion occurs and I cry out in spite of myself. When the convulsions subside, I lie still for a moment, catching my breath. Then I quickly look around and am relieved to find that no intruders have witnessed my moment of abandon.

The sun begins to sink below the horizon and another breeze comes up but this time there is a slight chill to it, so I gather up my towel and lotion and wander down to the house. Inside, I put on a tape of John Coltrane's ballads, fix myself a margarita and sit on the couch, wrapped in the towel, watching the last bit of orange and pink light fade. I feel content and relaxed.

But my reverie is soon interrupted by the intrusive ring of the telephone. At first I debate whether or not to answer. After a few more irritating rings I do.

"Hi," says a familiar male voice. "How are you?"

A conflicting wave of anxiety and happiness collide inside me when I hear this voice, but I try to answer in my most confident and relaxed manner. "I'm wonderful. How are you?"

He tells me about his work, we chat about a mutual friend. I avoid any potentially volatile topics. Over the past few months our relationship has taken a turn for the worse, and the foundation is now strewn with hair-trigger time bombs. The slightest jostle could set one off and blow me to smithereens.

"I miss you," he says, and I detect a slight tremor in his voice.

"I miss you, too—in fact, I was just thinking about you." I continue to try to affect casualness in my tone, a bravado I don't feel.

"Oh?" he says with a nervous laugh. "Nothing bad, I hope."

"Quite the contrary. I am sitting here watching the sunset, listening to Coltrane, and thinking about how much I desire you. Sometimes the desire I feel for you is so overwhelming it scares me and I become paranoid about scaring you with its intensity . . . overwhelming you with my overwhelming desire."

I pause for a moment but there is only silence on the other end. Chances are he is feeling equally awkward and self-conscious, maybe even more so, but consumed as I am with my own anxiety, this never occurs to me. So I try to fill in the void with a stilted monologue, attempting rather foolishly to explain the inexplicable: irrational, primal lust.

"Sometimes, I feel such a rush of desire, emotion and terror all mixed up together that I panic. I'm afraid you'll be repulsed by its excessiveness. When I was a child, I learned by necessity to be stoic; I come from very stiff-upper-lip British stock, you know."

I chuckle at my own joke, but again, the silence on the other end is almost deafening. "Are you still there?" I query, starting to feel a bit annoyed.

"Yeah, I'm here," he answers tersely. I think I detect a subtle change in his breathing but I am not sure. Wondering to myself why I am doing all the work in what is becoming an increasingly one-sided dialogue, nevertheless I plunge fearlessly ahead.

"Well, anyway, as I was saying, at an early age I learned to tone down my ardor—god forbid anyone should find me undignified. Little girls are to be seen—preferably with their legs crossed at their ankles and their hands folded demurely in their laps—and not heard. That's why I've never revealed to you just

how much I long to caress every part of you, to lick and penetrate every orifice, to merge all of me with all of you . . . but
that's what . . ."

Suddenly I'm out of breath and my voice falters. I'm feeling
too agitated to continue—in fact, if I weren't still wrapped in a
towel, I'd be sitting in a pool of liquid that would undoubtedly
leave an embarrassing stain on my friend's white sofa. Once
again, I wait for him to say something to relieve the tension. It
is quiet for what seems like an eternity. Then, in a voice barely
audible, he asks, "Can I come see you?"

Slowly exhaling, I skip a beat before responding with a per-
functory, "Please do."

An hour has passed and his mouth now has me in its thrall,
could probably keep me mesmerized indefinitely: the shape of
the lips, delicate yet full, elegant and succulent like a tropical
fruit begging to be eaten. With the tip of my tongue I trace the
edges, memorizing the shape, probing under the lips inside the
moist, warm cavity, feeling the smooth, even teeth; tasting his saliva, inhaling his breath into my lungs, sucking and licking, delir-
ious with sensuous pleasure. I continue the journey with my
tongue, exploring the crevices of his throat, his clavicle, marvel-
ing at the silky texture of his skin as he lies beneath me, passive
and subdued yet alert and watchful. Every so often a groan res-
onates from the deep cavity of his chest and his eyes roll back
in his head. I too am watchful, measuring his response, attuned
to the intake and exhalation of breath, the rapidity of pulse beating faster and faster. My tongue and mouth probe every orifice,
travel to all the nether regions, again memorizing all the details.
I am hungry for this memory as if I am about to go to the electric chair and this is my last supper. I am anxious to carry this
memory to my grave, to eternity.

For a moment, I revel in the grandiose notion that I am in
command of my own destiny and maybe even his. But it doesn't
take long for this reverie to be turned inside out, for him to grow
tired of the passive role. In one quick motion he roughly throws
me off him and onto my back, pinning my arms behind my head
and pushing his groin hard into mine. I gasp for air. His body

covering mine, his mouth to my ear, his deep, resonant voice murmurs, "Submit to me."

"Submit to me," the voice repeats with grave insistence, and the man who is making this demand presses his groin even more roughly against my pubic bone.

"Yes," I whisper. "Yes, I will submit to you. Completely."

"But you don't even know what I want yet," he says, his temple pressed hard against mine, his groin continuing its relentless grinding, rubbing raw the skin of my pubis.

"That is true submission," I say with calm assurance. "If I say I will do anything you want without knowing yet what it is."

His breathing intensifies; my unquestioning acquiescence clearly excites him.

"Yes, it is," he groans, biting my earlobe so hard I gasp at the pain. "You're right. Not to know but . . ." I can no longer make out his words. He yanks my arms harder behind me and continues in a voice I can now decipher. "While you were talking to me on the phone I was masturbating."

This is the most arousing and provocative thing anyone has ever said to me. I suddenly feel faint.

"Whatever you want I will do it," I say again. And as I speak these fateful words, a shiver of fear runs up my spine. I don't know why I reveal my desire to be dominated by this man, nor do I understand it, but somehow I instinctively know it is time to give myself up. I have been waiting for this moment for what seems like a lifetime.

Serena Moloch

Behind the Mask

I. Maid and Mistress

Sometimes it begins like this.

I follow my mistress as she makes her way through a crowded train station. I carry her bags for her. Her bags are very heavy, so heavy they dig into my hand, and later, when I look at it, there will be a rough red mark where the bag bit my hand with its toothless mouth. My mistress is dressed in a pale travel costume, the latest style with billows and ruffles that come right down to her heels, and she is clean, so clean that I can track her even in this mass of people simply by following in the wake of her stupendous shining cleanliness. Her hair glows with it, her skin gleams with it, her clothes remark loudly on the absence of any disfiguring spot.

I, on the other hand, am dirty, so dirty that even in this filthy crowd I can feel people turning to stare at me. I am remarked upon. Perhaps, I imagine, someone will mistake me for a spittoon or a rubbish tip and absentmindedly make me the receptacle for some choice piece of garbage. I feel the impulse to protest: it's not my fault, it's my duty that coats me in dirt. The servant's life: up at 5:30 to clean the grates and fill the coal scuttles, out on the steps at 7:00, bucket and soap and brush in hand, to wash the house clean, to kneel on their marble and try not to imagine how everyone who passes can look at my legs, will look up my skirts, insult me in language as foul as the chamber pots it is my duty to clean at 9:00.

Nine o'clock, when I must attend on my waking mistress. I bring up her breakfast tray, I sniff the aromatic chocolate steaming in the dainty, oh so dainty china cup, as thin as her calla-lily neck and just as easy to snap if one doesn't take the proper care. I carry the hot rolls and the linen napkins; gingerly, I bring her the chamber pot and watch her piss and shit into it and then I prepare to wash her clean. First she tosses off her sheets and grabs her chocolate, sucks it greedily down—there are times I've seen when I can tell you, she's no lady—and then she points at the tub. She isn't ready to speak, yet. I trudge up and down and up then down again to get enough hot water to satisfy her and then she undoes her night frock and I know my duty, I pick her up (like a stack of pillows, she's so light) and lower her gently into the tub, so gently she'd never suspect how easily I could crack her head against its edge.

Then I get to work, I know my task: with a bar of the best French soap I begin to clean every bit of her body, sliding the soap under her armpits, down along her back, by the sides of her neck, in between each one of her toes, skimming along her downy calves, up to her heavy breasts where I take special care, sliding the soap round and round, down to her belly, rubbing it up into a fine lather, until she shows how impatient she is with me by arching her back and thrusting her cunt toward my face. Because even she has a cunt, my mistress, though certainly it's pinker and pearlier than mine or any other one I've seen, and quite, quite clean, thanks to my daily labors.

So I begin, soaping her fleecy hair, rubbing my fingers between her lips, pulling up the hood of her little knob to clean beneath that, prodding her opening with the soap, cleaning her little brown hole until I feel it open beneath my fingers so that I can reach in and clean deep, deep inside. And if I dared to look up to her face I know I'd see her eyes hooded with mean enjoyment of the pleasure she feels when I kneel outside the tub and my hands swarm all over her and my fingers probe inside her and she wallows in the sweet hot water. And when the pleasure gets too strong and I feel the heat in her asshole penetrating to my finger's very bones and the skin around her pearly little cunt goes taut and tense, I hear the voice that always comes: "What's the matter with you, you sluttish thing? Don't you know your work? Get this soap off me, now."

I do know my work. I lower my head and begin to lick her soapy cunt, lapping up the lather with my tongue, which is as strong and muscular as the rest of me, dipping my head into the water to spit out the soap and fill my mouth with fresh hot water so I can pour it out of my mouth and over her mound. My finger is still up her ass, I push her buttocks up so I can lick her cleaner and cleaner, and as I clean she thrusts herself toward me so that her lips smack into my teeth, oh, I've come to learn she likes it a bit rough, so I rasp my tongue harshly across her until she convulses, smothering the sides of my face with her greedy thighs, then pulls away from my fingers and my face so she can loll back in her bath and throw her washcloth at my still-bowed head so as to let me know that she wants me to fetch the towels and dry her off.

What I wish for more than anything during my mistress's bath is to take my hand, my soapy hand with the dirt well worked in under the nails, and ram it up her foaming cunt, my whole hand right up her, clean up to the top of her head, show her what a real going-over is, not these pretty little games with soap and water and scented oils, but she knows better than to give me a taste of her insides. The one time I tried to put my fingers in her cunt instead of her bum she slapped my hand hard and said, "Filthy thing. You know your hands are too dirty to go in there—and anyway, that's for master, not for you. I'm afraid we'll have to have words about this later."

Words from her always mean one thing, of course—me, kneeling on all fours with my face touching the floor and my hands tied together in front of me, my skirts lifted up and my knickers pulled down, being whipped by my mistress's pretty lash or hairbrush, or worse, one of master's belts, all to remind me of my place. Then I'm forced to gawk at my red and welted bum in the mirror behind me while I tell her how sincerely I repent of my sinful, soilful ways.

But I do know my place and when I've finished dutifully cleaning my mistress with my tongue I wrap her in clean white towels and help her to dress. And on days like today, when she is about to make a voyage, I pack her clothes and toilet things and I scurry around trying to finish my household tasks—washing, dusting, scrubbing and oiling—so that I might at least snatch time to do up my hair and wash off my arms before I accompany her through the streets to the station. It's a race we run, she and I. I know she wants me to look as filthy as possible as I follow her through the streets, so that people will remark on us, my shameful grime lagging behind her haughty self, and it's a race she always wins.

And so here we are, as we began, in Victoria Station, waiting for the train to accept passengers. I stand by her luggage, my hands clasped before me and my head bowed low, while my mistress scornfully looks over the crowd and then prods the ground with the tip of her umbrella. I quiver and turn hot and cold when I feel people stop near me and whisper to each other. I can imagine the spectacle I must make for them, standing in the middle of the station, my face and hands streaked with coal marks and dust, greasy strands of hair flying about, my dress hopelessly soiled, my shoes caked in dirt, and as I imagine their eyes, some skimming over me and turning away in disgust, others staring in fascination at my impossible dirtiness, I hear my mistress hiss, "You hopeless wench! Look, look, *look* at that!"

I keep my head down but turn in the direction to which her umbrella points, at her feet, her boots, made of the finest kid leather with pointed toes and a high heel sharpened almost to a stiletto point. And what she points at are little specks of dirt, splattered on no doubt as we walked through the streets, but the umbrella points accusingly first at her feet, then toward me, as if to say—which she soon does—"Is this how you work for me?"

I know what comes next. I pick up my mistress's bags and follow her to the place we've always used in this situation, a retired part of the station where there is just enough danger of being seen and just enough certainty that we won't be. I gently place her bag on the floor and admire her endless spirit, the nobility and panache with which she pulls a handkerchief from inside her sleeve and drops it so that it flutters to the floor beside me. She lifts her skirts just above her ankles and says to me, "On your knees, and be quick about it. I want these shoes spotlessly clean before I board my train."

And so I kneel, and as I've always done, I pick the handkerchief up from the floor with my teeth and bring my head down so that I can move the cloth about her shoe with my mouth. But there is so little, little time that very quickly I let the cloth drop and simply go to work with my tongue, taking all the little spots off and working the soft leather into a respectable shine with my spit, all the time wondering how soon someone might come along and find us at our shameful game, so I work even faster, grabbing my mistress's leg just above the heel so that I can lick the bottom of her boots clean, as both she and I love, feeling the bits of grit work down my throat, and then the moment of supreme bliss for us both as I suck her heel into my mouth and gently, so gently, she slides it in and out of my slippery hungry mouth, and as I think of how useful and obedient I am, how I would do anything for my mistress, even take her dirty boot proudly into my mouth, I feel my cunt contracting, its slimy juices squirting out of me as I come and come and come, so hard I don't even notice how brusquely my mistress's foot has been jerked from my mouth.

Then I hear the voice. It's what we've always dreaded—the educated and indignant voice of a young man come to interrupt our seedy pleasures with his outrage and his testimonials. A poorer man we could bribe, an older rich man would be charmed and in any case hardly shocked, old rich men being what they are, a woman would merely scurry away—or stay to join us. But this man, I can see, will not be nearly as simple to handle, as I stand up and smooth down my dress. His sandy mustache is quivering with conceited pleasure at having someone to save, and that someone is me.

"What do you mean, my good woman, performing such an abominable act in the middle of Victoria Station?"

"My dear sir, I would hardly call this the middle of the station and any act I may be performing is certainly no concern of yours."

"I should think it is," he said. "I'm an active member of the Domestic Reform League and this past month we've been particularly concerned with the abuse of servants. Why, I've been on the committee that's been drafting a bill to present to Parliament on this very question. And I won't stand by and see this poor woman abused without interceding." He turned to me. "Can I help you, my dear?"

Before I could answer, my mistress laughed and said, "I would love to draw you out more on the subject of servant abuse, but I really must run to catch my train. Do stay here with Hannah and rescue her, by all means, if you see fit. I wish you all the best in the endeavor. Good-bye, Hannah dear." And with that, she leaned over, kissed me full on the mouth, picked up her heavy bags and teetered away unsteadily. I wiped my mouth and turned to my sputtering savior.

"It's unspeakable," he said. "Unthinkable. Never have I seen such a thing. Most of our young women's troubles are with the masters of the house, not the mistresses. But such, such . . . perversity is simply unheard-of. My dear young woman," he said to me forcefully, each word a wedge, "you must let me help you. Follow me to my club, and perhaps from there I can find new accommodations for you."

And having nothing better to amuse myself with, since my lover, my playmate, my pretend mistress, my beloved partner in crime had fled, follow him I did.

II. The Offending Member

For the third time that day—though by now it was night—I was kneeling, this time inside a tub rather than outside one, and the person I was cleaning was none other than myself. Some strange circumstance had dictated that my rescuer's club was closed for the evening, though he had a key and let himself in. He had led me to the basement, to a marvelous tiled bathroom, the latest in sanitary reform and engineering feats, he assured me, with hot water and cold water both running out of taps into a deep and delicious tub that drained into pipes laid underground.

It had been a pleasure to wash myself once he left me to my own devices with a bar of scented soap and some rough cloths. I watched dirty water run down the lustrous copper drain and clean, hot water fill the tub up again, I felt my skin begin to pucker up and the room fill with aromatic steam. I cleaned beneath my nails, scrubbed under my arms, washed my hair, soaped my breasts carefully, tended to every hidden fold. And then he knocked, my crusading hero. I snatched up a towel and tied it around my breasts to cover them, then called to him to enter.

He came and sat in a chair, an enormous stuffed chair, by the tub.

"Do you have everything you need?" he asked solicitously.

"It's wonderful," I sighed. "Delicious. Luxurious. Absolutely continental."

"Continental?" He looked startled but avoided looking at me directly. Under cover of his bashfulness, I stared at him hard. He seemed transformed from the earnest prig at the station to something more dissolute, looser about the mouth. Had he been drinking?

"Missus always says her bath makes her think of France and such, sir."

"Your mistress," he said, "seems to be all too familiar with the sorts of viciousness that we know tend to insinuate themselves into this country from abroad. Particularly from France." He rose from his chair and knelt by the tub. How pleasant it was to float in the water while someone lowered himself before me.

He took my hands, keeping his eyes averted from my face. "May I?" he asked.

"Lord, whatever for?" I tried to pull them away. He held fast.

"You can tell so much about a person from their hands," he murmured, a touch maliciously it seemed to me. "Their future . . . their past." He turned my hands palm up and began to trace lines on them with his finger. "Here is the path of love, and here is the path of life. I can see that you've loved loyally up until now, that your line of life is curiously . . . ruffled. I can see a difficult past . . . a troubled future . . . and here," he said, suddenly raising his eyes to mine and digging his nails into my hand, "here we have the unmistakable sign of the deceiver. Because these," he said, shoving them away from himself, "these are not the hands of a servant. These hands are not calloused, these hands are not hard, these hands are not marked with years of labor. These are the hands of a lady. A lady given to strange amusements and curious pleasures."

"That is correct," I said, leaning forward in the water, "and very penetrating of you. And now," I said, undoing the damp towel I had knotted about my breasts, dropping it along with all pretense of modesty, "if you permit me, I will demonstrate how very amusing those pleasures can be." And while his eyes were riveted on my now exposed breasts, I pressed on his mouth a hot and very hungry kiss. I climbed out of the tub, pushed him onto the capacious chair, and straddled him, water streaming down my body onto his, raising a musty but not unappealing odor from his suit.

"You're fascinated by these, aren't you," I murmured, bringing his hands to my breasts and to the rings that pierced my nipples. "You're staring at them. Go on, touch them. Pull on them." Tentatively, he tugged at the golden hoops. "Hard," I ordered before bruising his mouth again, sucking his tongue between my lips, gently biting him, running my hands under his jacket, loosening his tie, unbuttoning his shirt. I pulled away from him to better feel the strain on my breasts. A tense thrill ate me up. I ran my hands over his face as he put his hands flat up against my breasts. He grasped the nipple rings and pulled, as though guiding a horse by a bridle. I opened my legs so that I could rub my cunt and clit against his trousered thigh. I let my weight fall on him. Now I was riding him; my breasts led his body. I shoved his head against my tits and forced him first to suck one ringed nipple, then the other. I grunted with pleasure, grunted because he didn't deserve to hear me moan or cry out. When his licking, pinching and pulling had excited me as far as they could, I roughly opened his trousers and took out his cock. It was hard enough for me to be able to push it inside me, and so I did. Then I began to ride him in earnest, diving up and down on his prick, one hand grasping his shoulder, the other busy working my clit into a frenzy, until, almost too quickly, I came in resisting spasms. I pushed his mouth and hands away from me then, and got off him though he tried to keep me in place. I rose and stood before him and watched while he wrapped his own hand around his cock and frantically pulled a climax out of it.

I reached into the tub and pulled the stopper to let the water drain. There is nothing I detest more than a tub filled with cooling, dirty water.

"Take off your clothes," I told him. "I would like some company in my nudity."

He stood up and wrestled out of his costume. Then he pulled me to him and back down on the chair, in a parody of a domestic embrace. He stroked my hair and planted a kiss on the top of my head.

"I too have a confession to make," he murmured.

"I have made no confession for you to add to," I haughtily corrected him. "You made a surmise which I have as yet done nothing to confirm. But by all means, do confess."

"I am not a reformer. I am a scoundrel. I did not bring you here to rescue you."

"How refreshing." I smiled, trying to duck out from under the hand that held my head down.

"In fact, I brought you here on a wager."

I stiffened beneath the increasingly strong pressure of his hand.

"You see, every week the chaps, the members, bet on whether one of us can lure a woman into the club and have our way with her. That's why it's shut. To leave the field clear. Not everyone wins, but I always have. Though this time my trophy is of extraordinarily unusual—shall I say quality? interest? What word would you use, Miss . . . ?"

I snapped my head away from his heavy hand. "Wouldn't you rather have to say that it is I who have had my way with you?" I looked coldly into his face.

"Ultimately it's immaterial. Evidence, ocular evidence, is what counts, and in the end, that evidence never reveals who took who. My fellow members are not particularly imaginative men,

my dear Miss—shall I call you Hannah? Such an unsuitably ple-
beian name for one so perniciously refined. And when my fellow
members see you buried up to the hilt on my stalwart tool, they
certainly won't hesitate to hail me as the conqueror."

"And what is this ocular evidence to which you refer, pray
tell? Do you have spies hidden in the next room? Trick mirrors
on the walls?"

"Oh, nothing so primitive," he said. "The club has a camera,
the latest thing, doesn't require that one stay still for nearly so
long as those old daguerreotypes did. Almost instant. And you're
going to pose for some pictures. With those lovely rings of yours.
I'd heard they were all the rage among society women lately, but
this is the first time I've had the pleasure. Tell me, did it hurt?
How and where did you get it done?"

Hoping to disarm him, I said, "The woman you saw me with
at the station is my lover. You caught us, I'm afraid, playing one
of our favorite games—maid and mistress. But when we're not
at play, we're New Women. I take courses in political economy
at the University of London, and my friend studies medicine.
She is also the daughter of an eminent surgeon, whom she often
assists in his operations. She obtained the necessary instruments
and anesthetics and performed the piercing herself."

"Capital," he said, rubbing his hands, "absolutely capital. I
knew right away you were no serving girl. A veritable decadent,
that's what you are. Tell me, did she use ether? I've heard
women become the absolute devil when they're under the influence of ether."

My swain was beginning to reveal a most annoying incorrigible
disposition.

"Aren't you," I asked, taking his hand, "going to show me your
picture camera?"

The photographic apparatus was in a miniature laboratory,
filled with flasks, retorts, acrid vapors, heaps of papers, scraps of
material, mineral specimens and odd fleshy objects floating
about in jars like last season's pickles. I had wrapped myself in
a robe that had been lying about in the bathroom, and stood by
while my hero, now metamorphosed into a young man eager to
prove himself to someone more advanced than he in the school

of corruption, rustled about looking for old photographs to show me. He pounced on a pile in a corner. "Here they are!" He waved a sheaf of thick paper at me. "Come look."

I stood by him while he flipped through an apparently endless series of pathetic portraits, each girl looking more embarrassed and put out than the next, breasts flapping to one side, legs awkwardly parted to reveal a hairy slit, one arm stretched before a face in a wretched attempt at anonymity, the other arm stretched forward toward the camera as though to balance an eminently precarious act.

"That's Helen," he said enthusiastically. "She was a virgin and we paid her mother ten pounds to have her. She lost her virginity twenty times in that one night! And each time screamed as though it hadn't just happened before. By the time I had her, the jism was pouring out of her. Fred, he's the president of the club, he wanted to etherize her like they do in the specialty brothels, but we couldn't get hold of any. Maybe *you* could get us some," he mused. "And that's Kitty. You see the stripes on her legs? That was Harold, he likes to whip them. Has a special cat-o'-nine-tails for it. That's what comes of too many beatings at Eton. He's a regular devil. But Kitty was a sport, she was always happy to suck on one gentleman's member while getting fucked by another. She brought a friend along, too, where's her picture"—more furious flipping—"there, Phoebe, I think her name was. Phoebe was terribly fond of Greek love, if I remember rightly. Had three or four of the members' cocks up her asshole that night. You see," he said, "on the outside we call this the Sportsman's Club, but amongst ourselves we're the Randy Bohemians. Most nights it's a collective proposition, but Wednesdays, as I told you, it's more of an individualistic endeavor. Are you ready for your pose, Lady Hannah?"

"Soon," I said, leaning into him. "Show me some more so I have an idea of how to arrange myself."

"Of course," he obliged. "Lovely of you to be so agreeable. Most girls put up a horrible fight, we usually have to threaten to turn them into the police for prostitution. Well, that's if they're working girls. In your case I suppose blackmail would be more the trick."

"Won't be necessary, dear," I answered breezily. "Do show us some more."

He returned, engrossed, to his pretty pictures. "There's an awfully good one of an old hag named Hermione. She seemed pleased to have someone taking such an interest." As he searched, I undid my robe, working loose the belt that tied it. I wrapped each end tightly around my hand and stood poised, ready to seize my moment.

When it came, I had the belt tied round him quicker than even I could apprehend, and soon I had his arms completely immobilized, pinned tight against his sides. A pained expression overtook his features.

"I say, this isn't very sportsmanlike of you."

"Well, darling—what did you say your name was?"

"Arthur," he pouted.

"Dear Arthur," I hissed, pulling some rope from a mound of odds and ends, turning him round to secure each of his legs to the handles of the drawers behind him, "I am many things, but I am not a sportsman and have never claimed to be one." I took the pictures off the table and dropped them in front of his feet. "And neither, by the looks of *these*, are you." A match came easily to hand and I used it to set the pile aflame. "I'm afraid these have to go. And you'd better not move to save them, or you'll get a nasty burn."

"The work of years," he moaned, "years and years of planning, research . . ."

"They're easily replaced, Arthur."

"They are not."

"Oh, yes, they are," I said, "by some stunning portraits of you, a martyr to your own lust and your too, too trusting nature. Do maintain that look of agony, and strain at your bonds a little bit more." I picked up his camera and stood at the requisite distance, fiddling with the various knobs and buttons. Emma had attended the Ladies' Photographic School for a bit to learn about medical pictures and she'd told me some of what she'd learned. How amused she'd be when I showed these to her and told her everything that had happened after she left me at the station. "If you'd arch your back and turn your head to the left, you'd look very much like that delightful Spanish oil of Saint Sebastian in the National Gallery. With the fire blazing at your feet it's really quite wonderful." I shot and shot until the flames went out. Then I stepped through the ashes and delicately took hold of Arthur's prick.

"Why, here it is," I said, clasping his limp cock. "The offending member." I tugged at it a bit. "You really should be more careful, Arthur, whom you pick up in Victoria Station. I could be anybody. I could be that mad Ripper who keeps cutting people open. Of course, he's only been cutting open women till now, but one can never be sure . . . perhaps that's all been a ploy to make fools like you feel safe." I wanted him to tremble. Instead, of course, I only made his cock swell and rise up in my hand. I dropped it in disgust, then began to slap it from side to side. "You see, Arthur, you're terribly unaware of your true nature. You think you want to come between women, to conquer and capture them as trophies and possess them for all eternity, but really what you've always wanted is just this, to be tied up with some female bandying you about"—I slapped harder—"holding the power of life and death over you." My robe had opened and my breasts brushed against his shirt front. I grabbed his cock and squeezed it hard. "Don't you love the helplessness, the danger?" Silence. I squeezed harder. "Don't you?"

"Yes," he gasped. "It hurts."

"Good," I said. "I like that. And so do you, don't you?"

"Yes," he choked, "yes. Please."

I relaxed my grip. "Such a good boy. So obedient. Perhaps you're not really a boy at all." His cock got harder than ever in response to these taunts. "Perhaps you're a girl. Perhaps you'd like me to perform a little operation on you to help you be a girl." I pressed against him so that his cock was smashed between us. "Would you like that, Arthur? Would you like me to cut off that offending member?" I gestured toward the preserved specimens. "We could put it in a jar for you to look at from time to time." I felt his hips straining as he writhed against me. I let him. I even helped him along. "Take it out to play with now and then. And you'd be free to be the girl you really are, wouldn't you?" He was pushing faster, and whimpering. "Why, if you weren't so dirty and I weren't so nice and clean, I'd turn you around and fuck you right now, just to get you in the habit, Arthur." I pulled away and his cock bobbed helplessly up and down. "But I must go now, Arthur. I'm sure some trustworthy club member will find you here tomorrow and set you free. And an evening spent in bondage is an invaluable lesson in submission. You'll only thank me later. And you'll think of me every time you look at our photographs of tonight, which I promise to send to you here." I leaned over and kissed him on the forehead. "You will remember me, Arthur?"

"Yes," he gasped.

"Yes, ma'am."

"Yes, ma'am."

"And you won't interfere anymore when you see girls playing out of doors?"

"No, ma'am."

"Well," I said, gathering my robe regally about me and sweeping out the door, "good night then."

And I descended once again to the basement, where I found and donned my clothes. I assumed a grand gray mantle pillaged from the cloakroom and stepped out through the club's ornate and narrow doors. I stood poised for a moment on its marble steps, then made my way into the waiting city square, radiant in the misty, illuminated night.

Christine Beatty

❧

The Secret of Her Success

The gutter was a grotesque mixture of the repulsive and crude, a microcosm of this blighted neighborhood. Along this stretch of curbside was an assortment of cigarette butts in varying lengths and stages of decay. One of them was still smoldering. Shattered glass from bottles of cheap wine and hard liquor lay strewn in the pitted and stained concrete channel. Spent condoms, wrinkled and rotted from exposure, peeked out from beneath charred and tattered newspapers, junk-food wrappers and defiantly discarded parking tickets. In a clear section of gutter lay a used syringe clogged with blood, its spike askew, testimony to the lack of needle exchange in the city.

Lifting away from the dying cigarette was a pristine red leather pump, size eight. This shoe held a well-shaped foot clad in shiny new support hose surrounding an equally attractive leg. A red spandex miniskirt fell just an inch below the woman's firm, round buttocks.

She was a striking woman, apparently in her early twenties, with long straight black hair worn with no styling. Her hips and butt molded the tight skirt into an excruciatingly attractive curve that tapered into a thin waist and almost perfectly flat stomach. Firm, high breasts strained maddeningly at a white, pucker-knit tube top that showed off her smooth pale torso. Her face was devoid of foundation, but she wore heavy eye makeup, blush and lipstick. She could have posed for any men's magazine she wanted to—she was that kind of beautiful. Other women envied and hated her.

Her eyes were the most unusual thing about her—alive and sparkling with mischievous energy, greener than the glass of a Seven-Up bottle. But her most striking features were also her best-kept secrets.

She idled along this stretch of downtown sidewalk, illuminated by the multicolored neon of the shops and the yellowish orange of the sodium-vapor streetlamps. Her eyes scanned the approaching traffic warily, searching for the police cars she was trying to avoid and the customers she hoped to attract.

A dusty old Nova slowed for her; it was at least ten years old and wheezed blue smoke. The driver was not a day under fifty; even in this light she could see how disheveled he looked, as if he'd slept in his clothes. His eyes were wide and his mouth leered.

She tossed her head and looked away. A guy in a car like that wouldn't be good for more than a twenty, and he didn't look like he was worth taking for less than her usual fifty or sixty. Besides, a guy that creepy sometimes made her physically ill. There were plenty of fish in the sea on a Friday night, Tanya didn't have to settle. There had been times when she was so desperate that anyone would do—but tonight she was able to hold out for what she wanted.

Tanya passed two other hookers walking in the opposite direction and smiled to herself at the change in their conversation. She was the new mystery woman on the stroll, and everyone was trying to figure her out. She didn't mind if they talked about her. Everywhere she had ever gone, people had done that.

No one had seen her arrive: she'd just turned up in the Tarrington one day. She'd registered in that dismal lobby just before dawn several months ago, so her neighbors hadn't seen her check in. Tanya hadn't made a secret of her existence, but it took more than a week for the other residents to even notice that someone was living in 212. Nobody had even known her name for almost a month. She was polite when spoken to, but very close-mouthed. Mostly she didn't stay in a conversation long enough for anyone to learn anything about her.

It was hard for people to figure out what she was all about. She had no obvious needle tracks on her arms, legs or neck, so people assumed she smoked the pipe or did pills or drank. Oddly, she never seemed loaded. She hadn't asked anybody about getting drugs, which gave rise to the theory that she had her own connection. Most everyone in her hotel believed she had to be *some* kind of addict. After all, why would a girl *that* pretty be hooking *on the street* if not for a fix? And, like some addicts, you only saw her at night.

Ten minutes after she brushed off the Nova, Tanya's patience paid off. A metallic blue BMW pulled up. The guy, apparently a professional of some sort in his early thirties, dressed for success, rolled down the passenger side window. She favored him with a wide-lipped smile as he signaled for her to come over.

"What can I do for you this evening, darling?" she asked in a light, almost musical voice.

"Are you dating?" he returned.

"Most certainly," she replied in her cultured voice.

"How much?"

"Let me in and we'll talk about it."

He pulled up the lock and cracked the door for her. Tanya looked left and right out of habit to make sure no cops would witness this, then gracefully slid into the passenger seat and shut the door. Soon they were cruising down the street at fifteen miles an hour.

"I can't believe a girl as pretty as you is working the streets."

"I like being my own boss," Tanya said, "and I'm not cheap."

"How not cheap are you?"

"Well, we can do a quickie right here for a sixty, or you can get us a room and spend a hundred for half an hour."

Staring at her luscious cleavage and firm young thighs, he licked his lips and, with a slight quaver to his voice, asked what they could do for that long.

"Anything you want to do, honey," she smiled. "I'm open-minded."

"All right," he said. "Where do we go?"

In only a few minutes he had the car parked in one of the slots of a budget motel on the edge of the neighborhood.

"I'll wait for you out here. Okay, baby?" she said as he got out. "I'd prefer not to disturb the management. They'd frown at the idea of me plying my trade in their rooms."

"Good thinking, doll. I'll be right back."

After a few minutes he returned, jingling the keys triumphantly. With a generous, knowing smile she smoothly left his car and strolled over to take his proffered arm. He escorted her discreetly up the stairs to the second-floor balcony.

"So how long you been dating?" he asked quietly as they searched for the room.

"Couple of years," she replied.

"Why?"

"As I said, I like being my own boss. Nobody tells me what to do and I come and go as I please. I can pick and choose who I date, and I do quite well for myself."

"Where are you from? I notice you have an accent—Eastern European, I'd say."

"I don't know. My people have been on the road so long, I really have no idea where. We really kept to ourselves. I'd probably still be with them, but a girl can't stay at home forever, you know?"

"I guess," he said, and let it go at that.

With trembling fingers, the guy opened the door and ushered Tanya into the motel room. Intoxicating fantasies played through his mind as he began taking off his clothes. Tanya sat on the edge of the bed, slowly peeled down her pantyhose and wriggled out of her tube top. Her high pert breasts popped forth, nipples already swollen.

She sat there waiting for him in her red spandex skirt. His libido in overdrive, his cock astir in his shorts, he sat next to her and buried his tongue in her mouth. She eagerly, passionately returned his kiss and ground her bosom into his furry chest. His hands flew to her breasts and the crotch of her panties.

He slid his fingers beneath the hem of her underwear and found her vagina moist and open. Tanya sighed loudly, feeling his finger snaking into her lubricated pussy, and she sucked eagerly at his mouth, writhing her crotch against his hand.

The trick stood and pulled off his shorts while Tanya wiggled out of her skirt and G-string and lay back on the bed. She drew her thighs wide open to part her labia for him. The pink wet lips glistened slightly, and she wiggled her hips sinuously. She was a little taken aback by herself: it wasn't often that a client affected her like this.

Tanya wasn't a hooker because she liked anonymous sex. The best tricks came and went, and the sooner the better. Like most whores, her motto was "get 'em in, get 'em off and get 'em out." Of course, she occasionally had a john who was a good lover, but that created other problems for her.

As the trick pulled himself onto the bed he couldn't resist a closer inspection of Tanya's pussy. Her scent, wild and musky, sent a heady wave of desire through him, and before he knew what he was doing he found his lips poised over her cunt.

Tanya knew what was coming, but for some reason she didn't mind; in fact, she was primed for it. Maybe it was just something about this guy, but she responded to his touch almost immediately. The feel of his breath on her mound made her want to thrust her crotch into his face.

Tanya groaned in delicious surprise at the sensation of his tongue sliding up her juicing vagina, and she gasped when it brushed her electrified clit. She felt a heat growing in her belly, and knew it was about to happen. Quickly she grabbed him from beneath his arms and pulled him up so they were face to face.

"Wow! You work out or something?" His face registered surprise as well as passion.

"Let's do something else," she said, hoping it wasn't too late, that he hadn't aroused her too much. She scissored her legs together and tried to think about bank vaults, about blank brick walls—anything to distract herself.

"Hey, baby, c'mon," the trick said, insinuating a hand between her clenched thighs. "We're just getting warmed up here!"

Suddenly he froze. His fingers had encountered something unexpected. But he had *seen* her pussy—had *tasted* it. Maybe she was some kind of transsexual or hermaphrodite? He wasn't really sure, but he knew the hard cock he now felt in his hand was definitely attached to this beautiful . . . woman?

Now he knew one of her secrets, and he tried to pull back.

Knowing she had been discovered and that he wasn't into it at all, Tanya grabbed his arms and held fast. The trick felt her inhuman strength as he tried to struggle from her grasp, and became horrified. No woman—not even a man—should be this strong. And while he was trying to comprehend his powerlessness, he suddenly felt the stubble of heavy whiskers grate against his face. Where had *they* come from?

Tanya's trick fought to get away, struggling to free himself, preparing to shriek out in fright. Then she opened her lips wide, showing him her full smile for the first time, and he almost fainted. He tried to make sense of her other secret—her inchlong incisors—as she sank them into his shoulder.

He kicked and flailed, but she held fast, sucking greedily at the blood that pumped into her waiting mouth. Dizzy and weak, he noticed that the five o'clock shadow that had rasped against him had disappeared. As he felt his consciousness beginning to ebb, he reached back down to her crotch and recoiled in shock: he knew he'd felt a penis there just a moment ago, but there was only smoothness now.

Tanya stood unsteadily over the trick's lifeless body and collected herself. She shimmied back into her pantyhose, tugged her top back on and tiptoed out the door. She was in luck; there was nobody outside on the balcony. She headed for the stairs.

There were times when Tanya almost regretted being the way she was, even though she couldn't help it. She'd hated leaving her clan five years ago, but they couldn't abide her sex-changing ways.

There were definite advantages to being a shapechanger. The other transsexuals out here relied on all kinds of hormones, silicone and surgery to become women, but all Tanya needed was fresh blood.

By the time she reached the street, she was ready for another trick.

Annalisa Suid

After the War

I notice him as soon as I walk into the lobby, sitting there at the far corner of the bar. He has very short hair, almost a crew cut, bristly like an animal's fur. It works well with his eyes, and though I can't tell their color, they glitter like a tiger's in the early jungle evening, glitter and shiver in the gold dim light of the hotel bar.

I sit down, diagonally across from him, and watch the band, but I turn back to the counter when I feel a soft tug on my sleeve—the bartender trying to get my attention.

"Miss, this gentleman," he says, pointing to my animal man, "this gentleman would like to buy you a drink."

I smile, first at the bartender, and then, graciously, at my short-haired friend, and I say, "A beer would be wonderful." The bartender places an ice-cold bottle in front of me, and I lift it in a quick toast, my head bowed, and sip.

He watches me hold the bottle, watches my hand slip down its long, icy neck. I swallow the foam of the first sip, and he watches my throat contract on the cool liquid.

When the band takes a break, I wend my way through the throng to where he's seated.

"Thank you," I say. He nods.

We talk. I learn that his name is Jesse Miller, that he's a

twenty-seven-year-old air force lieutenant, was divorced after the war, and has no children. I learn that he hangs out at this bar and drinks tonic water every Friday night, and that in his year and a half as a regular, he has bought exactly one drink for one woman: me.

I notice how his green eyes catch the light from the chandelier above us, how the music, once the band starts again, seems to vibrate through his body, and he rocks, gently but right with the beat, in rhythm to the large black singer's whiskey voice.

I notice.

At two a.m., when we've done all the chit-chat you can do at a bar, I ask if he will walk me up the stairs to my hotel room. He seems happy that I've asked, and agrees, but he doesn't take my hand or touch me. In my room, we sit on the sofa and talk some more. Then, in the middle of a sentence, he leans over and brushes a wisp of hair out of my eyes. His cool skin chills me deliciously. I notice again how his eyes glitter in the dimmest light.

"Are you frightened?" he asks at the first pause in our conversation. I know he's trying to read my expression, the slight worry lines that have wrinkled my forehead as I fight within myself.

"You want to be with me, don't you?" he continues when I remain silent.

I smile and nod, because I do, but shouldn't.

"I promise that we won't 'go all the way,' to use a phrase from high school," he says, interrupting my thoughts.

I sigh, relieved. Now we can play.

Jesse kisses me softly on the lips, and I'm surprised at how excited this makes me. I shift slightly, feeling my panties clinging, thrillingly wet, and Jesse watches me move. He says in a voice like a lullaby, "You are the sexiest woman I've ever met."

I laugh. I don't see myself as sexy, though I know that men do, and while my lips are still curved in a grin, he pins my body back against the sofa and ravishes my neck and shoulders. I shudder as he pulls my blouse aside and covers my collarbones in hot, feverish kisses, slides his lips along my shoulders, bites me. I shudder again, and he understands instantly, knows that I want him to overpower me. He holds onto my hands, keeping them flat on the sofa while he suckles my breasts through my blouse, nips and bites the tender skin.

Then he moves his fingers up the split of my body, trying to touch my clitoris, but I don't want his hands there yet. I struggle until I can arch my back and press crotch to crotch with him. His cock throbs against me and grows harder still when he leans in to nibble my earlobe. He whispers to me, "What's the kinkiest thing you've ever done?"

"Ever?"

"Uh-huh." His lips are against my neck, so I feel his words more than I hear them.

"I was tied up once," I say.

"Yes?"

"Tied and mastered."

His grip on my wrists tightens.

"You?" I say in a rush of breath.

"I shaved her." He's husky. "Have you ever been shaved?"

I nod.

"I shaved her and then ate strawberries and whipped cream off her naked pussy. Would you like that?"

I nod again.

"Would you like to feel my flat tongue on your clit, licking you, probing you, then moving up to kiss your lips?"

"Yes."

"Don't you love the taste of sex, the smell of sex on your skin?"

"Yes."

"Do you like it if a guy eats you after he cums inside you?"

"I've never done that," I sigh. His hands wander over me, his hands and his eyes, and his lips and his breath, and his smell, and his sex.

He runs his fingernails all the way down the inside of my legs, setting my skin on fire. Then, with his hands on my nylons, he says, "Take these off."

I do, and he presses his sweet lips to the lips of my pussy, sheathed in damp white cotton.

"Would you like me to eat you through your panties?" He does this as he asks and I wriggle and squirm and stroke his

short hair, like animal fur, that rubs against my thighs. He licks
me and bites me, rips my underpants aside, and slips two fingers
deep inside me. He spreads my juices over the tattoo on my ankle and sucks it clean. Then he pulls my panties down all the
way and licks in circles around my clit until his lips are slick with
my honey. He reaches up and grabs my shoulders, forcing me to
bend and kiss him.

"Do you like the way you taste?" he says into my mouth.

"Yes."

"I do too."

I shift on the sofa to turn off the light, and while my back is
toward him he picks me up and carries me to the bed. The lamp
is still on, and I leave it, wanting to see his glittering eyes, to
watch his serious face change as he cums.

Quickly, I pull off my blouse and undo my bra while he takes
off his oxford shirt and jeans. He's wearing silk boxers, decadent
for a lieutenant I think, though I have no experience with members of the air force. The silk caresses my naked skin as we press
our bodies together, joined from the chest down.

"I want to taste you again," he whispers, and I lie back on the
pillows and let him. This is something he's good at, something
he's obviously had practice doing.

He eats me slowly and effortlessly, moving his tongue in and
out of me like ocean waves, kissing and licking and sucking until
the rhythm of his mouth becomes the rhythm of my blood, of
my body.

Probably because we've decided not to "go all the way," I am
dying to feel him inside me, and I tell him.

He lifts his mouth off my pussy just slightly. "Do you want my
cock here?" he asks, rubbing the right spot. "I'd like to tease you
until you beg me to fuck you."

But he's not going to, and that fact, along with his words,
makes me even hotter. I slither down on him and unbutton his
boxers to reveal his cock. I leave his boxers on, and open, while
I take his cock in my mouth, sip from it, drink from it in the
same fashion that I consumed the beer in the bar. He talks to
me while I perform magic tricks with his cock, making more and

more of it disappear down my long, cool throat, while my tongue flicks out to kiss his balls.

His voice caresses me while his hands smooth and stroke my hair, press firmly on the nape of my neck to help me release that catch that opens my throat even wider.

"You are sweet," he tells me, his voice husky again. I rub my cheeks against his silk-clad thigh in answer. "A kitten," he says, and then, when I swallow hard and take the last inch of his cock down my throat, "A panther."

I like that he sees me as feline and I wonder if my brown eyes glitter as hungrily as his. I look up at him, a question in my eyes, and he tries to answer by opening his wider. I feel that I might lose myself in his eyes, and I look away, concentrating again on that hard, pulsing rod deep in my throat.

"After the war," he says, in a sad voice that makes my skin tingle, "After the war I stopped sleeping."

"Mmmmm?" is all I can manage, too filled to respond appropriately.

"Just an hour or two a night—no dreams, no colors, just an hour or two."

I keep my motion steady, working him, drinking in his heady pre-cum.

"I couldn't make love to her," he continues, and his voice sounds as if he's crying, though when I glance up quickly, I see that he's not. His eyes are hard now, shiny and sad.

"She didn't understand." He shrugs with his entire body, and the movement pulls his cock from my mouth. I am quick to recapture it, and he strokes my cheek very gently as I start my steady beat again.

"But I understood, and I let her go."

I am watching him now while he talks to me. His eyes are hypnotic, his voice sad but urgent, as if he is forcing himself to tell me this, as if he has told no one but himself, over and over again. The words are simple, the pain most certainly intensifying the pleasure I'm giving him.

"I came home two years ago," he says. "And I only sleep an hour or two a night. I'd like to make love to you, but I haven't been able to do that, either."

Suddenly he moans, and I feel the first delicious drops of his cum slip down my throat. I'm startled enough to back away, letting the rest shower his chest and flat belly. He has an amazing amount of semen, and I rub it into his skin, delighting in the warm satiny glaze it forms on my hands and fingers. I bend to taste the salty-sweet cider, and he strokes my hair again, as if petting an animal.

"So much," I whisper.

"I haven't been able to cum." He pauses, and shakes his head as if angry at himself before continuing. "Not for a long time."

When I look up, hearing the tears in his voice again, I see that they are real, sliding crystal-like down his fine cheekbones. His grip on my shoulder is exceedingly firm, as if he needs something to hold on to. I move up his body into his embrace, but somehow it shifts, it turns, and I'm the one holding him. He lets me, resting his head on my naked breasts. He falls asleep in my arms.

I watch peace steal across his features, watch from beneath the black panther hair that falls over my eyes. I stroke his tiger fur and run the tips of my fingers up and down his cheeks, wiping away the tears. Then, hardly moving, I click off the light on the bedside table. I, too, feel peaceful as the first rays of sun filter in through the blinds and dance over the bed, slowly warming the body of the still, sleeping soldier cradled in my arms.

Mary Maxwell

The Café of the Joyous Women

The restaurant was tucked away on a side street, just a block away from the school that Jennifer's two children attended. On her way to a PTA meeting late one afternoon, she noticed the newly painted facade, the gold lettering on the door. The sign read LE CAFÉ DES FEMMES JOYEUSES. She had taken two years of French in high school and she remembered just enough to translate: The Café of the Joyous Women.

It was a tiny place: no more than a dozen small marble-topped tables set quite close together. On each table, a white candle burned beside a bud vase that held a single red rose.

The first time she passed the restaurant, she noticed a woman sitting alone at the window table—the one that commanded the best view of the street. Jennifer was struck by the expression on the woman's face—a broad and contented smile. That smile intrigued Jennifer. What delicious food, she wondered, could inspire such an expression.

For special occasions, Jennifer's husband, Kevin, usually took her to dinner at the country club. But for her twenty-fifth birthday, Jennifer suggested that they go to Le Café des Femmes Joyeuses. "It would be fun to try something a little different, don't you think?"

He frowned. "That's not one of those places where they serve fish raw, is it?"

"No, dear. You're thinking of sushi. This is a French restaurant."

Kevin shrugged good-naturedly and agreed. From his expression, Jennifer knew that he would have preferred the country club—where he knew that his steak would be well done and the portions would be generous—but he was willing to indulge her.

Kevin had been her high school sweetheart; they had married shortly after graduation. Right out of high school, Kevin had assisted in his father's plumbing business. Now he owned his own business—a successful plumbing supply store. They had two children—Nicole and Jason.

Jason, the younger of the two, had just entered kindergarten, leaving Jennifer, for the first time in seven years, with time to herself. In the afternoon, when Jason was at school, Jennifer sometimes found herself afflicted with a strange restlessness. There were many things she could do—wash clothes, make a cake, read a book—but none of them seemed worth the time. It was on just such an afternoon that she had ordered new lingerie from a mail-order catalog: a white lace teddy and matching garter belt, sheer white stockings. The lace, a glorious impracticality, was her birthday present to herself.

On the night of her birthday, she dressed carefully, starting with the new lingerie. For years, she had worn practical cotton underwear and Maidenform bras that could stand up to machine washing. The silk and lace of the teddy felt so fragile, as soft as rose petals. She slipped the teddy over her head and fastened the snaps at the crotch. The silk felt strange against her skin—so light, as if she wore nothing at all. She pulled the garter belt over her hips and gently pulled on the stockings. So sheer, so delicate.

She stood before the full-length mirror, studying the effect. Her full breasts pushed against the teddy, the rosy nipples visible through the lace. Between the tops of the stockings and the teddy was a band of naked flesh.

"Honey, the babysitter's here," Kevin called through the bedroom door.

"Okay! I'll be ready in a minute!"

She thought about wearing a slip, but all her slips seemed wrong with the simple elegance of the silk and lace. Instead, she pulled on the blue silk dress that she had worn to her sister's wedding three years before. She strolled to the vanity to get her evening bag. Without a slip to hamper it, the silk caressed her legs as she walked.

They had reservations for eight o'clock. A smiling waiter greeted them at the door. "Welcome to *Café des Femmes Joyeuses*. My name is Jacques, and I will be your waiter tonight."

It was early and only a few tables were occupied. The candles were lit and a fire burned behind the grate in the fireplace. He seated them at a table by the window.

"Isn't this beautiful," Jennifer said. "Candlelight and roses."

"The tables are kind of small," Kevin commented. He opened the menu and his frown deepened.

Jennifer opened the menu. The dishes were listed in French, with no English translations. "Oh, it's no problem, dear. I got an A in French in high school, remember?"

While Jennifer was examining the menu, Jacques returned, leading another diner: a self-assured young woman wearing a black silk dress. Her hair was short and dark, cropped close to her head. He seated her at the table beside them, just a few feet from Jennifer's elbow.

Jennifer glanced at her, curious. It seemed odd for a woman to be dining alone in such an elegant restaurant. The woman caught Jennifer staring and smiled. Her eyes were dark and they reflected the candlelight. Jennifer quickly looked away, embarrassed to be caught looking.

Kevin was puzzling over the menu. "So what's this?" he asked, tapping his finger on an entree: *Le Lapin au Thyme Frais*.

Jennifer frowned. "Well, I know what thyme is, but I'm not sure about the rest. I wonder if the waiter would help . . ."

"Perhaps I can be of some assistance?" said the woman at the next table. "I could not help but overhear. The food here is delicious, but the seating . . ." She laughed softly and waved her hand in a gesture of helplessness.

"I'm not sure," Jennifer began, but the woman was already leaning toward her.

"*Le Lapin au Thyme Frais*—oh yes! That is the rabbit cooked with cream and thyme. Quite nice, I think. And this—" She reached out and tapped a selection on the menu. "*Ris de Veau en Croûte*—that's veal sweetbreads cooked with vermouth, mushrooms, and cream in a pastry crust. A specialty of the house."

Kevin made a face and the woman laughed. Her hand fluttered and then came to rest, just for a moment, on top of Jennifer's hand. Her skin was cool and smooth, and Jennifer caught a slight whiff of perfume, but then the woman was pointing again.

"*Le Filet Mignon au Béarnaise*—that is, perhaps, more to your liking. A simple cut of steak, with a delicious sauce." She smiled at Kevin, but her hand once again rested on Jennifer's. "It sounds so much better in French, don't you think?" Her voice was soft, as if she were whispering secrets.

"Well," he said, softening a little. "I do like a menu I can read."

"Of course," she said. "But the food is exquisite. I come here often. It's truly worth these small inconveniences. I promise that you will both be pleased that you decided to come."

"It was Jenny's choice." Kevin shifted his eyes to Jennifer, perhaps realizing that he sounded rather rude. "Happy birthday, honey."

"It's your birthday. How wonderful!" She smiled at Jennifer. "Jenny—is that short for Jennifer? Such a romantic name," she said. "My name's Maria. Very plain and ordinary."

The waiter returned with a bottle of red wine and two baskets of rolls. He showed Maria the label and she lifted her hand from Jennifer's to wave toward the wineglass. "And some for my friends," she said. "This is an occasion to celebrate. It's Jennifer's birthday and, I think, her first visit to the restaurant." The sensation of her touch lingered on Jennifer's hand.

"I don't ordinarily drink," Jennifer began, but Jacques had already poured the glass.

"It's your birthday, Jenny," Kevin said. "Go ahead and have a glass." He was already buttering a roll, happy that the food had arrived.

"Of course," Maria said. "This is not an ordinary occasion. I regard it as a personal responsibility to welcome you to my favorite restaurant."

Maria helped them order: filet mignon for Kevin and, after some discussion, sweetbreads for Jennifer and herself. While Kevin was examining the wine list, Maria leaned close to Jennifer once again. "You must be careful with sweetbreads," she mentioned in a confiding whisper. "Some say that they are an aphrodisiac." She lifted her eyebrows and smiled to indicate that she was joking.

The food was, as Maria had said, excellent. And Maria was a fine dining companion. She asked Kevin about his business and he was quite willing to explain recent innovations in plumbing fixtures. "I used to have three kinds of kitchen faucets, and now we stock over fifty. And you've got your choice of pipe: your polyurethane, your copper . . ."

Jennifer was content to listen to Kevin's recitation, a familiar litany of hardware. She found herself looking out over the restaurant, admiring the way the flickering candlelight reflected in the tabletops, in Maria's dark eyes. Maria kept Jennifer's wine glass filled.

Jennifer was sipping her wine when Maria touched her hand unexpectedly, making some point about the value of plumbing. Startled, Jennifer jumped, splashing a few drops of wine on her dress.

"Oh, I'm so sorry," Maria said.

"It's my fault," Jennifer said. "I'm so clumsy."

"Come." Maria stood up and reached out for Jennifer's hand. "We must take care of this immediately, or it will stain. You will excuse us," she said to Kevin. "Women's business."

Without thinking, Jennifer put her hand in Maria's. Maria led her toward the restroom. As they made their way between the tables, she called out to Jacques in French too rapid for Jennifer to follow. He disappeared into the kitchen, then reappeared with a bottle of club soda. Maria took the bottle and waved Jacques away.

She escorted Jennifer into the powder room. There were two rooms: a small outer room with a vanity, a sink, and a single up-holstered chair; an inner room with a toilet.

"Come, come," Maria said. "No time to waste. Turn around." Jennifer obeyed automatically, and felt Maria's cool fingers on her neck as she unzipped the dress. "Take it off now." Jennifer slipped the dress over her head. The air was chilly, and she clutched her dress, feeling foolish and exposed.

"Here," Maria said, taking the dress from Jennifer. "A quick rinse with club soda and the stain will come right out." She turned to the sink and busied herself and then turned back with a damp but unstained dress. "Now, we must give it a moment to dry." She blotted it with the towel and draped it over the towel rack. "There now." She turned back to Jennifer with a rustle of silk. "Sit down, *ma chérie*. No need to stand. You look cold."

Jennifer had crossed her arms over her breasts, partly for warmth and partly for modesty. "It's a bit chilly," she said.

"Sit," she said, and again Jennifer obeyed. She caught a glimpse of her reflection in the mirror. Her nipples had hard-ened, and were pushing against the thin lace of the teddy. She felt exposed, vulnerable.

"It is my fault you are cold, and I must help to warm you," Maria said. She knelt on the carpeted floor beside the chair. "And how might I do that?" she mused, as if to herself.

"I'm fine," Jennifer protested. "It'll just be a few minutes."

"What lovely stockings," she murmured, as if she hadn't heard a word. "So pure and white." Jennifer felt her touch, a hand run-ning down her leg from the thigh to the ankle. "Beautiful legs in beautiful stockings."

"I don't think . . ." Jennifer started to say, but Maria's touch on her leg stopped the sentence before Jennifer could finish it.

"Of course you don't," Maria said. "This is no time to think. Don't think at all. We have a few minutes now, while your dress dries. But no time to think." With a rustle of black silk, she shift-ed her position so that she knelt at Jennifer's feet, looking up at her with a sweet smile. One hand held Jennifer's foot, gently yet firmly, encircling the ankle. The other hand traced a path up the inside of her leg. Her touch was very soft. At the top of the stocking, her fingers hesitated, playing with the reinforced edge. "There is nothing more romantic than a garter belt and stockings," she said. "Panty hose are so . . . pedestrian, I think. Don't you agree?"

"I think . . . perhaps . . . we should . . ." Jennifer was finding it difficult to speak. She knew she should stop this, but she said nothing as Maria's fingers delicately caressed the sensitive skin of her inner thigh just above the stocking's edge.

"Oh, don't worry, *ma chérie*," she said. "I have already locked the door."

"I mean we shouldn't . . ." She stopped, unable to say exactly what they shouldn't do.

Maria's fingers had moved higher. They played now with the silk crotch of the teddy, sometimes pressing against Jennifer and sometimes toying with the small curls of hair that had escaped around the cloth. "I'm afraid that . . ." Jennifer didn't finish the sentence, unable to sum up her fears while Maria's fingers continued their teasing.

"You are afraid that I will ruin your lovely stockings." She finished the sentence for Jennifer. "Oh, no, I would not do such a thing. I will be very careful. Very careful." One careful finger had slipped past the silken edge of the teddy and was softly stroking the outer lips of Jennifer's cunt. "But perhaps we had best undo these snaps. What do you think, *ma chérie*?"

She did not give Jennifer time to respond. Jennifer heard the click, click, click of the three snaps in the crotch of the teddy.

"Ah—no need to think. They are undone." She had moved closer, and Jennifer felt the warmth of Maria's head resting against her inner thigh. The air was cool on her exposed cunt.

"And here is a treasure," Maria said softly. Her breath warmed Jennifer's cunt. "Such beautiful curls you have," she murmured, parting the pubic hair. Jennifer felt both hands now, teasing the outer lips of her cunt, stroking down in an insistent rhythm.

"You are not thinking now, are you, my sweet? Not thinking at all." Maria's fingers explored the inner lips. When one questing finger stroked her clitoris, Jennifer's hips moved involuntarily, pushing toward the hand, and she exhaled suddenly.

"Not thinking at all," Maria murmured, and the finger traced tiny circles with the clitoris at the center. For a moment, the finger dipped into Jennifer's cunt and she moaned.

"Softly, *ma chérie*. Very softly." Her finger, now wet with the juices from Jennifer's cunt, returned to its place, rubbing harder. "Here now, this will help." One hand left Jennifer's crotch to lift her foot so that it rested on the vanity before her. Jennifer's other foot came up of its own accord. Her legs were spread wide. In the mirror, she could see her face and two high-heeled blue shoes. The rest was hidden by the vanity.

Maria's hand returned to Jennifer's cunt. While one finger continued teasing her clit, another finger pushed between the lips. Jennifer raised her hips to meet it, but the finger withdrew as she pressed toward it.

"What do you say, *ma chérie*?" Maria's voice was as rhythmic as her rubbing. "What do you say?"

"Yes," Jennifer moaned. "Oh, yes."

"You want this now, *ma chérie*? You want this."

Jennifer's nipples rubbed against the lace of the teddy. Her clitoris was a hard knot under Maria's finger. Her cunt was aching to be filled. "Please . . . oh, please."

"So polite," Maria whispered. "Are you still afraid?"

"No. Not afraid. Please."

"Good," she whispered. "That's very good." Jennifer felt Maria's mouth on her clitoris, kissing her, her tongue teasing the hard knot of flesh. Gently, she slid a finger into Jennifer's cunt. "Yes," she whispered. "This is what you want, isn't it, darling?" She looked up at Jennifer with those beautiful dark eyes. The scent of her perfume filled the small room. "You want me to fuck you."

"Yes, fuck me. Please fuck me."

Maria laughed and moved her finger slowly, pressing into Jennifer's cunt, then pulling back just a little. Involuntarily, Jennifer's back arched, bringing her hips to meet the hand. "Yes, you like this," Maria murmured, pushing again. Her mouth returned to Jennifer's clit, now sucking hard. Maria pushed a second finger into Jennifer's cunt, pressing hard against her, filling her.

The orgasm took Jennifer in a great rush—a natural force, like gravity, like magnetism, like lust. She was picked up and shaken and tossed back in the chair, limp and exhausted.

"Softly," Maria murmured between her legs. "Softly now." Still kneeling on the floor, she smiled up at Jennifer. Her hair was tousled; her face slick with the juices of Jennifer's cunt. Still smiling, she slipped her fingers from Jennifer's cunt and she stood, looking down at Jennifer. "I think you are warm now."

Jennifer didn't move. Yes, she was warm. Very warm.

Maria shook back her hair and washed her hands and face in the sink. Jennifer watched her dry her hands on the towel and smooth her hair into place. She knelt again and neatly snapped the teddy closed. "A good girl always puts away her toys," she said brightly. "And I am always a good girl." She stood and took the dress from the towel rack.

"Voilà! Your dress is dry, you are warm and happy. And it is your birthday. What could be better? Come now." She pulled Jennifer up from the chair. Jennifer stood passively while Maria dressed her, dropping the dress over her head, zipping it. "There now!" She stood behind Jennifer. "I do love quiet women. They always seem so surprised."

"I am surprised," Jennifer said.

She laughed and kissed Jennifer's cheek. "Come now."

Jennifer followed her back into the warm restaurant, filled with the scent of coffee and pastries. The plates had been cleared from the table. Jacques stood beside the table, chatting with Kevin about basketball scores.

"I ordered coffee," Kevin said as Jacques retreated. It seemed odd that Kevin was still there; it seemed to her that they had been gone for a very long time. He smiled at Jennifer indulgently. "It took you a while."

"Ah, yes," said Maria. "Wine stains can be tricky. But you see . . ." She gestured. "As good as new." She glanced over her shoulder. "And here is Jacques."

Jacques emerged from the kitchen bearing a small cake decorated with candles. "Happy birthday to you," he sang. Maria joined in. "Happy birthday to you!" After a moment, Kevin sang as well. "Happy birthday, dear Jennifer. Happy birthday to you!"

After the cake and the coffee, as Jennifer and Kevin were preparing to leave, Maria took Jennifer's hand in hers. "I hope you enjoyed yourself."

Momentarily flustered, Jennifer glanced at Kevin.

"Sure," he said affably. "The food's fine, once you figure out what it is. Could use bigger portions, but that's all right." He patted his stomach. "I could lose a few pounds anyway."

"We have ladies' luncheons here every Wednesday afternoon at one," Maria said. "Perhaps you'd like to attend, Jennifer?"

Jennifer hesitated. Then Kevin said, "You ought to, honey. It'd do you good to get out of the house more."

Maria smiled and Jennifer nodded. "I'd like that," she said softly.

"Until Wednesday, then," Maria said. She squeezed Jennifer's hand and smiled brilliantly. "I will look forward to it."

On her way to the door, Jennifer caught a glimpse of herself in the mirror. She was smiling like a woman with a secret.

Francesca Ross

❦

Giving and Receiving

Dorset, 1820

She never let him give her gifts. That disconcerted him, for ordinarily he was the most generous of lovers. He liked women, and liked pretty things, and liked giving women pretty things. And usually they liked accepting them from him; he was wealthy and had impeccable taste.

But Katerina maintained the edict as fiercely as she maintained her independence, and he not unreasonably became obsessed with disobeying it.

After the first week they spent together in the cottage in the Dorset hills, he sent her an elegant little bracelet—six hundred pounds' worth of pearls and sapphires in a white gold setting. It came back by return post, with a cool note: "Sir. Thank you for the bracelet. Regrettably, I am unable to accept it. Remaining always yours respectfully, Katerina Garrick." It was not, as he first thought, a dismissal. No, she would accept his visits, and his kisses, and his passion, and respond in kind. But she would not accept his gifts.

"I am not your mistress," she told him once when he had the effrontery to slip an Indian silk shawl over her shoulders. "I am not your mistress."

And of course she wasn't, in the sense of being kept by him. Her husband had left her well off; she had a manor home in Devon and a town house in London as well as the little ivy cottage; she had a tragic past in a foreign land, a lost family she couldn't speak of; she had a child, a circle of eccentric artistic friends who knew nothing about him, a life of her own. She was not his mistress.

"What are you then?" he asked.

Folding up the shawl, she gave him that slanted look from those exotic Eastern eyes, the look that told him he would never truly know her. "I am my own. Nothing more."

"Then what am I?"

She had come to him then, her hands gentle on his face, her voice husky with love and longing. "Oh, Eric, you are my joy."

Aye, he was that, and only that. He was not her husband or her protector or her employer, her owner or her friend. He could not live with her or tell his friends about her or take her to meet his children. He was her private diversion, and she was his, and their connection was kept hidden from the world. He was only her joy, a secret reward she allowed herself when she had been very good.

And it was enough for him; he wanted to be no more than that. He had his own life, his own past, a wife he still mourned years after her death. He was as wary as Katerina of that sense of betrayal that would come of greater intimacy. They had both loved before, had learned, somehow, to live with loss. Now they had each other—but only in joy, never in sorrow, never in sadness.

That was enough for him, truly. He didn't want her sorrow; he had enough of his own. He wanted to tantalize her, and be tantalized by the mystery that was the center of her. He wanted to slip into her life as he slipped into her bed, bringing pleasure, reminding her to laugh and tease and love again. It was just—oh, he wanted to leave something with her when he left, something more lasting than the taste of him on her lips, than the trace of his kiss on her skin, something of himself.

Katerina, no less than any other woman, had her inconsistencies. She wouldn't let him give her gifts, but sometimes she would let him give her pleasure. She could not resist French chocolates or French scented soap or French champagne—by the bottle, at least; she refused the case. She was a sybarite of the first order, and she loved delicious things. So he could bring a box of bonbons, bite one in half and put the other half in her mouth, and laugh as she sighed and surrendered. As long as it was momentary, as long as it was mutual, she would shake her head and kiss him and accept.

So when he returned from voyages to the West Indies, he brought her Jamaican coffee for their breakfast. When he came down from London, he brought raspberry jam and crumpets from Gunters. She would taste and close her eyes and he would think, ah, at least you will take pleasure from me, if nothing else.

It wasn't until the third year that he thought of the cottage. After that, he thought of it often, when he was sitting in meetings at the Admiralty, when he walked on his quarterdeck hearing the sails sing in the wind, when he lay alone in his oceanic bed at home. The cottage was not the only place they met; there was a discreet little London flat near the new Regent's Park, where they could walk in the mist at dawn, holding hands like children, and a lodge within an hour's drive of town, where they could ride headlong across the heath. The cottage was reserved for those summer weeks when she took a holiday from the duties of running an estate and rearing a son. Their affair had started there, and he sometimes thought that one day, when he didn't expect it, it would end there. So he thought of it with a mix of longing and loss, of triumph and trepidation.

That third summer he came early, a month, in fact, before their appointed time. The sun was high, the breeze light off the lake, as he circled the little house, his boots leaving crescents in the soft grass. The yard was overgrown and the garden lush with May's abundance. The ivy climbing the old brick walls was glossy now, with tiny white flowers strewn like stars through the green. The windows shone in the sun with that peculiar blankness that said there was no one home. But the memories were there, drifting through the garden where they had their breakfasts, rising from the lake where they swam naked in the moonlight. Would she see the memories if their inconclusive affair concluded this time, or would she, with her gentle ruthlessness, dismiss them as she had dismissed him?

Of course, she had never dismissed him, never spoken of an end, never suggested they might not go on like this for the rest of their lives. She had no other lover, he knew that, and after the first few months neither did he—what point would there be in others? Sometimes he thought they could go on forever in their private world, making love a holiday from care. But they couldn't; he knew it. Joy was all they shared and joy can't last forever, not even with all the goodwill in the world.

He crossed the empty terrace in a few long steps, imagining her here painting at her easel, her brow furrowed in concentration, a spot of paint on her cheek, her sable hair pulled back in a long braid down the sweet curve of her neck.

"My mother painted birds," she told him once, watching the birds fight for space in the bath. Her eyes were opaque, her head tilted to the side, her paintbrush held suspended near the canvas.

Mother and daughter could both have painted the marble birdbath today. It was full of rainwater and white petals from the crabtree, the pedestal a dusty gray against the rich green ground. A motley flock perched on the fluted edge—a finch, a wren, an oriole, a bright and dark collection of song. The birdbath was an oddity in this humble setting, a block of marble elaborately carved like an Ionic column. It must predate the cottage by a half-century, installed when this plot was part of the gardens of a larger estate long since partitioned off when the mortgage couldn't be met. The great house was gone, along with the gardens, but the birdbath remained to testify to some earlier grandiosity.

It came to him then. He would give her something too big to send back, something too impressive to ignore. Something permanent. Something imbedded. Something to make her laugh and give in and accept, because she had no other choice.

A bath. He would make it a Roman bath, because she collected ancient artifacts, and because it would be big enough for them both. He would make it opulent, because he had always been extravagant. He would add on the most newfangled equipment, because he was a man of vision. He would sink it deep into the foundations of her cottage, so she would never be able to make it go away.

He was a navy man, used to acting with dispatch, and he had sources at all the docks. A block of Italian marble and its Florentine carver had just arrived at Southampton, to be used for a pedestal for some garish statue at the Brighton Royal Pavilion. A hundred pounds slipped to the king's contractor was enough to have the shipment condemned as flawed, and the carver was pacified with the promise of better pay. Eric arranged for workmen to meet him at the cottage while Katerina was still in London. Of course, difficult little Katerina had never provided him with a key, so he had to break a pane in the front door to unlock it. The workmen only looked down and shuffled their feet as he committed this felony, then trooped in after him carrying their tools. They excavated the small second bedroom easily, there being only dirt beneath the plank floor, and then the craftsmen moved in.

The plumber, having lately worked at the Brighton Pavilion, blanched when he saw his latest assignment. But like the Italian carver, he swallowed his professional pride and invented on the spot an innovative piping system flowing from a rainwater cistern on the roof, as well water lacked the requisite softness. Of course, the roof had to be reinforced to hold the cistern, and the walls replastered over the pipes, but that was a small price to pay for running water. Most impressive of all was the stove and water-tank contraption, through which a copper pipe traveled. When the stove was lit, the plumber assured him, hot water was only a matter of turning a tap. He produced from his pocket taps fit for just such a purpose; solid gold they were, with rubies in the handles, meant, he assured Eric, for the king's personal bath. The Florentine carver nodded his approval and went back to etching laurel vines in the steps that led up to the bath. And so the copper piping ran to solid gold taps, which spewed hot and cold water at the slightest urging.

Katerina could not refuse this gift.

The last workman swept up the debris and left Monday afternoon. Eric stood in the doorway, surveying the new addition. It was worthy of any Roman emperor, six feet by four, with a marble shelf running along one side, steps leading up and down into it, all of it carved of the creamiest Carrara marble veined in deep purple. Heavy gray towels were stacked on a low bench, a crystal decanter of bath oil nearby. Hand-painted gray and blue tiles covered the walls to chest height. The hearth was tiled in the same colors and stocked with beech logs. A bay window looked out onto the garden—eventually he would have to add a wall, for privacy's sake.

For a moment he sat on the step and let himself imagine Katerina's response when she saw his gift. Would she be angry at his high-handedness, declare that her rustic hideaway had been ruined? No. No. He ran his hand over the curve of the marble, cool and smooth under his touch. She would rise out of the soap bubbles like Venus from the sea, all naked glory, and welcome him home.

Katerina unlocked the front door and let the coachman carry the baggage in and set it down before she entered. As she tipped him, she noted with some distant appreciation that the cottage smelled not at all musty. Perhaps Mrs. Glover, the caretaker, had come in to air it out.

There was a white square on the floor of the tiny foyer, a note that had been pushed under the door. She opened it as she walked into the sun-filled parlor, savoring that sweet fluttering she felt at the familiar bold scrawl, the endearing misspellings: "Kat—The last time I was here I left something for you in the back bedroom. I shall be there as pledged Tuesday. E." The door to that back room was shut, but an unprecedented amount of light poured through the inch-high crack underneath. Alarmed, she flung it open, then stepped back instinctively, blinded by the sun shimmering through a new window. Once there had been an old four-poster bed here. Now there was an ocean.

An empty ocean. "Oh, Eric," she murmured, rubbing her forehead with her fist, "you are *impossible.*"

The tub took up most of the small room. The rest was filled with a merrily burning stove—what a waste of fuel, and in

June—a great expanse of window and window seat, and hundreds and hundreds of exquisite tiles, tiny gray triangles laid in a herringbone pattern. She almost turned and walked out again, but steeled herself and went to touch the shimmering taps. Just as she expected, real gold. No brass for Eric.

It was all new, the walls, the ceiling, the flooring, the window. And it was better suited for some glossy modern town palace than this old cottage. No doubt Eric thought of this as an improvement over the tin bath in the kitchen. But how could she sell this cottage now, if she needed to? Only one bedroom, but an acre of bath. You might have asked, she accused silently, and imagined his injured reply, *But you would have said no.*

With a sigh, she perched on the edge and gazed around. His presence lingered there with his extravagant gift. He had been here recently to light the stove. And the ice in the gold bucket was still melting around the champagne, next to a bouquet of yellow tulips from her own garden, stuffed into a lead crystal vase.

Idly, she turned one tap. First a trickle and then a stream of water emerged, only to pour down the open drain. The waste offended her frugal nature, so she cut off the water and looked about for something to stop up the drain. When nothing more promising revealed itself, she bent over to shove her balled-up handkerchief into the gold-rimmed drain. Like an inquisitive child, she turned on one tap then the other, letting the warming water cascade through her fingers. When it grew too hot to touch, she switched to the other stream, which was pleasantly cool and smelled of rain, like Eric when he came in from sailing.

It was very like a miracle. Katerina had heard, of course, of the advanced plumbing installed in new homes, of nabobs returned from India who insisted on hot running water. She had never expected to see it in her simple holiday cottage. But then, she ought to know better than to underestimate the grandiose Eric Radcliffe.

Extravagance proved contagious. With a generous hand, she poured in the fragrant bath oil, producing billows of suds. It was too inviting to resist, like its giver, and after a moment's struggle, she gave in. Twisting her hair up, tossing her gown and stockings into a heap in the corner, she climbed naked up and then down the marble steps into the welcoming water. The side opposite the taps was curved precisely to fit a woman's body, her body, in fact. Did he take measurements? Or did he know her so well? She slid down the slick marble, imagining Eric's square, capable hands sketching their familiar path along the slight curve of her back, the gentle slope of her hips, the length of thigh, while the stone carver nodded thoughtfully and measured the arcs left in the air.

The water rose, sluiced over her belly, through the valley between her breasts, over her shoulders, the suds tickling the sensitive nape of her neck. The oil made silk of her skin; she ran her hands along her sides, thinking of Eric and his designing ways. He had corrupted her, as she always worried he would, with his extravagance and ardor. He knew too well all her weaknesses.

She always found it hard to let go, to let the tight control slip, to give in to the simple joys of a man, a summer holiday, a love affair. She had always been tempted to live too narrowly, to focus her life too tightly on one source. Since her husband's death, she had not made that mistake again. Painstakingly she built another life, this one strictly apportioned. She had her literary friends in London, and her artistic friends in Devon; she had her charitable works and her paintings and the routine business of running a home and estate. Each part was separate and detachable from the others, replaceable.

Only her child and her lover broke through the boundaries. Her son, of course, was central; she was tied to him with a thousand knots. But she had no illusions; he would slip those knots someday, as he must. The process had already begun. Yesterday she had held her boy tight, seeking a reason not to leave. Once he would have cried and clung to her, and she would have wept too, leaving him. This time Jack had squirmed out of her farewell embrace, taking off after his little cousin without looking back. A child knew no loyalty, only love, and that love was limited no matter how unconditionally it was returned. She knew that, else she wouldn't have let him go; she knew all about the borders to love, and the loss that accompanied their crossing.

Eric didn't know that, she thought. He couldn't help himself;

he had a generous heart and couldn't help giving it away. She could be so generous only in passion, and only because some trick of nature had given her a sensualist's body along with a Puritan's heart. That, at least, she could give him—a passion to match his own. But someday it wouldn't be enough.

She thought hard of him, conjuring him up as if his spirit lurked nearby. She thought of his calloused sailor's hands, felt her nipples harden under her palms. She had left the door off the latch, and soon enough it opened. She heard Eric call her name, heard his footsteps moving surely, too surely, through the hall to her new sanctuary. At the door he halted, his expressive face the picture of surprise. "Kat, what have you done? A Roman bath here? What a sight!"

"You can't fool me, you rogue. Come here."

A little wary, he approached the tub. She reached out a hand to touch his leg, looked up and saw that he wondered if she liked his gift. She curved her fingers around the leather boot, felt the taut calf underneath, wished she could caress his tension away.

"I rather hoped," he said wistfully, "that you would rise to greet me. Like Venus. Merely for artistic demonstration, I mean."

"Like this?" Both hands on the sides for security, she rose, the water streaming off her, soap suds clinging in suggestive places. He was so close she could hear the quick intake of his breath, sense the instinctive flex of his hand toward her. She slipped back into the water, away from him. But then she held out her hand. "Will you join me?"

That merry smile that always lingered at the edges of his mouth broke through, and he yanked off his boots and stripped off his riding clothes. He was a beautiful man, fair-skinned and dark-eyed, restless and lean and mercurial. She wanted to tell him so, to tell him that she loved the laughing curve of his mouth, the sweet boyishness of his slender waist—but all his life women had marveled over him, and he disliked it. So instead she waited until he ducked under and came up, soap suds frosting his shoulders, and praised what no one else ever thought to praise in him—his wickedness. "You were very clever, my darling, having all this done without my knowing."

The irony in her voice only made him laugh—he was in the clear, and they both knew it. He stretched out beside her, his long body slippery against hers, his hand sliding sensuously along her hip and up to her breast. He just skimmed the tip, as if by accident, and cupped her face, his thumb going to stroke the bow of her lower lip. Her tongue flicked his thumb; then slowly, tantalizingly she sucked it, her teeth gentle on the callus at the end. He bent close and kissed her, their mouths meeting as his thumb withdrew. "Were you surprised?" he whispered against her lips.

She pulled away to search for signs of guilt in his eyes, but no, they danced with laughter, pride, triumph. "Surprised. Yes, you could say that. I think I have never been so surprised in all my life. The bath, the window—the bath oil, in my favorite scent. How ever did you arrange all this? How did you get in?"

His dark lashes swept down to hide his eyes—he was guilty after all. He was also aroused; she felt him stir, rise warm and intimate against her thigh. But they had time yet for that, time to let the desire gather as they learned each other again. Time to let him explain himself, and absolve himself, and time for her to forgive him his sins and let him sin more.

"I had to break a pane in the door. It worries me, kitten, that it's so easy to get in here. I think my next improvement will be a solid oak door. And bars on the window. Not this window, I don't want to spoil the view—I had a locksmith take a wax impression of the lock and craft me a key." A bit sullen, he added, "I left the key there on the side table in the hall."

"Oh, keep it, Eric, do. This new addition without doubt cost more than I paid for the entire cottage, so I think we must consider you half-owner now."

That impulsive offer surprised them both, because she was never impulsive. But she would not take it back; it was a gift to match his own. He liked that, though he tried to conceal it, shrugging as if it were of no consequence. "It was worth every penny, just to see you surrounded by bubbles." He twined his legs around hers, holding her fast against him, her breasts pressed against his chest, his arms tight about her waist. "You do like it, don't you?"

"Yes. Thank you."

He had the grace to confess, "Oh, I did it for me, too. You know that."

"I still thank you."

"For what?"

"For reminding me of the occasional felicity of the universe."

He didn't want to be thanked, but he didn't want the gratitude going elsewhere either. She traced the sulky droop of his mouth with a tender finger as he said, "I don't know what the universe has to do with it."

"And the felicity of you. Ah, Eric, you remind me every moment—" She couldn't find the words, had to let her hands trace the thought on his chest, her lips trace the sentiment against his.

But he slipped away from her kiss—the bath oil made them slippery, she realized with a shiver of anticipation. "Katerina, my love, do cultivate a bit of patience."

He reached out a long arm for the bottle of champagne. "Let us toast to our Roman pleasure before you start on all that Russian pleasure you have in store for me." Effortlessly he popped the cork, then looked around, frowning. "I forgot the glasses."

"We can drink out of the bottle, Eric."

"But then how will we toast?"

"I can think of a way." She took the bottle from him, tilted it up and let the froth run into her mouth. Then, lying against his chest, she kissed him. His tongue pushed her lips open, slipped inside, made a sensuous circuit of her mouth.

"I love the taste of champagne on your lips," he whispered. "Kat. Kat."

They got through half the bottle that way, Katerina thinking that she could never take another lover after Eric. Surely no other man would waste so much time on lips and mouth and tongue while his hands lay gentle on her back and his erection pulsed patiently against her inner thigh. No other man would settle for just kisses while the water cooled and the champagne warmed, would let his tongue brush rough then soft against hers, catch her lip in a gentle suck and then release it, let her tease him with tiny bites and ask for no more than this moment and these mouths.

It was she finally who ended this coupling of kisses, for her hands ached to touch him, to trace the hard living form of him. Her awareness was intense but narrow; she could not kiss him and touch him too, not if she wanted to experience either. So she rested her head on his chest and closed her eyes, let herself be mesmerized by the steady surge of his heart, and detached her hand from his to touch him.

In the months they had been apart she had forgotten how different a man's body was from her own; now she remembered that his shoulders broadened where hers left off, that everything soft in her was taut on him. By memory, not sight, she found the tattoo on his upper arm, tracing the masts of the ship with three fingers—his first love, he had told her once, the HMS *Defiant*. He was entirely alien to her, this man, and entirely familiar now that she could touch again this body she knew far better than her own. Up past the hard swell of his chest, with its thicket of damp curling hair, her hand found out those felicitous paradoxes—the roughened cheek and the suggestion of velvet on his eyelids, the silken brush of his long lashes against her wrist, the generous curve of his mouth. Somewhere under her touch was the secret of him, some essential knowledge denied to her vision and reason. All of her followed that quest of sensation her hand traced, and all of him waited in the silken darkness to be discovered.

Now he became restive, as she drew her fingers across his lips, down the square-cut chin, parting the water to trail down the chest to the heavier tangle of hair below his belly. She closed her eyes tighter, listening for that quick breath that told her she had come too close, and traced a circuit around, sliding her fingers into the water-soft curls, feeling under her fingertips the very pulse of his life. His patience was nearly gone; the muscles and tendons in his loins were gathered tight under her touch, ready to spring. She waited, suspended in her search, until he moved, shifting slightly so that her hand could close gently over his arousal. "Ah," he whispered, and she could feel, hear, the vibrations in his ribs lying ridged against her cheek. She slid her hand along the shaft, not to arouse him, only to explore him, the velvet skin, the pulsing ridge of vein, the power embodied there, the secret of him.

And then his hands were at her waist, pulling her up along his thighs, and she had to let him go to take him another way, her legs going around his waist to tuck against the marble wall. His entry was inevitable in that intimate position, his withdrawal an anguish, this action echoing in the core of her as she slid back and forth across his wet legs, until his strong hands held her there, body to body, her ragged breath mingling with his.

There it was, the border. He drew her across it, and she rested her cheek against his damp neck, her lips on the surging pulse in his throat, her own pulse surging in answer, and she felt the careful construction of her self dissolve. There would be time, she told herself, to build it back up again, time to cross back again that border.

But for now she let him carry her with him, hold her against him until the shimmering stopped, pick her up shivering from the chill water and wrap her in a gray towel, his arms wrapped around her too. The bed linens were cool, but his body was warm.

"Thank you," he murmured against her hair.

"For what?"

"Oh, for that occasional felicity of the universe of yours. And for you."

And for the joy, and the sadness it leaves behind. One day she would accept that too.

Barbara DeGenevieve

My Mother's Body

I have this memory. I'm not sure where it came from. I don't know if it's a dream, I don't know if it ever happened. I don't think it did, but I'm not sure. I wonder how you'll feel hearing this. I'd hate to complicate or confuse our relationship, but I'm desperate to talk about it. It frightens me, but it excites me more.

We're in my studio, talking, sharing a bottle of wine. I tell you that you have a perfect body, the body I've always wanted, the one I inhabit in my fantasies, the one I watch in my fantasies, the one I fuck while my lover makes love to my other body. You sit there staring at me, not understanding what I'm talking about.

I ask if I can tie you up. You say yes, but you might resist. I say, good. We know each other. We are in the same body, the same mind, the same fantasy. When we ask each other questions, it is only to confirm what we already know, to play the word game, to hear the desire in each other's voice.

We move from kitchen table to couch. Rather than undressing you, I tell you to take your clothes off, slowly, for me. At first you are uncharacteristically shy about it, but by the time you've slipped off your shoes and jeans, the script begins to interest you. You stand in front of me in a long-sleeved orange velour shirt that fits tightly over your breasts, your black thong underwear barely visible beneath. Watching my eyes watch your body, you unfasten the 14 small buttons and slide the clinging fabric from each of your arms, letting it drop to the floor. As you reach to unhook your bra, I tell you to stop, that I'll do it later. For now I just want you to stand there. I want to take in what I have only been able to imagine. I can be the aggressive voyeur, the solipsistic pervert now. You don't mind. You like it. Your desire to be desired feeds my compulsive fixation on your body. You tempt everyone around you to fantasy. You want everyone to want you. Well, I do.

I ask you if I've ever told you about my mother. Only that she committed suicide, you say.

Oh. Your breasts are beautiful, like my mother's. It's odd when I think about the ease with which she dressed and undressed in front of me. She was so uncomfortable about every other aspect of sex in relation to her daughters, but not her body. I was fascinated by her breasts. They were large and very dense with nipples in perpetual erection. The thought that my body might one day look like hers thrilled me. I watched in awe as she put her bra straps over her shoulders, bent over and shook all of that pink flesh into the white cotton cones of her 36C Maidenform.

Bend over and shake for me.

Freud had it all wrong. It's the mother/daughter relationship that's so titillating. Women are either lesbian or bisexual; how can we be anything but, when our first and primary love object was our mother? Freud never got very far with his ideas about women because he was so hung up on the dick thing. It's the breast that's so powerful—for everyone.

I tell you to close your eyes and I lead you into another part of the studio where two heavy braided leather ropes hang from a ceiling beam. I quickly fasten you into the wrist restraints at the end of each rope, place a thick wooden dowel behind your back, and clamp your wrists close to your waist. In this position, your back is straight and your breasts display themselves to me. Your eyes are open now watching me prepare. I go to the toy box and pull out the blindfold.

Please don't make me wear that, you say. I want to watch you.

It's more delicious when you don't know what to expect, I say.

You stop protesting because you are as much into your own pleasure as I am into mine. I put the blindfold over your eyes and tie it behind your head. Touching you for the first time, I run my fingers through your long hair, down your back, down the crack of your ass.

Lightly I kick your feet to spread them almost a yard apart. I walk around to the front of your body. I want to gorge myself on what I see. I move my face within a fraction of an inch of your smooth, browned skin. You can feel my breath as I exhale your scent back onto your flesh. I smell your whole body—up and down each arm, under your hair, around your face, down your back and left leg, across and up your right, circling around your waist to your belly and breasts and finally down to the place where I know you want me to be. I pull your panties away and nuzzle the dark, damp hair, breathing in deeply and blowing out into your separated lips. Your smell is strong and I linger only to tease you with the weight of my breath.

I move away silently as your body chills from the absence of my warm face. Where are you, you ask.

I don't answer, but I press my body into your back as I begin to peel off my clothes. I unbutton my loose, silky pants and let them fall down the back of your legs; I pull my shirt over my head and dangle it between your breasts before letting it slide down the front of your body. You can feel the soft leather corset I'm wearing, my breasts pressed against your shoulder blades. I turn and rub my ass against yours, letting you know that our taste in underwear is similar.

I take another tour of your body, my gaze focusing again on the beautiful breasts quivering inside a black lace bra. My lust embarrasses me and I'm comforted by your blindness to my lechery. I want to work your body into the same frenzy I feel in mine. My cunt is throbbing. I stick two fingers into my wet and swollen hole and bring them up under your nose. You smile and your tongue darts out so quickly that my attempt to tease you is foiled. I wipe my fingers on your chest as I slide my hand down to your breast and pull the bra away. I lick your nipple and you moan, the first indication of increasing heat. I suck hard for a few seconds then move away, leaving you with one breast hanging over the bra, the other still in place. You look quite helpless, an unusual situation for you.

Shake your breasts for me.

I continue the story about my mother. I don't know why I was so focused on her body. I never thought of it as sexual until I started telling you about it. When I was a kid, I compulsively drew breasts and high heeled shoes, usually without attachment to a body. When I got mad at one of my girlfriends, I would draw a picture of her naked and pretend a group of kids gathered around to watch and laugh. My mother found some of my pictures and was so upset she slapped my face and made me kneel in the corner with my hands behind my back for two hours. The next day, she took me to confession and stood outside, listening to make sure I told the priest what I had done.

I pull the other side of your bra down and run my hands across those exquisite tits. I take a nipple between thumb and forefinger of each hand and squeeze. Their immediate erection provokes a tighter pinch. Your head rolls and your shoulders sway back and forth as if teasing an audience in an erotic dance. I squeeze harder and your mouth falls open. I stick my tongue inside, probing the open cavity, then slide it over your lips and chin, licking your cheeks and ears while you squirm to move away. I pull you back by your nipples and with one last rough tweak, I release you.

I make another trip to the toy box.

The scissors are old, the ones my mother kept in her sewing box. They're beautiful—long shiny blades with a delicate incised pattern decorating the finger holes. I press them against your throat and you flinch from the icy coldness. Dragging them down your chest, I open them just as they pass your bra. I catch the fabric between the blades and slice. You draw your breath in through your teeth, making a hissing sound. I've heard it before. I know what it means. I move the scissors across your flesh to one strap—clip, and then the other—clip. The black lace falls to the floor.

Shake your breasts for me. You lean forward this time.

The hallway that connected the three bedrooms in our house was carpeted with an ugly green and brown fake oriental pattern. I knew how to negotiate the design to avoid the creaking of the old floorboards beneath. My mother never closed the door all the way when she undressed for bed at 9:30 every night.

Shake your breasts for me.

Your legs are still spread from my earlier positioning. Another two clips and the small piece of black cloth that covered little more than your pubic hair and cunt is lying on the floor near your bra. I pick it up and bring it to my face. It is as wet and aromatic as I expected. I put the scissors down but within reach and begin to roam your body.

It's not cursory this time; I'm no longer teasing. I take off the corset and cover the front of your body with mine. We move to a center point as if gravity begins where our bodies collide. My hands grab your ass, spreading your cheeks and exposing the puckered hole to night air. Our tongues enter each other's mouths and taste the wetness, feel the teeth, lick and suck lips, cheeks, chin, neck, shoulders, while our bodies remain glued together.

I finally break away to focus again on your breasts.

Take the blindfold off. I want to watch you want me, you say.

Your arrogance and voyeuristic desire arouse my exhibitionism. I slide the mask off your head and say, shake them for me.

You grin and lean forward, enticing me to play. I kneel down to face them, to return to a place of familiarity. I lift them in my hands, study them, and sink my face into their fullness. I learn them with my hands and every part of my face. My nose follows the contour of each, my tongue tastes and makes them wet, my mouth sucks your nipples, my head thrashes back and forth between them. You lean farther into me so I can have as much as I want. You love it—both what I do to your body and the frenzy you see in mine.

I pull away, knowing I can never be satiated but wanting to bring you to this same place of desire. I move the scissors over, place them next to your foot, and sit back on my heels between your legs. You look down and know what I'm going to do. Oh, no, please don't, you say.

Why not? I ask.

I feel so naked and exposed, you say.

That's just how I want you to feel, I answer.

But before I start, I lean into the hair and explore the flesh beneath. I spread your lips with my fingers and my tongue makes a slow deliberate pass over your clit. Your whole body convulses. You've been waiting for it all night. My fingers find the tunnel and burrow in while my tongue continues its slow but firm navigation of the center of the universe. The name of this game is desire. I want you to want me as much as you want to be the object of everyone's lust. My fingers move faster and harder in and out of your slippery cunt. Your whole body is trembling now and you are moaning loudly. The walls of these studios are paper thin, and I like the thought that the people in the three adjacent units are all hearing you.

I stop, leaving you very close to an explosion. You plead, don't stop. Please. Finish me. I want you back inside me, I want your tongue. At least hold me. This is cruel, you cry.

I pick up the scissors and touch them to your cunt lips. The coldness startles you but you are subdued for the moment by any stimulation. I grab some hair between my index and middle finger and shear it away. You wince. I do it again and again, pulling it away from your body but leaving only short stubble. I move a light close to your body so I can see your cunt mouth. The danger of the situation instigates new whimpers and moans. You like it. You like all attention paid to your body.

When I finish cutting, I brush and blow away the loose hair. I'm not going to shave you. This is much more abject, much less tidy, a contrast with the rest of your body. I'm reminded of the photographs of women whose hair was cropped to stubble because they were accused of being Nazi collaborators during World War II. I was fascinated by those pictures; it's only now that I can understand the sexual implications of being held down against your will and having your hair, part of your identity, chopped away. I want to feel the stubble on my face, let it prick my tongue and lips. I want to gag on the hair that gets stuck in my throat.

Shake for me.

My thoughts exhaust me. Your moans fill my head and I plunge back into your nearly bald pussy. This time I don't stop. I don't want to. I'm as close as you are.

I can see what you want me to do. I'm in your head and I understand the three spots that need attention. My fingers, tongue and face move from clit to cunt to anus. I think my heart is going to pound through my chest.

Your voice rises. The couple next door turn on their stereo to drown out the screams. With one hand occupying your clit, I reach up and unclasp the restraint on your right wrist. I hold you to keep your balance while you undo the other wrist, and we both tumble to the floor. You get on your hands and knees and I follow like a male dog after a female in heat.

I lie on my back, head under your cunt, and bring you down on my face. From here I see your breasts moving above me as I lick and suck and penetrate this hot wet mass of sex between your legs. I want to slow down again, to catch my breath, to take a drink of water, but you won't let me.

All my energy now focuses on your clit. Your hands squeeze your breasts and you move yourself rhythmically over my mouth, maintaining just the right speed, just the right pressure. Within minutes your legs start to quiver uncontrollably and you stop rocking. You stop breathing. You become totally unconscious to anything but the sensation that is erupting in your body. I watch it happen. You suck in your breath three or four times. Your screams are feverish. I continue to work your engorged bud until your body jerks away from my mouth and you collapse in convulsive spasms on top of me.

I have this memory. I'm not sure where it came from. I don't know if it's a dream, I don't know if it ever happened. I don't think it did, but I'm not sure.

Karen Marie Christa Minns

❧❦❧

The Muse Comes

*I felt her before I saw her, the summer blanket whisked from my
sweating body, the cooling night washing over me like fine mist.
Still fog-bound from sleep, I hardly knew what was happening.
Before I could cry out for help, the bed groaned, and then there
was the scent of her, like fresh peaches, like grapes ripened and
ready to burst. I listened as my stomach growled.*

*"Don't worry, honey," she crooned, laughing into my hyper-
sensitive ear. "You aren't the first."*

"It's your own fault." Kim rolled her eyes in deep disgust. She
put the cigarette out in her Diet Coke.

"Give me a break," I pleaded, trying to clean acrylic from a
brush. It kept me from facing my roomie's accusations.

"Orleans, I've sent over at least five students—each of them
has a couple of years of modeling experience. You tell me what
is wrong with any of them, for chrissakes."

I kept stabbing the brush into the cake of Ivory. Kim didn't
relent.

"Just because they don't meet some abstract scale of perfection! Jesus, O, all this shit about your 'muse' is just that. *Merde.*"

The P-town sea breeze of early spring was crisp, tangy, almost
edible. Still off-season, we'd soon enough be invaded by summer

throngs. Then there'd be full-blown, rowdy, ripening flesh a'plenty, all more than willing to pose—but that was later. My deadline for this last portrait was in three weeks. The naked canvas stared blankly at my offended friend. It had long ago tired of looking at *moi*.

"You know, O, you are the biggest looksist pig I've ever met, and that includes the last man I slept with in college. Yuck!" Kim plopped her lithe frame into the overstuffed and much duct-taped easy chair.

"Wanna go for my jugular with an Exacto blade?" I put down the now denuded brush.

"For the past nine months I've watched an entire parade of women pass through this studio, O. And now, the one painting that is of a fictional character, and could, ergo, use anybody at all as a model, you go bonkers—nobody is good enough. C'mon, the other portraits were of real women, O, but this is a made-up character—you know—like the Greek myth books in grammar school. Or your imaginary friend. You did have an imaginary friend, didn't you? Shit, I don't even see why you need an actual model. I think it's the old excuse to get laid—being horny can do strange things to a woman."

"Will you stop already?" I dropped a bottle of Simple Green on my foot.

"See! You can't even talk about it. Put the paint away and come to the club with me tonight. People think I've buried you at sea, it's been so long." Kim stretched and cracked her knuckles, then her entire body, joint by joint, like a giant Tinkertoy.

Wiping the cleaner off my Nikes with the back leg of my jeans, I tried to explain, yet again.

"When men write encyclopedias about the wonder of their muse nobody bats an eye, but let me strive for my little ideal, my little piece of perfection, and I'm a pig. This is the final piece in my first solo show, may I remind you. You're my alleged friend. I'm not supposed to get flak from you. Call that fair?" I leaned heavily against the sink, still rubbing green cleaner from my sneaker laces.

"There's going to be an Etheridge wannabe from Boston at the club tonight. Come with me, O. Lai-Sau is coming, too, and you know how Lai takes it personally whenever anyone tries to cover M. E.'s material. We have to protect the singer—I need help." Kim stood, five feet five inches of loose and beautiful.

"Maybe."

"Yeah, tell me something I don't know. Well, I tried. See you later, roomie."

I watched Kim open the attic door and head downstairs, the sound of her cowgirl boots the most lonesome music I'd ever heard.

Okay, I'm a pig—maybe. Perhaps, I'll admit it then, at least when it comes to this one issue: *The Muse*. Mine. Her first public "out-of-my-psyche" appearance just had to be perfect. It was my metaphorical ass on these canvases, *my* frigging muse. The other portraits were all "Women Close to the Artist"—not exactly a Shakespearean title, but passable. All of them were simply themselves. But the Muse—she was everything I thought, dreamed, felt or hoped about art and life, and most especially, about women. She was "The One" I'd been chasing all of my adult career. How many times had I fallen into heavy thrall with some incredible female only to fall out of love the moment the muse left her body? I'd paint the babe and, boom, muse gone south, affair *finito*. The woman hadn't changed. I hadn't changed. The only difference was the fickle timing by that most fickle of all capricious spirits—*La Muse*. And I honestly never saw it coming until the spirit split.

Not the best way to build a reputation—as an artist or otherwise. So, okay, I'm a pig. And I've racked up major karma. But why did paybacks have to kick in right before my first major exhibit? Kim was right; I'd gone through every beautiful woman in Provincetown who would even remotely consider a sitting.

Word was out—avoid Orleans at all costs. Secretly I blamed Lai-Sau, who was the first to accuse me of being an "unrealistic, unrelenting bitch-painter-in-heat" right after I'd politely turned down her offer to pose. It just wasn't the right look—the four-foot-eleven flat-topped Lai didn't possess much in the way of "musability."

Now I was up the proverbial creek without a paddle.

* * *

"I did warn you. Tell me that I warned you." Kim sipped her Heineken with delicate know-it-all grace.

I was busy stretching canvas, Goddess knew why. I had enough ready for the rest of my no-good life.

"Maybe, well, maybe there is one more student I can bribe." Kim was interrupted by a knock at the studio door.

"Come in, it isn't locked," I shouted across the attic.

The door swung wide. This was a good thing, since the woman standing behind it needed the space. All the space.

"My name's Melina. I heard down at the pharmacy that somebody over here is looking for a model—a painter's model?"

Kim spat up Heineken. She jumped up and ran for the bathroom.

"Asthma," I tried to cover.

"Really? At the beach?" Melina didn't wait for any sort of confirmed invitation. All six feet, two hundred and fifty-plus pounds stepped into the studio.

I backed up into one of the empty easels, knocking over a jar of acrylic glaze.

"Shit! I mean, never mind, sorry," I sputtered, dumping rags into the sopping mess. "Why don't you sit down somewhere."

Melina looked around, decidedly unimpressed. "That's okay. I have a dental appointment in half an hour so I'd like to get through this interview as quickly as possible. Is that realistic?"

Kim emerged, thank Goddess, her golden face tinged with fuchsia. "Hi. I'm the roomie. Sorry about my exit—beer down the wrong pipe, you know." Kim stuck out her slender hand.

"I'd heard it was asthma." Melina's fist swallowed Kim's tiny paw as she shot me a knowing look. I was not on her A-list.

"So, you live here, with her?" Melina dropped Kim's hand, nodding in my direction.

"Yeah. Downstairs. But she's the painter. I'm just a lowly art historian. Really, we aren't related." Kim grinned stupidly.

"Yes, well, I gathered you weren't sisters. Tell me what, exactly, you are looking for—in a model, I mean. I brought my portfolio. Actually, I'm only in town for three and a half weeks. Just finished a big underwear campaign—'Large Lady Fashions'— maybe you've seen my work? I needed a break so I came here to stay at a friend's summer place. Now I'm antsy. Not too much to do off-season, is there? I was talking to the pharmacist and she mentioned there was an artist in town looking for a model—desperate for a model, actually is what she said—said you were legit. Neurotic, but legit. Well, I've never done this type of modeling. Just ads. Well, actually, there is that commercial—'Heavenly Momma Pantyhose'—did you see it? Last fall?" Melina rose to her full height, stretched mightily, and then moved to the line of windows overlooking the sea.

I wondered if I wouldn't have a real asthma attack from lack of oxygen. Desperate, neurotic . . . maybe—but this desperate?

"Wait!" Kim was across the room and by Melina's side. "I did see the commercial! It won all kinds of awards, didn't it?"

"How nice of you to notice. Yes, it did. You *are* an art historian." Melina turned around abruptly.

Like a ballerina gone ballistic, I dove for two canvas panels I was sure she would knock through the windows. But it wasn't Melina's bulk that smashed them; I tried to pick up the broken easels and my own clumsy self.

"Are you sure she's the painter?" Melina looked suspiciously at Kim.

Kim merely smiled, enthralled.

Melina pointed at me again. "Does she do drugs or what?"

"Just caffeine and white sugar." Kim looked disgusted.

"That explains a lot. Well, ladies, do you want a peek at my portfolio? It's getting late."

I crawled to the duct-taped easy chair, my head still spinning from the stupid pratfall.

Melina reached into her tote bag and came up with a leather-bound portfolio. There was more invested in that binder than in one month of our rent. I was gasping and Kim was ready to genuflect. Melina only smiled demurely.

Gingerly, Kim reached for the English bridle-bound book and began to carefully turn the pages.

I was mostly dumbfounded.

Hundreds of Melinas—all in see-through nighties and peek-a-boo bras. Melina, earthbound, pinkly glowing, running rampant amid cherubic children, all sporting shorty p.j.'s; Melina in lace teddy and feather boa, striding wickedly atop stiletto heels. I had to stop.

Kim, however, was emitting a long, low wolf whistle, the likes of which I was sure Lai-Sau had never heard.

Suddenly, from behind us, we heard the soft thump of discarded shoes and clothing. Turning, I found our entire universe had shifted.

Not four feet away stood Melina—stripped. Ready, I suppose, to pose, or to fight. She was an amazing mountainous confabulation of Amazonian wonder, a mighty woman, a woman of might.

Firm as California foothills, buffed, waxed, shaved and shining. Rounded out, thickly ribald, undulating—all Melina. Her flesh was the perfect saturation of roses and cream. It was eggshell sprinkled slightly with golden dust of minute freckles— almost Victorian, and just as provocative because one knew these freckles only a spring sun could bestow upon the most careful of Northeastern skinny-dippers.

O Goddess!

O mother!

Kim and I fell back on top of each other.

Melina, well, she did not stop there; no, she began to "work." I guessed it was years with those hyped-up photographers on fashion shoots that made her move the way she did—or maybe that was just Melina—but she seemed to almost float over the attic floorboards, all the while undulating like the swells off Hawaii's North Shore.

Kim shoved an elbow into my spleen, but even the pain wasn't enough to shut my mouth. Melina was beyond voluptuous, beyond overload, beyond anything I had any contact or words or feelings for. I was in a place of absolute shock and disarray. Was it her pure animal sensual side, or just her size in comparison to any image I'd ever imagined about my muse? At that point, who could tell?

Finally, Kim sputtered, "Melina, really, that's fine. Thank you."

Melina stopped mid-flight, looking mildly surprised. Then she broke into a wide grin.

"It's so nice working with other women," she gushed, picking up her clothing as she went.

Kim dumped me unceremoniously from her lap and jumped forward to help the rerobing model.

"I knew we could work together," said Melina. "Now, here's my card and the number where I can be reached in town. You call me just as soon as you need me, but remember, don't wait too long. I'm only here for three and a half more weeks." She finished dressing, then planted a juicy kiss on Kim's cheek.

"One last thing." Melina turned before her descent to the street. "I've never had a problem with your 'tribe'—I mean, eighty percent of the people I work with are gay. But there are some folks in this town with way too much time on their hands. I know you know what I mean. I told my neighbors there won't be any more over-the-fence comments about 'the lesbos in town.' You both just should know where I stand. Toodley-oo!"

The attic stairs seemed to call out a wooden-voiced chorus as she descended.

"Don't say a word, Orleans. I mean it. This is a gift from heaven and you don't deserve it. You call that woman, you call her right back. You call her or so help me, I'll have Lai-Sau sit on your face."

Kim raved on. "Did you see those hips? That skin? Have you ever seen anyone move like that? Jesus H. Christ! Look at me, I'm sweating. I never sweat. Can you imagine what kissing her must be like?"

I sat back in the duct-taped embrace of the old chair and wondered.

But what about my muse? *My* muse was slender, ebony-tressed, closer to five feet than six. Her eyes were ebony, not delft blue, not shifting in the spring light like Melina's. *My* muse had a rich tan and would never move like that. *My* muse was an angel, a subdued lady, an intellectual who would have to be coaxed, after long hours of growing intimacy, into shedding her clothing. Her basic skin tones were woodsy and earth-infused, not peaches and roses. Kim's ideal (much to my, and I was willing to put money on it, Lai-Sau's surprise) was zaftig. But my ideal?

Kim took one look at my contorted face and shook her head in quiet disdain. Once again I was treated to the cowgirl rendition of "Lonesome Blues," as she clomped downstairs and slammed the door behind her.

I went to the window. I needed a fresh perspective on this strange spin. Across the street, the waves turned from palest peridot to deep emerald. Thoughts of all the women in whom I had seen the muse flashed like the light on the water outside. All the women I had been attracted to—later to find the Muse moving through them, filling them with inspiration to guide my hands, my eyes. There was the Gypsy, and Ginny, Medora and Melissa and Mary Jane, Katharyn and Catherine and Kathryne and Kathy and Cate, Lenore and Liza and Teresa: where did Melina fit?

Half an hour later, with the sun gone down in its celestial sputter, I dialed Melina's machine.

"So this 'muse' stuff, you take it seriously? For real? Kim told me you absolutely believe it. Huh?' Melina was fiddling with the bath towel I insisted she wear.

"Melina, look, if you talk I can't draw your mouth, okay?" I hid behind the canvas, grateful for its small refuge. I was in no way convinced that the experiment of Melina-as-muse was going to succeed.

"Right. Sorry." Melina grinned, then shut her mouth tight.

"You know, Orleans, these portraits of your friends, you've really got something here." Melina moved in that floaty way which defied the laws of gravity and totally unnerved me. She knew the effect it had on me—and relished it.

I was trying to focus on mixing colors before the light changed. She was not helping my concentration.

There was something about her skin—marvelous or terrifying. As an artist I had never had such a challenge presented to me. The light shifted upon her and, within milliseconds, the hue changed. Where there had been an amber cast it was now rose—or rose would cool to lavender, then suddenly, up to a warming gold. Maddening. Complex. Almost as infuriating as she was. She was getting under my skin.

"Have you looked at them?" Melina was insistent.

"Of course. I painted them, didn't I?"

"Look, honey, photographers need art editors to pull one good picture from a hundred rolls they've shot. Just because you drew these women doesn't mean you can see them. Take a break and come here for a second."

I made no move in her direction.

"Look at this one of Kim. I've only just met her but she's becoming a real friend—so smart and funny. I just love her little blush. And her friend, Lai, well, they took me by your club and it was a trip! I had the best time line-dancing. I forget how much fun women are. Anyway, this painting of Kim, just look at those eyes! Not only did you get the exact color of brown there, but you have the, well, the *expectation* of brown. You know what I'm saying?"

Okay, I'll admit it, by this time I peeked. "Expectation of brown?" I was confused.

"I don't know what you artsy-fartsy types call it, but you know, like even if I hadn't met Kim yet I'd still know what her eyes would look like, outside, near the ocean, or inside, at the pool table at your club. You got it down, in the paint, girl, can't you see?"

Melina had crept up and was not more than three or four inches from my face. I felt her hot, sweet, vanilla-scented breath as it poured over me. I noticed, too, the musk of her perfume. Sweat trickled down my sides and across my shoulder blades.

"It's a God-given gift, Orleans. I hope to hell you don't take it for granted." Melina stood there, hands splayed on her hips, like Athena.

I felt the blush burn, bad as Kim's.

"Isn't this what you're supposed to be doing in the first place? Showing people what they can't see for themselves? Like a poke in the eye with a sharp stick? Kim's loaning me some books and that does seem to be their point." Melina moved back. Suddenly, I could breathe regularly again. The air cooled down. I could continue to paint.

◦ ◦ ◦

"Well, it looks like something." Kim moved around the canvas.

"Care to be more specific?" I was swabbing titanium white into cerulean blue, trying for another generation of "Basic Melina Flesh."

"Well, it's just . . . face it, O, she intimidates the hell out of you." Kim stubbed out her cigarette in the empty ashcan.

"What?"

"Even Lai-Sau sees it and she hasn't seen you in a month. You aren't dealing with the real Melina yet—no understructure, no surface tension. What are these supposed to be?" Kim pointed at Melina's hips.

My face burned. I sputtered but couldn't come up with a quick line.

"Aren't you the artist who 'carves paint'? Isn't that what they said at the last juried show in New York? An artist who can go through half a gallon of 'Mars Black' just to get some model's pubes right? What's the matter, O? Is Melina pressing a few buttons back there, or what?"

A sudden image of what it might take to get Melina's pubes right flashed across my deadening mind. Kim was right. I was totally thrown by all my churning reactions to the model. Who the hell was I? All my old standards were being reset and I wasn't ready for it. Wasn't even sure I wanted the overhaul.

"You know, O, if you believe in your muse as intensely as you claim, you should be treating Melina with a whole lot more respect than you have so far. What if she *is* the muse, come down to play with your mind, as well as your other parts, huh? Better tread mighty carefully, Orleans. Listen, if you feel halfway human later, stop by the club. Melina might even be there. I'd say you owe her more than a few drinks."

Almost midnight. I'd cleaned every brush in the place. There was enough canvas for an entire flotilla to set sail. Only the still unformed, unfinished portrait of Melina remained to accuse. I grabbed my denim jacket and fled the haunted attic.

◦ ◦ ◦

The bar wasn't crowded. From the back I heard the high, happy sound of a drunk Lai-Sau and knew immediately where they all were.

I walked up to the bar and ordered a beer. Toni smiled, passing the foaming bottle along with a crack about me coming back from the dead. I took a long swallow.

And then I choked.

There, on the middle of the dance floor, in the arms of the bar owner—probably the most sought-after dyke in Provincetown—twirled and dipped my model, Melina. To the strains of Ronstadt's "Blue Bayou," Katherine Ann Maple, a Sharon Stone look-alike if ever there was one, moved the amazing Melina across the dance floor, totally absorbed and enraptured.

I couldn't catch my breath. Toni banged me on the back, trying to help. Finally breathing, albeit raggedly, I slipped from the bar stool, somewhat dazed. When had all this occurred? The way Melina was holding on to Katherine, this was obviously not the first time they'd locked legs. And it wasn't a "straight girl good-time dance with a friend"—not by a long shot. Score one for our team, right? Another freed-up straight girl finally on the right track. Right? So why did I feel so damned depressed?

I left the bar, meandering my way back to the studio, under the blaze of stars.

It must have been around three a.m. when I awoke, and then I felt her. Like cool air against my feverish skin, like a fine mist washing over me, causing me to shiver, still fog-bound, sleepy, unsure of what was happening.

"Your roomie let me in." Melina's husky voice ripped the remaining shreds of sleep from my consciousness.

I sat upright. She pushed me back down. I stayed there.

Before I could holler for help, the bed sagged and then, like a fine rain, like good light pouring all over and around and into me, her scent—ripe peaches and fresh berries. I listened as my stomach growled.

She laughed. "Don't worry, honey, you aren't the first," she crooned, her ruby lips descending and then locking on my gaping mouth.

The folds of her hot flesh enveloped me, velvet and wet, so

wet against my own moistness. Her leg was thrust harshly, exciting me with the shock, causing new wet to rise from between my thighs. Our breath mingled, then hers overtook mine, like a friendly bellows, feeding me clean air.

My arms came up of their own accord, floating weakly. I felt the large muscles buckle and shift beneath the firm flesh, felt the slick and slithery movement as she squirmed against me, the sliding curl, the happy dance, the gentle moans. She was crying like a dove, like a doe, like a dangerous angel.

As if on an air mattress in a swimming pool, warm, cushioned, suspended between two worlds, I surrendered to this magnetic ride, uncrushed, unrelenting, all hardened nipples and rising clits, all pounding hearts and smashing pulse.

Melina thrust again and again, releasing then recapturing me between the trap of her powerful legs. I was weak and groaning, taken for the third time, almost wrung out and yet she kept on. Wet, wet, so very wet, the delicious friction made me erupt volcanic, shuddering against her, inside her, through her. It was as if she'd been taking lessons on the side, as if she'd learned not only what to do but when to do it. My model turned muselover, beginning the slow, insidious grind that was blowing out into explosive fuck. Her hands reached inside me, kneading me, working me like the first time she worked the studio in front of Kim, and I was as taken—more, Christ, so much more. My throbbing clit, engorged as a cherry, ready to go off yet again, she carefully ignored, maddening me to prayer, praying for just one more touch, one more brilliant caress. But the maniacal nerve-maddened Melina just laughed and huffed and thrust yet deeper, moaning that she would take me the way I'd taken so many women all my bratty butch life. She could take me as deep as I could stand, maybe even deeper, making me burn in that obliterating place of black hole hunger, making me babble and speak in tongues, making me buck like an animal. Her fist almost wholly inside, her mouth only leaving my lips and tongue alone long enough to come up for sobbing gulps of air, she would take me, almost break me until, when I thought surely I would die, she brought me back up, buoyed me and started all over again.

Each act was given with such magnitude. Before I could ask
or even groan, almost before I could gasp, I was totally engulfed,
encircled, shaken; one with the heaving bed, almost lost to myself; every orifice filled with Melina. All hands and toes and
tongue and breasts, fingers churning cunts and cunts lapping at
lips and lips bit and reddened and teased into screams; clits ripened in voluptuous suck, bursting as if they could shoot, soaked
and swollen and fully engorged, all meltdown, all high and magnificent gush.

Melina, Melina—when had there ever been such a powerful
one? Melina my model, my lover. My muse.

"You know I'll never forgive you." Kim passed a glass of cheap
Chablis in my direction.

All around us the crowd parted like water between stones in
a stream. Nobody knew I was the artist, unless introduced. Nobody but my friends.

"I swear, I didn't make a single pass." I blushed, still thinking
of Melina's scalding mouth as she went down on my clit again
and again.

"Just this one night, you hear me, you artist hound-dog, you,"
Melina had whispered.

That's all it had been. She'd slipped away by dawn.

"Well, I'll believe it the day Lai-Sau proposes marriage," said
Kim, reaching for the melting Brie. "You have to admit, it's the
best portrait in the exhibit. The hit of the show."

My roomie was right—as usual.

I sipped the weak wine and toasted the health of my muse.

Bonnie Ferguson

Amazing Grace

"The harvest is *ripe*, look out in the *field*," Wilette Jefferson sang as she moved among the bean rows toward Ruby Hawkins. She bent down on the word "harvest," her hands seeking out the slender green shafts hanging among the leaves. She picked the string beans, one after another, at the precise place where branch and stem joined, until her hand was full. When she got to "field" in her hymn singing, she straightened her back and released the beans into her bucket.

Wilette moved closer to Ruby, ahead of her in the next row, and continued to sing the song that signaled it was time to run away—to go off and hide, play a game, tell a secret, conspire, ask a question, or confide a fear that only a girl of fifteen could have.

Ruby continued to pick beans until Wilette's voice was just a breath away. She didn't turn her head until their hands brushed, offering beans to the same basket.

"I can't go tonight," Ruby whispered so their mothers in the row up ahead wouldn't hear them.

"Who's going to watch me then?" Wilette whispered back.

"Watch what?"

"What I got to show you," Wilette said, grinning.

Every Wednesday night that summer, each girl left her home at dusk to meet at a certain crossroad, then follow a path to the

Zion Methodist Episcopal Church that bordered the Hawkins property. Before Wilette and Whistler got to courting, the girls would creep to the porch and watch the service through the window together because Ruby was afraid, being a white girl and seeing what went on inside.

Just for devilment, Wilette would sometimes leave her alone and go inside. Then Ruby would have to watch by herself as Wilette raised her arms among the others, all their hands fluttering in the air like low-flying starlings promising rain. Ruby would watch Wilette wail and sway among the men and women caught up in shouting spasms, arching their backs, jerking and swooning.

Sometimes before Wilette came to herself, Ruby would have to run home, her feet stuttering on the path in the dark. There she would slip into bed and lie trembling, in fear of the place where nothing was covered and nothing was still.

"I'm going by myself then and you just have to do without my secret," Wilette said, thinking about Whistler, and about spreading and waving her arms and legs, making angels in wet night grass.

Wilette left her field work and walked down the path below the Hawkinses' house where she and her mother lived as sharecroppers for Ruby's family. She took a bucket of cool water into the bedroom and washed herself by the window, enjoying the little licks of late afternoon sunshine on her body, thinking about Whistler out there waiting for her. She lifted the flowered dress from the nail by her bed, put it over her head, and let it hang like a canopy over her body, thinking of how Whistler could suspend himself above her. She let the dress fall down, past the brushes of her hair, catching at her hips, swirling around her sturdy brown legs. She pulled the top up over her breasts, pausing when the moving cloth made her nipples sing as she had recently discovered they could.

When she was ready, she grabbed a cold biscuit from the kitchen and went out the door, humming and singing. Her mamma was on the way in.

"You going to prayer meeting, don't go sashaying past the Hawkinses'," said Mamma. "Don't go showin' yourself."

Passing the Hawkinses' house, Wilette began to sing "Swing Low, Sweet Chariot," then changed to "When the Roll Is Called Up Yonder" because it was louder. She was gratified when Mrs. Hawkins came onto the porch to hurl a pan of dirty dishwater toward a slip of crepe myrtle, her eyes directing a strong rebuke at Wilette.

Wilette passed by with long strides, unaware of the soft white shape of Ruby slipping along behind her like a shadow. She climbed the hill above the creek, rushing, the blood rising in her face. When she reached the cemetery in the glen behind the church, Whistler was already lying on an unoccupied piece of ground, wiggling his bare toes, whistling a tune that was connected by nothing except cheer. He had gathered pine needles into a thick ground cover.

She ran, laughing, and he turned his head to watch her approach.

He was long on the ground. She towered over him—the only time that she could.

She put her hands on her hips and looked down on him.

"Jesus didn't never look *down* on who He was standin' over!" boomed the preacher's voice from the church. On a night as still as this, the straining voice of the preacher and the congregation's moans and shouts encouraged Wilette and Whistler, and hid their cries. That was why they continued to meet there.

Wilette worshiped him. His head was noble, the way he held it. His neck was thick and tender. The muscles of his arms were complemented by the range of his shoulders. His chest was wide and hard, narrowing to a waist that she could enclose when she circled her arms around him. His pelvis was quick and flat, his legs shafts of tendon and muscle. He was territory, and she claimed him sprawling, finding both with her legs, her arms, and all of her fingers.

As soon as she was settled, Whistler began on her dress, admiring the flowers on the cloth, capturing a scrap near her neck, rubbing it between his thumb and forefinger.

"Waas *blind* but *now* I see," the congregation sang.

Whistler never took his eyes off Wilette's face. When it was open and soft, he began his predictions, studying the shift of her expressions while his fingers moved with soft urgency.

"Your face is going to fall apart first," Whistler promised. "Your eyes are going to brighten and spring forth in tears."

"Amen," someone said inside.

A drift of breeze played across Wilette's back. She let Whistler move her with his hands and with his voice. It was one of the best parts, the slow run of his voice like sugar syrup, over her head and around her ears. When the prodding upon her from inside his britches became more insistent than his fingers, she eased off him and walked away, swinging her hips, knowing he was watching. When she reached the honeysuckle tangle, she slipped off her dress and bloomers and hung them there. She returned to him with her head bowed before his hungry gaze.

She let him take her by the arm, bring her down and back. She let him cup her head with one hand, to pillow it until he had her settled upon the bed of pine needles where his workingman's hand explored her deeper. When he finally reached down to undo his britches, she was ready to help him. He chuckled at her haste to expose his lively coil and let it spring. Astraddle her, he put his hands around his cock and hammered her folds. She raised her pelvis as if her hungry mouth down there could close upon him, take him in, and give suck. He let his cock nuzzle and part her until she moaned.

"I am *climbing*!" the preacher's voice inside asserted. "*You* are climbing!"

Wilette's brown legs climbed Whistler's back as soon as his first glide and thrust filled her. She panted, opening her mouth wider each time he delivered his drive, squeezing around him, sucking and pulling him with the mouth between her legs, eating and drinking him before he could withdraw.

"Enter into His gates now," the preacher inside told the crowd.

Wilette panted, opening her mouth wider and closing tighter around his pounding shaft until she barked as he called up the sharp deep animal woman sound she had inside her, the sound that made him come—filling her, emptying him.

"Lord, Lord," she murmured.

"Oh, mercy," he breathed, his words falling over her like baptism.

A gust of wind whipped up, carrying "Oh, For a Thousand Tongues to Sing" through the trees in peculiar harmonies.

Whistler slipped downward and Wilette caressed his ears as he licked up her wet place, he the mother cat, she the kitten newly born, he making her shudder and cry with pleasure born again.

"Wilette?" The cry on the air sounded like hope. Wilette raised herself up and looked toward the sound. She could almost hear Ruby in that cry, almost see her slipping away from the honeysuckle, hurrying to the churchyard, holding herself the way she did when she was worried or frightened, her arms clutched around her waist.

Wilette rose, gathered her dress, and went to the creek to wash. When she returned, Whistler dried her off with his arms and kissed her mouth before he walked her to the churchyard where the lights beckoned. Leaving her there, he slipped back among the trees.

Wilette walked toward the church where silhouettes swayed on the window and the sounds of singing rose again.

"The harvest is *ripe*," they chanted. "Look out in the *field*!"

Wilette moved closer and looked through the window, half-expecting Ruby to join her. She saw Old Brother Peterson dancing in his own circle in the aisle, his arms spread-eagled, all eyes beholding his ecstasy. She took the chance, and eased herself inside the door to join them, sitting down in the last pew, as if she had been present all the time, waving the fan beside her.

Lisa Rothman

Commuter

I am sitting in the kitchen surrounded by the chaos of splattered tomato sauce and dried-out cooked spaghetti strands courtesy of my considerate roommates when the phone rings. It's David.

"I'm really tired from my bike ride."

Damn, he doesn't want to see me tonight. I guess that's what I have to expect when I go out with a man sixteen years older than I am.

"But I still want to see you."

Ah. Hope springs eternal.

This guy is not exactly a whiz at saying what he means. The first time he invited me to his house he said, "Want to meet my cat, Samson?" Although I'm allergic to cats I said yes immediately—I guess that doesn't make me too straightforward either.

Tonight David asks, "Want to come over to watch *Northern Exposure?*"

What would happen if I told him the truth? David, I don't want to haul my lazy ass to Oakland from San Francisco to watch *Northern Exposure.* I could watch it very easily from the comfort of my housemate's flea-infested bedroom. The real reason I'm going to Oakland is for the privilege of stripping down to my gray lace bra, pushing you against the kitchen counter, unzipping your Levi's Dockers and licking the length of your big cock until it stands up to your navel and you beg me to fuck you.

Instead of speaking my mind, I deal with logistics. How am I supposed to get to Oakland by nine?

"I'll pay for a cab to BART."

Though I am tempted, I take MUNI to the BART station instead. I'm just not comfortable having David treat me. It would feel too Holly Golightly.

My Victoria's Secret underwear slides and tangles as I cross my legs. Can the other passengers tell that I am going to meet my lover? At twenty the thought of having a regular lay still blows my mind. As the train enters the tunnel, plunging us below the bay, my ears pop from the pressure.

I get off the train and hastily tuck my billowy green shirt into my black jeans. David is leaning against the rail in all his six-foot-two-inch glory waiting for me. Taking my hand, he steers me out of the station. He opens the passenger side of his car first. What a gentleman. When David gets inside I stroke his red curly hair. He reciprocates by grabbing my inner thigh. What powerful fingers.

"Did you use the StairMaster today?" he asks.

"Yep. I need to keep in shape for the workouts you give me."

David unlocks the door to his penthouse apartment overlooking Lake Merritt. It's so soothing to leave my messy flat in the lower Haight, where the brown rug in the bathroom is shaggy with soapy water and mildew, where my housemates have been known to leave their dirty casserole dishes in the sink for five days.

We neck while we watch the show. David seems tired. I tell him he should get more sleep. "When?" he asks.

"I get plenty of sleep the nights that I'm not with you," I reply.

"I never have my nights off," he says. "I think about you all the time."

Right answer. As far as I'm concerned, he wins the car, the boat, the all-expense-paid trip to Jamaica and the ceramic dalmations.

But I've had enough of this idle chitchat. I slither my hand down his stomach to his penis, snake behind his balls, and press lightly on his prostate just the way he likes it. Groaning, he slides off the sofa and gets on all fours. I start stroking him from behind, running my hand from his ass to his abdomen. Occasionally I tweak his nipples. He keeps moaning and groaning. Staggering to a standing position, he leads me to his bedroom.

"I thought I was just coming over here to watch *Northern Exposure*."

"It's a package deal."

He pushes me down on the bed. As I swing my legs up in the air to wriggle out of my jeans he grabs my cunt with his palm. I gasp and flop my legs over to the side.

"You're so wet."

"It comes with the territory. I'm just a fertile, nubile twenty-year-old sex machine. You should have felt me when I was still a teenage thrill kitten."

David does a somersault off the bed and lands on the floor. I pull him back on the bed and push him onto his back. My tongue begins a long slow journey to his cock. I devoutly outline the ripples of his taut stomach. His penis is soft by the time I reach it. No matter. I cradle it in my hand and slither it into my mouth, using my fingers to lightly scratch his balls. It starts to grow and hits the roof of my mouth. Success.

David begins to pant. "Oh, oh."

I don't want him to get too excited too soon, so I stop sucking. Instead I firmly lick from the base of his cock to its big fat head. I alternate between lightly flicking the head and licking its entire length. Once again I stop. Then I establish a slow steady rhythm and caress his balls. I look up. David's head is thrashing from side to side and he's pumping his pelvis.

"Please, please. Don't stop." I love it when a man begs.

Enough teasing. David's cock is so hard that it slides easily into my mouth. I pulse the inside of my cheeks and start to suck—hard. I feel his penis contract as it goes ramrod rigid and he's coming and coming and coming in my mouth. Cum is in my hair and dripping down my chin.

David lies on his back without moving for a good five minutes. Finally I ask if he's okay. Slowly he lifts his hands and stares at them. Once again I ask him if everything is copacetic. It's all he can do to stare at his hands. Eventually he says, "My fingers are tingling. So are my toes. That was the longest orgasm of my entire life. I have never experienced anything like that. Thank you."

He switches position so that I'm on my back and he's on his side. Slowly he rubs my clitoris with his thumb. Back and forth. Nice and hard. Over and over again. I'm about to come.

And then his hand stops. I can feel his chest steadily rising and falling. He's just plain tuckered out. I guess that's what happens when you have the longest orgasm of your entire life.

Unfortunately, I am one hot and bothered young woman. And, quite frankly, I'm a little resentful. When I decided to date a man sixteen years older than myself, I thought he would go to extreme lengths to please me. Instead, David got the greatest orgasm of his life, and what did I get in return? A comatose lover and the sound of his snoring.

I waited for him to finish his silly bike ride. I waited for him to take a shower. I waited for him to call me. I waited for MUNI. I waited for BART. I waited for the end of *Northern Exposure*. My pleasure has waited long enough, Goddammit. It's high time I claimed what is rightfully mine. As I wriggle my hand between our bodies and start to stroke my clit, I am reminded of the saying, "If you want something done right, do it yourself."

The sound of David's snoring represents his weakness and defeat, I decide, and I am going to mock him by turning it into my own pleasure. I let the volume of his snores set the pace of my hand. It's fairly quiet at first—a quick inhale through his nose followed by a gasping exhale from his lips. I stroke my middle finger up over my clit fast, then slowly slide it down. Up and down. Up and down. I dip my other hand into my wetness and bring it, moist and warm, up to my large breasts and massage my pale pink nipples.

Oh, David, if you hadn't expended all your energy on the ridiculous bike ride, you would be able to revel in my wet cunt right now. I'd let you stick a finger or two inside me, and you would feel the rippling of the walls of my vagina. Instead, you are oblivious to everything, drool gathering in the corners of your mouth, while your voluptuous twenty-year-old girlfriend gradually strokes herself into a frenzy.

Whenever David makes a noise, I move my hand. When he doesn't, I stop. His snoring grows progressively louder. I'm surprised he doesn't wake himself up. I am aware of how hard my nipples and clit feel in contrast to the overall softness of me. My eyelids are half-closed, my head is tilted back exposing my long white neck, and I am panting through my moist lips. Ah, David, you are missing out on what I know, having watched myself in the mirror countless times, is a damned sexy spectacle.

My caresses cross the line from leisurely to urgent, and my legs begin to tremble. What if he shifts position and stops snoring? When I'm this close to coming, holding back is torture. I hover on the edge. Even David's stupid cat Samson jumping on my face can't stop me. My toes curl and my back arches into David's downy chest as I come.

Gradually, I stop moving my hand. David stops snoring. I drift into sleep.

The radio news show *Morning Edition* wakes me up. David is standing in front of me, doing what appears to be tai chi. In the middle of a low lunge he stops to run his hands through his hair.

"What step is that exactly?" I ask. "It doesn't look like red-crane-waiting-at-the-water's-edge."

"It's the Yanni," he says. Then he goes back to the lunge and breaks it up by scampering across the floor like a hermit crab.

"And what move is that?"

"The M. C. Hammer."

Laughing, I get out of bed, amble to the kitchen and take the frozen waffles out of the freezer. David starts the coffee dripping and takes a shower. Midway through, I join him.

"Is it a hair-care product morning?" he asked.

"No, I'm going to the gym before work."

David drives me to the BART station and kisses me good-bye. "I'll call you tonight."

Going down the escalator to begin the tedious trip back to San Francisco, I wonder if I should stop this commuting thing. I'm a resourceful gal. I should be able to find a lover closer to home.

Sonja Kindley

Make Me

There is a clammy, remote stairwell that no one thinks of using, and that is where we go, midafternoon, when I am done with classes and he has a coffee break. Today all I'm wearing is a short crepe dress and sandals, and my skin feels warm and steamy. I'm excited to be near-naked. He is wearing tan linen, white cotton, and tortoise shell glasses. He smells like foamy mocha, he smells like heat, he smells like he could screw me—but that is not why we are here. The stairwell is solemn and it is dangerous.

Turn around, he advises. I do, heart stuttering. He raises the hem of my dress and pulls my bare ass to his crotch. I feel his shaft pulse through pleated linen and I get dizzy, flower bulbs opening up inside me, nectar dripping. If I fall, will he catch me?

You have the stench of wench, Angie, he smiles, his dry palms creeping up my inner thighs.

Put your finger in my cunt!

He wraps his arm around my shoulder blade to hold me close and jams it in. My knees give; I am drunk with this; he holds me. He whispers, Your cunt's a little inferno . . . Yeah, I say helplessly, clenching onto the finger which draws me out, spreads me glistening over smooth white.

Tell me you wish we were fucking!

I am bent over the railing and his cock is out now, sliding between my trembling thighs.

I wish we were fucking!

Say it again.

I wish we could do it. I wish . . . I could have you . . . just once . . . inside me . . .

I mean this; my intensity is almost hysterical. I want to shove that erection inside me and have at it, to gasp and laugh and squeal, to get rammed by this brilliant, worldly, wicked fifty-year-old man who is my equal in deviousness and the sport of seduction. Leo, Leo Saxon, who is popular and respected and not unkind.

He will do everything but. Or not even that. He hasn't eaten me, nor I him. We are playing it safer than safe, which means no latex and the wedding ring stays on.

I am straddling the railing and its cold metal feels cruel and kinky. His teeth come down on my right flank and I yelp in surprise. Little peach, juicy thing. He kisses to make it better. I want to leave my mark on you. No, *I* do.

He zips his pants and I turn around, aggressively meeting his eyes. I like to get up close and stare at him because it's interesting how the intimacy unsettles his usually unflinching composure. We separate and watch each other. He is sitting on the steps, I am standing.

So tell me, he says, Why do you want to fuck your dad?

He became my dad when he said he was my mirror reflection, and that my swagger was affected. He saw how I don't trust easily, how I doubt my femininity. He told me I have great potential and will go far because I'm a truth-seeker and an adventuress and that is when I thought: a father. You see, he understands me.

I was tired of boys and their demands, their I-don't-knows, their wonder at warped sex, their fleeing. I was with a boy once who hung onto my back as a papoose, so timid, never voicing opinions. In bed he would thrust away arhythmically as if I were

a blow-up doll, and then come with a whimper and a sigh. Don't
tell me that can't hurt after awhile. I'm tired of boys.

Leo says boys are easy, too easy, when we compare tales of seduction. And: Men are dogs, women are cats. Woof woof, I say.
He smiles at me with curiosity. Who is Angie this time? That
time I was my little self, the one who says nasty words for a giggle, the one who flashes, the one who jumps up on him like an
untrained puppy. Leo thinks all this is a pose, the one I use to
manipulate people with, the sure-fire method for enchantment.
I am afraid he is right.

I thought the ring was a teaser, although I now recognize that
as desperate hope, not insight. I thought, he is the kind of man
who would wear a ring to attract only women who are looking
for trouble. This is still true, but it's not the reason for the ring.
Diane, the jet-setter whom I've never seen, is. She's a buyer for
Saks and hobnobs in Europe much of the time. Leo says their
marriage is quite good. I believe this; I would hate to believe
otherwise and feel destructive. The reason we don't fuck is that
their marriage is quite good.

No kids, thank God. I'm sorry but I could never let a father
of a person older than me grab my butt, it's too sinful.

Leo has all his hair, a strong jaw, and an energetic, fit body.
He was a drug fiend and hyper academic in the sixties. He now
rides a Harley, which he insists keeps him in touch with his feminine side—spread-eagled, a big warm machine between his
legs. He is proud of that feminine side and likes to feel gentle
sometimes. I don't think he knows jack about femininity, but I
won't say that to him yet.

We met because I originally wanted to set up a summer in-
ternship with the magazine but missed the deadline, so we were
just going to rap and he'd look at my résumé and offer advice.
I liked him when he said, "I think that bright, thoughtful, articulate young artists should be cared for." I thought he was referring to me. I knew the rumor about him, though, and wanted to
see if it was true: ladies' man or not? I could tell he was sincere
about his dedication to his work and fostering young talent—I
recognized him as a good man with heart—but I also sensed his

love of mischief, as he teetered between friendly professionalism and artful sleaze during the two hours we chatted.

A month later he revealed, "I had this flash of putting my cock in your mouth, but then went back to the business at hand. There was something about the way your lips curled . . ."

I scolded him—You shouldn't have been thinking about those things so early!—but he was more honest than I: I had had erotic dreams about Mr. Leo Saxon before I'd ever met him, and when he said that, I realized he was the first man I'd met who seemed to be as fascinated by sexual tension and its inner workings as I was.

How do you do it, Leo?

Even on acid he was pulling straight A's at grad school, four hours of sleep a night. He sold his services to a wealthy Mrs. Robinson—satin sheets, honeymoon suite, age eighteen; he had a pleasant and solitary homosexual experience in the early seventies; he has swallowed cum—he is braver than I. Leo, of the *ménage à trois*, the Why Not, the wake-up screaming scene—yes, it's in his past; no, he's never had "safe sex" per se but he might be persuaded to step into the phone booth and become Latex Man if, by chance, we feel compelled to do the deed.

Where are you, Leo? I'm waiting in the lobby, wearing your favorite dress, the narrow purple rayon with the buttons down the front. I want to feel your gruff hands on my hips. I wish I could kiss you but you don't kiss. I like you so much. You challenge me. You want me to succeed in life, to grow up without making your mistakes, to take risks.

See, I brought some photos from my childhood to help you remember me as a kid. My birthday was June 12, 1970. Gemini. I was a weird, ghostly thing before I became more confident and pretty. That is me when I was thirteen and had no real friends. I lived at Gramma's farm that summer and mucked around with the animals. The bandage is on because a horse stepped on my toes. As a baby I had enormous blue eyes and a pouty underlip.

You were twenty-eight when I was born, remember.

I am still looking at the photos when he takes a seat beside me.

Who's the babe?

Oh, I don't know.

Lemme see them.

He goes through the pictures quickly as if speed-reading, looking for a theme, the major points.

Even as a child you were into costumes and drama, he observes. You were cute and coy—enfant terrible. Collusion written all over your face.

He once said that he'd "smelled" it on me when we met. My nasty curiosity. I told him I am really quite inexperienced and he said, "You just think you're more virginal than you are, Slick." When I asked, he said I was neither a succulent nymphet nor a jaded woman of ill repute but a "succulent woman who wants to retain her nymphetishness while becoming more jaded."

He can describe me to me with astonishing accuracy. He knows what kind of transformations I have gone through to deliberately erase my family's influence, from the mild cautious bookworm to the shrewdly flamboyant femme fatale; he knows the image I desire will always elude me until I stop cracking the whip. He calls me a narcissist. He tells me we are made of the same mold, full of too much jive and power trips, only he is a face reader who ignores how he feels and I am a manipulator of faces.

I say these things to you with affection, he says. And I know you are strong and self-aware and will take what you want and chuck the rest.

His hand is on the top button of my dress. He opens it slowly, exposing my throat.

Leo says, I would hate to have you think I took advantage.

And another time: You should never reveal who you really are because people will take advantage.

And then: Why do you want to fuck me? I'm a happily married man.

I say, You are bad and like to get into trouble. You are the first man who has ever seduced me before I seduced him and the first man to make me blush. So, thanks.

I can't explain why I want to fuck him. Maybe I don't really want to go that far.

We're outside on the park bench now and I'm getting that feeling again, that daughter-dad giddiness which makes me act like a goofy girl, munching chips with my mouth open, sitting with my knees pulled to my chest. I'm happy. There is a sweetness between us. He tells me I am a kook; he is stimulated by my stubborn passion. Then he chides me for flashing my snatch—he calls it that; not very dad-like, I might add. I think I'd like to snuggle up to him. But we are across from his building and I understand the situation all too well.

His face does not look like mine. Though light-haired, he has a profile like Clark Kent. How can he be my father? I am soft and wispy and red-haired, with Swedish blood.

I ask him if he has five minutes for a rendezvous in the stairwell. He can't say no. I watch him and he has so much vitality and directness—it amuses me to note what a fine actor he is, looking so courtly and open when he's actually planning sleazy escapades.

I join him thirty seconds later inside. He looks at me sassily when I open the door, as if I had interrupted a meeting.

You want something, he says, knowing I am never satisfied.

I want to kiss you. Can I?

I lean over, put my hands on his shoulders, and try to kiss him but he opens his mouth wide and my lips fall in. He did that on purpose.

I hate you, I say.

I'm sorry. Hey, Angie, don't sulk.

You made me feel stupid.

I apologize. Sometimes I can't control my antagonistic tendencies.

You don't trust people—I trust more than you do. I make myself vulnerable but you're always playing games.

Give me your foot and I'll kiss it.

Yeah, sure.

Give me your foot.

I let my shoe clunk to the floor and he puts my leg across his corduroy thighs and pets it like a sleek eel.

There is something very intense about you, he says. If I were twenty-two you would scare me. Sometimes I wonder if you are a spy, sent out to ruin me.

As if your reputation could be ruined!

I drop my leg between his thighs and rub his crotch. I think corduroy is a funny fabric. He is gazing at me. When I touch him I feel powerful—it feels like trespassing and I do it with glee.

Now he's tracing my lips, now he's thrust a finger inside my mouth and I roll my tongue over this invader and tighten lusciously. I feel a charge in my cunt. He goes in and out slowly.

I would love to slide in from behind and fuck you.

I grab his hand and put it where it should be.

See how wet I am . . . I'm oozing.

I would even love to watch you with another man.

Put it in—please.

He is rough and I am caught off-guard. He forces my walls open with his index finger and it's not sensual, it's rude and frantic. I take hold of his wrist. I move my hand into his big hand and when I meet his amused eyes I look away, then brush the dust off my dress.

His theory is that when you really trust someone nothing they do to you will feel painful because you're so open to them. I fear ever reaching that point, even though it's considered good; I want to always be able to distinguish pain from pleasure. The lover I trust will not be someone who will ever hurt me.

Leo said, You must not tell a soul. So far I have told a couple of souls. My reasoning was that they don't really care who he is and besides, they would not be inclined to talk about this with anyone who cared. The secret was burning a hole in my stomach. I felt as if I were losing touch with the moral majority in my degenerate pursuit of intrigue.

I made my friends uncomfortable. I understood then that I really was all alone in this, that even if I were to confess to every friend I had it would still be my burden, and I would run the risk of serious self-incrimination. I hated feeling judged by a trying-to-be-sympathetic jury. I became defensive, spiritual: I said he was an angel sent to unnerve me and help me recognize my strength, and my receptivity to the message was contingent upon a sexual rapport. I was breathless. I gave up.

We're in his white, airy office overlooking the park. He has a hollowed skull of red clay on his desk which seems voodoo-ish but he can get away with it; there is nothing weird about him to the public eye. He tells his staff nothing; they can only guess.

So how would you explain my presence to someone? I ask, slyly.

You're an aspiring journalist and I'm taking you under my wing. I don't need to explain it to anyone.

Should we close the door?

Nope, don't need to. We've got an open-door policy here.

I want to show you something.

I lift up my blouse and flash my dainty breasts.

I didn't see anything. Do it again, slower.

I know what he's doing, he always does this: He takes my dare and ups the ante, making me exceed my threshold for scandal, scooting me past an already tainted decorum.

I have so many questions for him in the back of my mind about how he grew up, how he loves, what made him want to get to know me, why he's still with Diane. There never seems to be enough time. There's so much joking.

That's why I typed up the questionnaire. His laughter is a short blast; he can't wait to read it. "This is most excellent," he says. "It's so Angie. Direct, aggressive . . . academic."

Question one: What was your relationship with your mother like?

"I was her surrogate husband. I slept with her from age four to nine when my father would go out with prostitutes. Nothing happened, of course; I would just listen to her cry and complain and try to comfort her."

Question two: Should I trust you?

"You mean am I trustworthy? Yes, I am trustworthy, but I can't tell you whether to trust me or not. The choice is yours. You have to follow your instincts. Somewhere along the line a person you're close to is bound to disappoint you if that kind of promise is made."

After ten more questions to which he responds frankly—almost too frankly (I'd assumed he would laugh at some of them but he took each one seriously, which made me embarrassed for doubting his sincerity)—he puts his coffee mug down and says, I understand you so much better now.

I get off on the pornography my mind whips up, splices and dices; I am sometimes surprised by what I need: I like force, a hissing in my ear, a passion that makes me happy, helpless, a man who knows how to fuck me. Because Leo has me twitching, flipped out with desire, I think of him, always.

I see him following me up the stairwell, smiling and focused. I see him on his knees, licking me, murmuring, *You are so beautiful.* I let him lead. His hands smooth my body my skin tingles I am alert he says *Relax Angie I need to fuck you you're so sexy* and has me lean over the railing and OH he's in he's thrusting I hear him groan my wet walls clutch him hold him I need to come screaming I am losing control he's on the edge his breathing is shallow we will get to the same place at the same time . . .

I meet him for coffee and he asks, Are you wet? and yes, I am.

He's not going to touch me. I can see it in his eyes. He is thinking, "I should be more respectable. Maybe." But it's also possible that there are no shoulds in his vocabulary, as he is a spontaneous man.

He used to say "make love." Now he says "fuck" more than I do. I am inclined to call it "making love" now because I have these reverent feelings for him, but fucking is what we will do. Is this sad?

I tell him I think he has too much power.

No, he says seriously, I don't have any power. Maybe you're just not used to these terms?

Right, I'm not. But you can't deny that you dictated the terms, and that's power.

The choice was yours to accept or reject.

∗ ∗ ∗

The first time we touched: It was seven-thirty at my apartment and he was half an hour early for our breakfast date. He asked me to dim the lights. He asked me to come over. I went over to him, feeling curious. Closer, he said.

I stood between his legs, a little princess in sky blue silk pajamas, waiting. He breathed me in: His face brushed across my throat, memorizing my natural rumpled bed scent. I remember thinking: I am very young. I was quaking a little from the danger and my lust. His light brown hair was thick, smelling of citrus.

He said, I want to touch and not touch.

He said, If you could feel only one part of my body, what would it be?

I squeezed his thigh as I stared into his eyes and watched him respond. He took his turn and caressed my ass through the silk and I thought: I am younger. I lowered myself onto his thigh.

Look at my breasts.

Just look? He unbuttoned me, watching my face seriously. What would you like me to do?

I answered, in a small voice, shy: Feel me.

When I rubbed his erection it felt sacrilegious—what was I doing, touching an older man's cock?—then deliciously nasty. I felt empowered. I had never related to someone like him in a sexual manner. With each stroke I had my way with every male history teacher, every friend's handsome relative, every actor/musician/politician I have desired from afar. That is some kind of power. I accepted; how could I have refused?

Today I assure him, though, that if the sexual element in our relationship is causing any discomfort I would be happy as a platonic friend. He said the same thing to me the third day after the initiation, I remember.

A flash of relief appears on his face.

"This is good—it's good to have some nice options," he says. "I haven't made up my mind yet but I'm glad we're mutually respectful."

Then he sits back in his chair and describes a "secret position" he knows and he won't tell me what it involves but "one of these days we'll either find ourselves in it or you'll discover it on your own."

So I'm still dangling.

There have been times when I've wondered about Diane and felt rotten, but whenever the guilt comes I start feeling disgusted with Leo because he's older and should know better. Sometimes I want to reprimand him: You think you have the right to just fuck around with women half your age to do whatever you please when you're married? The thing is, I can't express this disapproval because I'm benefiting from his degeneracy. So we call each other "sleaze ball" affectionately.

We don't talk much about Diane, but when he brings her up he has compliments. I'm not jealous of Diane, actually; I think she's probably a great woman, a hard worker.

That's enough on Diane.

I'm blind.

I'm in his car and a cool, wet wind blows against my face as we go around curves, up these anonymous hills. A silk scarf is wrapped around my eyes, our agreement. He asks me if it's too tight and please tell him if I get too hot or cold. I touch the thick Pendleton wool of his blazer, I feel the heat of his jean-clad thigh, the softness of his shaved cheek. I am safe.

Tonight we are going to make love.

There is something thoughtful about him, something tentative. He hasn't made many jokes and there are more pauses than usual. He admits that he is going through a small debate, and do I understand why? Yes, I understand why. He wonders if the acting upon desire is less important than the desire itself, or the pursuit. This has all been good fun and I like you a lot . . . he explains.

But what happens once we get over the edge? I fill in.

Yes. I'm afraid of fucking things up in three people's lives, he says, simply.

He stops the car. We must be up in the hills where the big houses are. A minute goes by. A decision is made. He pulls back onto the road.

How are you doing? he asks.

Good. I love this mystery. I like feeling clueless.

Soon we park and he takes me gently by the hand. I take tiny steps but he will watch out for me. I feel like a gummy-eyed kitten, sniffing wildly, nuzzling. He picks me up and my black velvet coat falls open as he folds me into a furry zigzag. We go up steps. This may be his house, though he said it wouldn't be.

He lowers me onto a futon-feeling surface and spreads me so I'm lying on my back. The softness could continue indefinitely, wall to wall, a moonlit cushy rumpus room. I have no sense of space.

The door clicks and a second later I feel his body next to mine, a warm breath on my neck, a broad hand resting on my hip. I reach for him, purring. He puts his thigh between my legs and I hold on. He is pensive. I want to keep my blindfold on and go by Braille.

Nothing needs to happen, I say.

I know.

But you are serious. This is confusing to you.

Give me a minute.

I wriggle out of my coat. I unzip my dress. I don't know if he's watching me or not and the uncertainty relaxes me. I feel close to him. I strip until I am naked. I reach for him and affix myself to his body, feeling pleasant.

Suddenly he's on top of me, pushing my legs open wide and rubbing hard against me. There is anger in his movement. I try to adjust to it, hoping it is passion. He scrapes his fingernails down my skin, he bites my tits. We are breathing heavily. I pull off my blindfold to see his face and it is agonized: tight jaw, closed eyes. He is harsh. He flips me over and I hear a zipper unzip, pants pulled down. My face is smushed into the pillow and I'm soaking wet, terrified. He yanks my ass up to him and puts his raging hot cock at my cunt, grazing my clit, and I begin to pulse. If he fucks me I will be gone forever.

Leo!

Angie ... he slurs. Angie ... let me get to you ...

But I slither out of his grip and lean back on my elbows.

Tell me you wish we were fucking, I say.

Oh God, not this.

He runs his fingers through his hair, staring at me with disbelief. Without glasses, his eyes look vulnerable and aged.

Say it.

Angie, I won't do games. Don't be a girl.

He rubs my pussy, slicking me down. I feel like collapsing, running wet all over. He slowly drives two fingers inside, his face hovering above my belly, then lowering to kiss my inner thighs.

. . . Because you're not a little girl, Angie . . .

I'm opening to him, I clench his hair in my fist as his tongue flutters on my clit, one firm hand holding my tilting pelvis down. I shudder. Tears begin to pool in my eyes.

. . . and you don't need a father . . .

Leo! I cry, breaking the rhythm, We can stop, we can stop this! I want you to look at me.

I push myself up. I give him my hand, and he takes it. He waits for me to speak, his face softening when he notices the tears. We pause, watching, as the rain knuckles the rooftop.

I want to tell him about the angel. I want to say I got the message, I want to use the word *trust*, to say, Watch me fly from the cocoon, watch me leave you as a daughter. I got the message.

But my mouth is dry. I'm a slippery naked thing with wide spooky eyes, soft bones, and now I'll hold myself, waiting.

Michelle Stevens

Pornophobia

It was already dark by the time Emmy and I got home from the rally. I was carrying all the signs, since both her arms were tired from thrusting her fists in the air. She had a sore throat, too, from screaming so much.

Emmy and I had been together about three years, and these weekend rallies had become a way of life. Emmy was a member of NOW, GLAAD, Greenpeace, Eco-Feminists for a Non-Violent World, and about three thousand other activist groups. In the past six months she'd even added the ASPCA to her list.

Today's rally had been an antipornography sit-in at the Playboy mansion. Actually, it was held two hundred feet away from the street end of Hugh Hefner's driveway. There were about twelve of us sitting in the ivy, chanting slogans and holding up signs.

Hugh never showed.

When we got home, Emmy took off her boots and plopped down on the couch. I dropped my signs by the front door, along with a stack of the magazines we were protesting—used for display and educational purposes.

I sat down beside her and kissed her feet.

"I'm pooped," she said with the little bit of voice she had left.

"Saving the world is hard work," I laughed, and I kissed her feet again.

When she closed her eyes, I took the chance to take a long look at her. Just ninety-seven pounds with those tiny little features: a turned-up nose, little baby lips, and the same pixie haircut she'd had since I met her. With the Levi Strauss jeans and the Eddie Bauer shirt, I imagined she was the perfect genetic mix of k. d. lang and Katie Couric.

The brown eyes opened sleepily. The little baby lips gave me a grin.

"What are you thinking about?" she asked.

"Sex."

She giggled and rolled her eyes. "I'm too tired."

"I know." I got up and kissed her forehead. "I'll make you some tea."

Before I went into the kitchen, I quietly picked up the informative stack of *Playboys* and *Penthouses* and *Hustlers*. Emmy was already asleep.

I went into the kitchen and picked up the kettle, dropping the magazines on the table. The top one opened to Seana.

Seana. Beautiful, long-haired, long-legged Seana with the world's most perfect breasts. *Penthouse* Pet-of-the-Month, September 1992. Many a night had I spent with Seana while Emmy was at a meeting. And Brandy and Lacy and Maxine, Mistress of the Night. Oh, if Emmy only knew!

I was deep into Seana's thighs when the kettle brought me back to reality. I put the tools of women's imprisonment into their rightful drawer and brought Emmy her tea. She was still asleep, and I didn't have the heart to wake her. I put the mug on the coffee table, threw the afghan over her and went back to the kitchen.

Seana was right where I'd left her.

In the bedroom, I pulled out my power-packed Panasonic Massager 2000. It hadn't been designed for this purpose, but it did the job anyway. Emmy had a real vibrating dildo that she'd bought at the West Coast Women's Music Festival. It had two speeds and was shaped like a dolphin.

I lay down on the bed, put the Panasonic on my crotch and opened to the first page of Seana's layout. There she was, in her little white boots with her little white jumpsuit, smiling at me, flirting with me. "The Luck of the Irish," read the caption. I like to read the stupid captions.

As I turned the pages, there she was again and again. In her little purple business suit with the skirt missing. In her bad-boy leather biker jacket. Oh, Seana, you have the greatest . . .

I heard the doorknob turn. I barely had time to throw Seana under my pillow. The Panasonic was still on my crotch when Emmy walked in. She laughed when she saw what I was doing.

"Ah ha! Now I know what you do at night when I'm not around," she joked.

"I never outgrew puberty." I grinned.

"Why don't you use Flipper?" She grabbed my Panasonic, which packs a lot more power than our dolphin-shaped vibrator.

"Not enough voltage." I grabbed it back.

Then she jumped on top of me and gave me a long kiss while she nuzzled her hand between my legs.

"I thought you were tired," I said when we broke for air.

"I got my second wind," she said. She unbuttoned my jeans and pulled them off. "Let's do it Darwin style."

"Huh?"

"Darwin style. You know. Survival of the fittest." She pulled off my underwear and kissed me.

"Do you want to eat? Or be eaten?" I asked.

She started to laugh, so I tickled her to keep it going. Then I grabbed her by the waist and flipped her over. I jumped on top and started unbuttoning her shirt.

"Hey! What are you doing?" she laughed, as I wrestled with her bra clasp.

"There's no contest," I answered. "*I* am the fittest."

"Oh, yeah?" She picked up the pillow and hit me with it.

I tried to push the *Penthouse* behind the mattress, but it was too late.

"Argh!" she cried out, as she looked right into Seana's package. "Chris! What is—? Christine?!"

She looked at me with confused, pleading, angry little brown eyes—like any wife who has just discovered the other woman.

"Do you—were you *reading* this?"

"No," I tried to joke. "I only buy it for the pictures."

I turned my head away, unable to look Emmy or Seana in the eyes.

"I don't believe this!" She tossed the magazine against the wall. "I don't *believe* this!" She picked up my Panasonic Massager 2000 and threw *it* against the wall. "What were you thinking?"

"It turns me on," I answered feebly.

"It's perverted filth," she screamed.

"But I like it."

Emmy started pacing back and forth in front of our bed. "Chris," she said between gasps, "you cannot *use* that magazine. It's degrading to women."

"But I *am* a woman," I answered quietly. I could look her in the eyes now. I was getting *my* second wind.

"It's a tool of patriarchal oppression!"

"What about *Playgirl*? With all those pictures of naked men? Or the gay ones? *Honcho*? *On Our Backs*?"

"Porn is porn. It takes away the human being and objectifies the body."

"No," I said. "*I* objectify the body when I look at the picture. *It* doesn't do anything. *It's* an inanimate object. The issue is not pornography, Em. The issue is the person looking at the pornography. What's the difference between a naked girl in *Penthouse* or a painting by Manet? They're both just *pictures*."

"But one is meant for sexual—"

"Emmy," I interrupted her. "It doesn't matter what it was meant for. People will use whatever they want. Some people get turned on by the pictures in *Playboy*, and some get off on *The Wizard of Oz*."

"That's my point," she said. "It's wrong to get off on *things*. People should love each other."

"But everyone gets turned on by things. Everyone objectifies sometimes. It's a natural part of our sexuality."

"Not me." She shook her head and lifted her chin a few more inches into the air.

"Of course you do," I told her. "When we make love, don't you find yourself, sometimes, just focusing on one part of me?

Don't you forget I'm in the bed sometimes when you're sucking on my breast?"

"No," she said.

"But Emmy, you have to! You must! You're not being honest with yourself."

She gave me her long, pity-filled look. I hate that look.

I walked over to the far wall of our bedroom and picked up the crumpled *Penthouse,* brought it back over to the bed and put it right in front of her. I opened it to page 42. Seana.

"The Luck of the Irish," I started to read.

"What do you think you're doing?" she asked.

"I want to show you."

"No!" She slammed her eyelids closed and started to walk out of the room. I grabbed her just before she walked into a lamp.

"Emmy," I said, "you protest these magazines every weekend. But have you ever looked at one?"

"Of course not," she said. "They're garbage."

"How do you know if you've never even looked at one?"

She let out a long sigh and glared at me.

"Emmy," I kept up, "don't you think you should at least look at one? Just once in your life? You said yourself that these pictures couldn't turn you on."

"Of course they couldn't," she snapped. "Never."

"Then what's the harm in looking?" I grinned. "For educational purposes."

Another sigh and a glare. I opened the magazine.

"The Luck of the Irish," I read. Then I showed her Seana. Beautiful, long-haired, long-legged Seana. I took extra care to point out the world's most perfect breasts.

I showed her Seana in her little purple business suit with the skirt missing. In her bad-boy leather biker jacket. In her lacy little negligee two sizes too small. Then I showed her Brandy and Lacy and Maxine, Mistress of the Night.

Then I closed the magazine and I started to talk about Emmy's body. I told her how sometimes, when she was asleep, I would just stare at her turned-up nose for hours. How I loved her tiny lips and her pixie haircut. How sometimes when we made love I forgot who she was or who I was or where either of us were, because all I could think about were her perfect little breasts. How sometimes I got completely lost in her neck or her elbows or her ears. How I would fantasize about parts of her body. The parts that I loved. And how it made me want to make love to her.

As I spoke, Emmy started to cry. Soft and quiet.

I put my hand on her cheek and wiped a tear away. She put her hand on mine and we looked into each other's eyes.

"I'm sorry," she said, still crying.

"No, I'm sorry," I said. I kissed her forehead and wiped some more tears away.

She finally stopped crying and gave me a kiss. That turned into another kiss. Then another.

Emmy slid her hand down between my legs, and we were off.

The Best Whore in Hillsboro

"I hope you're available tonight. This call is going to be good."
It surprises Kitty to hear this much enthusiasm from her friend
Corrina. Of course she's available; who can afford to turn down
business the week after Christmas? But Corrina is really tired of
being a whore; she's gotten blasé or negative toward just about
everything, and Kitty can't imagine what she considers a good
trick. Corrina is way past thinking whoring is a grand adventure,
she doesn't like most of her clients, and because she feels like
she has to keep her work a secret from her straight friends, she
doesn't get much support. She ought to just quit the business.
But Corrina got caught by the IRS a few years ago and she's still
paying off the heavy fines. Pimped by the government, the
whores call it. Corrina is stuck, and every little thing that makes
her feel better about still working as a prostitute takes on great
significance. This client must be pretty special; Kitty appreciates
an intriguing sexual adventure almost as much as she appreciates
$350 outcall rates.

Kitty's also glad to be called for a double with Corrina because
she's turned on to her, and the feeling seems to be mutual. Kitty's trained ear can tell by the sounds Corrina makes when they
have sex that she likes it better than being done by a client. This

is a bonus, though. Only a truly homophobic whore would prefer to do a client alone when she could get someone to help.

Kitty gets out a very elegant black suit, high heels, and her most expensive lingerie, the crimson silk with black French lace.

Nice makeup, not too slutty. It didn't take Kitty long in the business to realize that most whores dress up, not down; signaling that your ass is for sale on the night streets of the Tenderloin is one thing, but slipping into the Fairmont to service an out-of-town CEO is quite another, and Kitty's bought more conservative clothes since she began whoring than she's ever owned in her life.

As she dresses she wonders what kind of date could make Corrina so enthusiastic. A wealthy submissive? Corrina would rather dominate clients than fuck them. The only client Corrina ever said she actually liked was a disabled man. Corrina felt happy about bringing him pleasure—she said most guys who paid for pleasure were too fucking rich and spoiled and Republican to appreciate it.

Corrina picks her up at nine.

"So where are we going? Who's so special?" Kitty asks.

"We're going to Hillsboro," Corrina says. A very wealthy suburb. "We're going to see a couple."

A couple! Corrina fills her in. These two called the escort service a couple of months ago looking for "someone intelligent."

"That's a switch!" Kitty squeals, and Corrina says, "Yeah, but they meant it. They're well read and cultured and didn't want to play with anyone they couldn't talk to. When they found out I'd been to law school it was like they were ready to ask me to move in."

"I shoulda worn my Phi Beta Kappa key," Kitty says.

"You should have. Maybe they'd want to pay you more." Corrina giggles. "I already told them you're a writer. If your book was published they'd have bought it already."

Kitty is wondering what to expect. Every new client is like a blind date—doubly so, this time. She's conjuring up well-preserved older literary types, just a little bohemian. No wonder Corrina's dropped her customary ill-feeling about her clients. This *is* an adventure.

There's another angle to her excitement: being called to see a
woman. Kitty is acutely aware that almost every dollar she makes
equals adultery. Maybe two percent of her clients are single; the
others don't tell their wives where they go on those long lunch
hours. If the Mrs. ever finds out, it's because there's been a stupid slip-up, an indiscretion with alcohol and resentment most
likely to blame. Kitty is not particularly devoted to heterosexual
monogamy either as theory or as practice, but she gets tired of
all the businesslike betrayal, the idea that men have to call her
because they think their wives are too pure or too "frigid." Kitty
hopes all the wealthy ladies whose husbands she fucks are lustily
consorting with their garden boys, but still, it's a weird job, shor-
ing up the illusion that married life is a functional state. It feels
more legitimate to do this date, and that makes Kitty think about
the fucking whore's stigma that she has to deal with. She wonders if this is the beginning of her own disillusionmnt with working, if this is how Corrina felt at first.

All this is flitting through her head as they walk from the car
to the door of the very tony Hillsboro house where the couple
lives.

The woman standing at the door is poised and wonderfully attractive. Kitty almost laughs—talk about what she does like
about the business, here it is: another stereotype shot to hell! It
takes a minute for Kitty to get introduced because the pretty
woman has grabbed Corrina and is hugging her and telling her
how fabulous she looks. A minute later the woman is embracing
Kitty and telling her how much she's been looking forward to
meeting her. She takes both their hands and pulls them toward
a big living room, where a giant Christmas tree sparkles.

Her name is Pamela and her husband's name is Tom, and Tom
has been waiting to meet Kitty too. He has been pouring them
all glasses of Remy Martin.

Jesus Christ, Kitty thinks, this is like a Victorian Christmas tale
where the whores get rescued by the rich people. Kitty has been
in a lot of wealthy houses (usually while the wives were away),
but rarely has she been made to feel welcome in them. Pamela
is only a little older than Kitty and Corrina. Tom is already offering to loan Kitty a book. They are creating the near-seamless il-

lusion for Corrina and Kitty that they are all affectionate friends, in the same class and enjoying the same life circumstances—that they are equals chatting about Christmas and sipping brandy.

It's the same thing Kitty does with her ordinary clients, in a way—part of what she's paid for is to create the illusion that she's their devoted mistress, even if it's the first time she's met them. They're supposed to feel like it's normal to be with her, that their behavior has an emotional context, certainly not that they're committing a misdemeanor with an expensive whore.

Corrina is eating all this up.

It's certainly understandable—the seduction here has nothing to do with the sex that will get underway once they have all finished their brandy. Maybe with Pamela and Tom, Corrina can feel good about what she's doing. Kitty feels pretty good about it most of the time, which gives her a vantage point to watch this rare situation work its magic on her usually reserved friend. Corrina is sexier than Kitty's ever seen her, laughing and at ease—she's seen these two several times already—and teasing Tom about being ganged up on by three women.

Kitty has already envisioned the bed. King-size, big enough for four to stretch and romp; expensive white linens, already turned down. Books on the carved Chinese nightstands. Pamela says she decorated herself; it took two trips to China to buy the antiques.

Kitty's glad for her silk lingerie. She's glad for the expansive bed and the pretty, lively woman she's being paid $350 an hour to go down on. She's glad they like Corrina so much; maybe they'll adopt her and invite Kitty over on weekends. It's so hard to believe Tom and Pamela are going to drop $1,400 (they will almost certainly go into the second hour) on this. Ironically the perfect illusion of comfort they've created makes it all seem surreal.

So Kitty concentrates on one thing at a time. Slipping half a dozen condoms out of her purse and onto the bedstand. Pamela's soft, pampered skin connecting coolly with hers as she slips up behind her, arms round her waist. Tom's lanky body emerging from his clothes; Pamela's ringed, French-manicured hand stroking his cock, already hard and high from all Corrina's giggled teasing. He'll please three women, he declares, or die trying.

Three women are going to please each other, Kitty thinks. She wonders if Pamela's the one the party was arranged for. Is it easier or harder to be bisexual if you're a married lady in a rich suburb? Why aren't these two throwing parties for all their decadent friends? Why are they hiring prostitutes? Kitty knows if she dwells on this too much she'll miss out on the fun; she'll be too busy deconstructing the best date ever to really appreciate it. So she puts a lid on the analysis.

Tom, Corrina, and now Kitty have Pamela laid out on the bed. Her silk bra and panties have been pulled off. She's wearing nothing but lots of gold jewelry—it gives the scene a slight Roman orgy feel. Her thick blond hair is streaked expertly, her pussy trimmed and starting to swell and get pinker as her husband strokes her body, then sucks on one nipple after the other. Corrina lies by her side and kisses her.

Kitty is never shy in situations like these: she lies between Pamela's slender thighs, breathing on her pussy, hot little blasts of air on Pamela's clit, and smiles when she hears her begin to sigh. At the price this woman is paying to get her pussy attended to, Kitty will lick it very well indeed.

Maybe Pamela's comparing it to a Roman orgy too. She is bucking and thrusting in no time, thoroughly hot from all the attention, being held down, and the wet heat of Kitty's tongue stroking and stroking her clit. Pamela is clutching Corrina and is very close to coming. Tom urges Corrina up onto Pamela's face, Corrina's pussy settling down on Pamela's lips and muffling her sounds in a way that inspires Kitty to lick her even better.

Corrina doesn't come very easily, Kitty knows, but feeling Pamela's mouth on her pussy, coming and gasping and then settling down to lick her as soon as her orgasm is over, has her very close. Kitty scrambles up from between Pamela's legs and reaches for a condom from the nightstand. Tom's erection is straining from rubbing against Pamela while she came. Kitty works the rubber over this cockhead and rolls it down the shaft—a nice big cock, which is what Corrina likes.

"Put it in Corrina's cunt," Kitty urges, "right over Pamela's mouth, Tom, that's right, let her lick your balls while you fuck Corrina." Kitty hopes Tom has a modicum of self-control; lots of her clients would fill a rubber just at the mere suggestion. Of course, most of her clients didn't have wives like Pamela. If they did, business would either die out or be hopping—Kitty isn't sure which.

Tom kneels behind Corrina and rubs his cock up and down her slit, already wet from Pamela's tongue. Kitty slips her hand between them with some extra lube, strokes it onto his cock and then lets go, hearing with satisfaction the very sincere noises Corrina starts making the minute Tom's cock sinks into her. Pamela is going crazy having both a pussy and Tom's cock and balls to lick. She pulls Corrina down to her pussy; now they're sixty-nining. Kitty slips a couple of fingers into Pamela's cunt. Tom's fucking Corrina. Kitty's fucking Pamela. Their faces are buried in each other's muffs. Kitty glances up and grins at the sight of Tom—he's beside himself. Kitty and Corrina both have bodies that look like Pamela's, small-breasted and slender.

But now Kitty loses herself pumping her strong right arm: she can feel Pamela's cunt opening in the last expansive moment before climax. As Pamela starts to come Corrina begins a muffled cry, one Kitty has only heard a few times—her friend's nonfaked orgasm.

Kitty has never faked an orgasm in her life, but she's heard and seen enough phony ones with her whore girlfriends to cherish the real ones. She's even run into a few men who fake it. She's not sure why she lets go into enjoyment more easily than her friends, but she's sure that's what makes it possible for her to like sex work. When Corrina comes it bridges the gap between their experiences as whores.

Tom almost loses himself, connected to two orgasming women, but not quite. He collapses on the bed beside Pamela and Corrina. Now Pamela takes over.

How inspiring, Kitty thinks, to see a pampered, wealthy suburban woman deep-throat like a succubus! In her fantasies women like Pamela never suck dick, but obviously Kitty's had the wrong idea, because Pamela is going to town on Tom. It's pretty to watch partners suck and play with each other—she's seen plenty of paid-for blow jobs up close, but this is very different. Pamela relies less on impressive technique (though her technique is plenty impressive, Kitty notes), and more on her pleasure in making Tom groan and shake. Unlike all the other wealthy suburban housewives (to hear Kitty's clients talk), Pamela *likes* sucking cock.

Kitty lies next to them, propped up on one elbow, and strokes her clit while she watches. Then she remembers how much money Tom and Pamela are going to fork over for the honor of their company and decides she'd better get back to work. "Nice job if you can get it," she reflects. Corrina is lying on the other side of Tom and Pamela. Kitty winks at her and then begins describing what she sees.

"Tom, I wish you could get right down here close to Pamela's hot mouth and watch her lips slide up and down your dick. It's slick with her saliva, baby, and I can see she knows all the places on your cock that make you go crazy. She's sucking your big cock with her eyes open, Tom, she's watching your face to see how much you like it. Give it up to her, baby, go ahead, let her take you, she knows how, let her take you there . . ."

Tom bucks and writhes with the effect of Kitty's words and Pamela's million-dollar tongue. She's slowing down; she won't let him shoot. He's thrashing his head back and forth and saying, "God, yes, honey, please, oh please, oh make me come, oh Pammie . . ."

But Pamela won't. She gets him down her throat one last time and then pulls her mouth all the way off him, hand around his balls and shaft like a cock ring, and says, "No, baby, not yet, don't you come yet, I'm going to fuck you, honey, you wait for me."

She straddles his hugely straining cock, rubs it on her pussy, croons as she slides slowly down his length, "No, baby, you wait for me." Tom is still thrashing.

Kitty watches admiringly. This woman is good. She is fucking him so slowly and with such focus, eyes locked on his, whispering to him, that Kitty wouldn't be surprised if he started to whimper. Pamela's voice gets a little louder, loud enough for Kitty and Corrina to hear.

"I'm going to fuck you so fine, Tom, just like I fucked that man who took me to the top of the biggest hotel in Denver and bought me all that champagne, baby, remember that story? That time he put me in front of the window with nothing but my high heels on, remember? What did he do to me, honey, you remember what I told you."

Tom is mesmerized, and he definitely remembers. "He fucked you where everybody could see, Pammie, he fucked you in front of the window, in the daytime, and everybody could see your tits, honey, and your pussy, and his cock in you, he fucked you."

Pamela is fucking him, oh boy. Kitty briefly considers moving between their legs and rimming Pamela; there's no plastic wrap in sight, though, and even though it may be the hottest trick ever, it isn't worth a possible case of amoebiases. Besides, she wouldn't be able to hear Pamela's story clearly, so she doesn't.

"What else did he do to me, baby? What else did I do in the hotel?"

Tom's having a hard time speaking. "He . . . he ate your ass . . . by the window . . ."

"Uh-huh, honey, where everybody in Denver could look up and see me, everybody could look up and see me holding my asscheeks open wide so he could run his tongue up inside."

Hmmm, Kitty thinks. Synchronicity. She gives an instant of thought to which position she'd rather be in—tonguing a beautiful woman's asshole high above Denver, or spreading her cheeks to the world. She really can't bring herself to pick just one.

". . . And you pissed . . . all over him . . ."

"He drank my piss, baby, he drank it right out of me." She's riding Tom like a galloping polo pony. His eyes are standing out of his head, drinking her in, totally keyed in to this story he's obviously heard many times. "And he paid me for it, too, honey, a thousand bucks for it, a thousand bucks so he could drink my hot piss . . ."

"Uhhhhnnn!" Tom is shooting, lifting Pamela up off the bed with the strength of his thrusts. She rides him like a mermaid on a dolphin. She has his nipples between her fingers, squeezing.

Corrina's eyes are wide. This is apparently a new wrinkle in her relationship with these two.

Kitty is ready to combust. This is just too much. But Pamela isn't finished. As soon as Tom has shot his load into her she pulls off him and spins around, presenting her creamy, cum-filled pussy to his mouth, and he sets to like a starving kitten, licking it all out of her. Pamela is beginning to shudder; now that her performance is over she can come again.

"Jesus, Corrina, fuck me!" Kitty is beside herself. When had she died and gone to porno heaven? She'll have Corrina's whole hand inside her within five minutes. Such kamikaze arousal with a client is rare, but this is no ordinary situation. Corrina's too happy to oblige; she's on another plane of existence herself, completely free of the pall of guilt and withdrawal that she usually carries when she tricks. By the time Corrina works her little hand into Kitty's over-amped pussy, Pamela has recovered from her most recent orgasm and gotten into the act; Tom still lies there panting while she licks Kitty's clit with slow, teasing swipes that build her toward a big explosive one. Kitty dimly hopes she won't break any of the small bones in Corrina's hand. Tom, just back from the over-the-rainbow place where she's about to rocket, reaches over and takes Kitty's hand.

After such a big come Kitty's brain is always a little fluffy. Pamela pads out and returns with the cognac. Afterglow in Hillsboro, Kitty mumbles to herself. Pretty perfect, with her head pillowed on Tom's belly and the hot waft of the Remy in her nostrils.

"Is this what folks out here do all the time?" she asks.

Pamela laughs and says if people were all doing this wouldn't the world *already* be a better place?

Sure would, Kitty says.

Corrina's eyes are sparkly. Kitty has never seen her so happy. Pamela goes off to the big marble master bath for a quick shower. Tom puts his arms around Corrina and Kitty and thanks them for the wonderful time. "It's really good for Pammie to be around girls like you," he says. "With our other friends she just can't really be herself."

He really does loan Kitty the book, a best-seller she'd never have bought on her own. "It's fabulous!" he says. "You have to read it. You'll be on the best-seller list yourself someday."

So will you, Kitty thinks. But no one will ever believe it.

Astonishing, the intimacy that comes with sharing the secrets of strangers. Pamela and Tom fondly kiss them good-bye. Tom has slipped Corrina an envelope. Kitty tucks the fat hardback under her arm and promises to have a critique of it for them next time, even though she knows that, as a whore, she's never guaranteed a next time.

In the car Corrina slits open the envelope. Fourteen hundred-dollar bills and a Christmas card. Kitty gets seven, then gives Corrina one hundred and fifty back—her courtesy fee for the referral. But Corrina is dreamy, not much focused on business.

On the way home they do a postmortem, even stop for coffee so they can linger over it. This is a whore's ritual, precious time for sharing secrets no one else wants to hear.

"Was Pamela really a prostitute once?" They both want to know. How did she get in that big lovely bed with a devoted rich man? Kitty is suspicious of Cinderella stories, though she knows she'll be an ex-whore someday who whispers salacious tales to her lovers. What inspires her about Pamela is that, unlike all the other working girls who graduated to marriage—which looks to her like full-time whoring with one inescapable client—she shares her secret. And Tom loves her for it. Smart man, stiff-dicked over the best whore in Hillsboro.

Kitty says all that to Corrina. She nods, but there's a faraway look in her eyes. She's just beginning to be able to believe what Kitty already knows: there's going to be life after whoring.

BIOGRAPHICAL NOTES

°"I've always lived partly in worlds 'out there,'" says **EMILY ALWARD**, whose early role model was Wonder Woman. She has just completed a novel, *Shimmer Spell,* set in the same culture as "Honeymoon on Cobale." Her published work ranges from environmental history articles to science fantasy and erotica. Emily currently shares a lakeside house in Indiana with her dog, Bonnie, and two visiting cats.

°**CHRISTINE BEATTY** is a transsexual lesbian author and musician. Her recent publishing credits include a collection of short stories and poetry, *Misery Loves Company,* and an entry in *Beyond Definition,* a gay-lesbian-bi-trans anthology from Manic D Press. She is also a staff writer for *TransSisters* magazine, and her work regularly appears in *Tapestry,* the *Spectator,* and the *San Francisco Bay Times* Letters section. She performs with Glamazon, a rock band she formed with her lipstick lezzie lover, Rynata.

°**ERIN BLACKWELL** is a Eurocalifornian who went to France to learn about love and was not disappointed. "Real Pleasure" is dedicated to her personal *"prof d'amour,"* Nicole Guenneugués.

°These authors' stories also appeared in previous *Herotica*® collections.

°**CALLA CONOVA**, a poet and short-story writer, found that the key to getting published was moving to San Francisco, where the readers are kind, the people are good-looking, and all the dogs are above average. She has another story in *Herotica 3*.

BARBARA DeGENEVIEVE is an artist and professor at the School of the Art Institute of Chicago, where she teaches in the photography program. She received an NEA Visual Artists Fellowship in 1988 for her photographic work and in 1994 was awarded another NEA Fellowship, which was revoked by the National Council on the Arts because of sexual content.

°**DEBBIE ESTERS** is the happy single mother of one and lives in San Francisco. She works as a health professional and writes whenever she can. She has been previously published in *Herotica 2*.

°**ANGELA FAIRWEATHER**, the recovered wife of several ex-husbands, lives her life as a colorful memoir. She has reinvented herself as the queen of vanilla and belly-dance goddess, and writes passionately of food and sex. She shares her life with abundant friends, a beautiful, adored daughter, and two tortoise-shell cats.

BONNIE FERGUSON of Benicia, California, is completing *The Intruders*, a short-story collection. "Amazing Grace" inspired her first novel, *Bloodroot*, the story of a biracial friendship between two families in the rural South circa 1940. *Vahine*, a novel of the South Pacific, will explore Polynesian taboos and will require leisurely field research.

JOLIE GRAHAM is a West Coast artist and writer. In her spare time she can be found hanging out at the local library—cooking up interesting new dishes.

°These authors' stories also appeared in previous *Herotica®* collections.

C. A. GRIFFITH left New York City and a career as a professional camera assistant and cinematographer five years ago for the challenge of writing and directing in *Cali*.

***JANE HANDEL** is a writer, visual artist, and publisher. In 1990 she founded SpiderWoman Press, which publishes limited edition artist-designed and -illustrated books and broadsides. She currently makes her living as an art dealer and curator specializing in vintage photography and other works on paper.

SUSANNA J. HERBERT has written professionally for television, films, the theater, and a number of magazines. She is thrilled to have her work included in *Herotica* and dedicates "Breaking and Entering" to her muse, Hondaki.

SONJA KINDLEY is a short-story writer, diarist, and poet with a degree from Oberlin College and a penchant for intrigue. She has been published in *Zyzzyva* and *The San Francisco Review of Books*.

JO MANNING's stories have appeared in *Imagine!*, *Fiction Forum*, *Just a Moment*, *Stuff*, *Nocturnal Ecstasy Vampire Coven*, *Romantic Interludes*, *Travel Erotica Anthology*, and *The Star*. An audio book, *The Prairie Princess and the Sanskritologist*, was released by Radio Books/Redwood Press. She finds writing erotica very liberating.

EVE MARIPOSA is a poet, drummer, and lover of everything she can sing to. She thanks all the warrior women who have lit her sky with their truth.

***MARY MAXWELL** was raised by wolves. In subsequent years, she has adapted reasonably well to the strictures of civilization.

***MARTHA MILLER** is a Midwestern writer. Her short stories are widely published in lesbian and literary periodicals and antholo-

*These authors' stories also appeared in previous *Herotica*® collections.

gies. She writes a monthly book review column for women and has had three plays produced by Mid-America Playwrights Theater. She has recently completed a novel.

*KAREN MARIE CHRISTA MINNS More Idgie than Ruth, more Vita than Virginia, this thirty-eight-year-old novelist *(Virago, Calling Rain)* continues to seek one special woman wearing pearls but hiding a rock 'n' roll soul. If you dream rebels and repartee or hunger to go "deeper," Minns invites you to write.

*SERENA MOLOCH currently lives in San Francisco, where she is enjoying the varied forms of public transportation, the weather, and the women—in that order. She is contemplating an epic romance about the erotic life of a large chintz sofa, to be written in the style of a dry-cleaner's bill.

*CAROL QUEEN writes stories that are often not untrue. Her book *Exhibitionism for the Shy* was recently published by Down There Press. Her novel-in-progress about the sex industry is called *Frugging at the Gates of Hell*. Since all characters but Kitty are composites and some of the things they do together are made up, any resemblance to persons living or dead is not surprising, but any exact description is a miracle.

*STACY REED recently relocated from piercing San Francisco to swampy Houston, but her nomadic lifestyle jibes with her editing and writing. Her writing appears in *The Daily Texan, Images, The Austin American-Statesman, Texas Beat,* and *San Francisco Live.* After three years of undulating, Reed quit the interactive sex industry in favor of the virtual one. Again, for Sheila.

FRANCESCA ROSS is the pseudonym of a widely published romance novelist. An editor of nonfiction books, she also teaches composition and literature at a state university. She lives with her husband and two young sons in the Midwest and communicates with other writers through computer networking.

*These authors' stories also appeared in previous *Herotica®* collections.

"Commuter" is **LISA ROTHMAN**'s first piece of erotica. She is currently working on a collection of short stories about ballroom dancing, the harrowing world of coordinating volunteers, and why dating assistant sous-chefs and computer consultants is probably not a good idea.

*SUSAN ST. AUBIN began writing erotica in 1984 and hasn't been able to stop. Her stories have been anthologized in all three volumes of *Herotica, Yellow Silk: Erotic Arts and Letters, Erotic by Nature,* and *Fever: Sensual Stories by Women Writers.*

MICHELE STEVENS's plays, including *Hunger* and *Diary of a Lost Child,* have been read at the Mark Taper Forum, the Pacific Resident Theatre Ensemble, Barnsdall Art Park, and the Gene Frankel Theatre. She is a graduate of New York University's Dramatic Writing Program and now lives in Los Angeles. Michelle subscribes to *Playboy, Penthouse, Hustler,* and the Victoria's Secret catalog.

ANNALISA SUID is a California-based writer of erotic fiction, currently at work on her second and third novels. She dedicates "After the War" to Anne Rice, her inspiration, and to Judy Cole, her mentor and friend.

*CECILIA TAN is a writer, editor, and activist in the bisexual and leather-SM communities. She is founder-publisher of Circlet Press, a book publisher specializing in erotic science fiction. Her work appears in anthologies and magazines, including *Taste of Latex, Bisexual Politics, Some Women, Looking for Mr. Preston,* and *Map of Desire: Asian American Erotica.*

*These authors' stories also appeared in previous *Herotica*® collections.

More...More...More!

In 1988, the first *Herotica* anthology forever changed our expectations and understanding of erotic literature. It became an underground classic and left readers hungry for more fine writing to tantalize and titillate both the libido and the imagination. To satisfy all of those ravenous readers we present

HEROTICA 2

A Collection of Women's Erotic Fiction
Edited by Susie Bright and Joani Blank

A completely new feast of spicy stories that celebrate sex and sensual pleasure. From hot, steamy beach fantasies to romantic encounters that are sometimes quick and dirty and other times exquisite matters of the heart, these tales are sure to delight. Uncensored and uninhibited, *Herotica 2* brings us all the nuances and shapes of love—be it candy-kisses sweet or razor-edge sharp.   (267870—$11.00)